If EVERYONE knew every plant AND tree

by Julia C Johnston

I hope you like it!
Love
Julia :)

Copyright © 2013 Julia C Johnston
All rights reserved.

ISBN: 1481914251
ISBN 13: 9781481914253

Library of Congress Control Number: 2013900510
CreateSpace Independent Publishing Platform
North Charleston, South Carolina
Author website – www.juliajohnston.co.uk

Acknowledgements

Many thanks to:

My Createspace Project Team, especially the cover designer, and my editor, Emily Havener; Nicola Morgan (author who read and critiqued an early draft); Penny Holroyde (literary agent for Caroline Sheldon Agency, who read and advised on a later draft); Jodie Marsh (literary agent for United Agents, who read and advised on a later draft); Alysoun Owen (editor of Writers' and Artists' Yearbook, who chose me as winner of a writing competition); Matilda Suadwa (friend who read my novel, gave notes, and cheered me on); Cathy Johnston (dear sister who allowed me to draw on aspects of her life for my novel, and who read and approved the finished manuscript); Demelza Monk (as yet unmet teenage reader/writer who made useful and intelligent observations), Martin Wren-Hilton (my husband who has supported and encouraged me through my writing in every way you can imagine).

CONTENTS

Prologue		vii
Chapter One	What's Wrong with Lily?	1
Chapter Two	Lily Laughing	9
Celia-mail 1		17
Chapter Three	Pratt and Prejudice	19
Chapter Four	Don't Blame Lily	29
Celia-mail 2		43
Chapter Five	What's Wrong with Nathan?	45
Chapter Six	Saved by Lily	53
Chapter Seven	Lunch for Lily	69
Celia-mail 3		80
Chapter Eight	A Homely Prison	83
Chapter Nine	The Great Exhibition	95
Celia-mail 4		106
Chapter Ten	Lily's Plants	109
Chapter Eleven	Flowers in Still Life	121
Chapter Twelve	Grandma and Grandpa's	129
Chapter Thirteen	Shopping with Lily	145
Celia-mail 5		156
Chapter Fourteen	Drama Club	157
Chapter Fifteen	London	167
Chapter Sixteen	Thomas	183
Celia-mail 6		196
Chapter Seventeen	Lily Love-Stone	199
Chapter Eighteen	Lily Still There	211
Chapter Nineteen	Always With Me	221
Chapter Twenty	Grave Rehearsal	233

Chapter Twenty-One	Lily Talking	247
Celia-mail 7		262
Chapter Twenty-Two	How It Is Now	263

Prologue

This book is not about gardening. Well, it is slightly, but hardly at all. Thing is, I love plants and trees. Dad's fault. He loves learning the Latin names of plants and flowers. It was he who got me obsessed with words and looking them up—well, him and my best mate, Kamal. But this is not about Dad or Kamal or words or anything—it's about Lily.

When my sister got ill, I went a bit mental with planting, I suppose partly so I could spend time with Poppy Teasdale, who worked in her mam's garden shop, The Fuchsia's Bright, at weekends.

Mam once said, "Why don't you spend your pocket money on a book *about* gardening, Oliver, instead of shed-loads of strange plants and seeds? You've planted a right bizarre mix. Blind people will enjoy the textures, I suppose."

That wasn't a compliment, by the way, because that was something alien to my mam at that time.

We used to converse, mainly swear, I suppose, using plant-speak—Poppy and me, that is, not Mam and me. Conversing was not Mam's bag (not with me anyway). When I was pestering Poppy in the shop and getting on her nerves once, she said,

"Bleeding hearts! You give me such a cactus head, you common dickweed!"

All I could say was "Brilliant!" which somehow annoyed her even more.

The most embarrassed I ever saw Poppy was when I said, "I love yew," and had to explain that it was a joke and I meant the tree and not 'you,' even though I probably sort of really did.

When Lily got very ill, I used more serious plant-talk like 'Feeling yucca today,' and when I needed to get my mind off my life, I used to say over and over in my head, 'Dizygotheca elegantissima'; I imagined the long, serrated leaves growing out of my brain.

I sometimes think if everyone knew every plant, flower, and tree in the world, yeah, we'd be experts on plants, but we'd also be experts at describing colour and texture and emotions and stuff... perhaps everything. Life. Once when I was at the hospital with my two brothers to see Lily, I said,

"Brugmansia blood looks like, seeping from her arm."

Even though the lovely Nurse Celia laughed and said I was a 'one off,' which I took to be a compliment, Sam told me to stop being irritating, and Nathan called me a nutter.

But if you *knew* that flower, that precise colour, the emotion it evokes in you... Before anyone rushes to their Royal Horticultural Society Dictionary of Gardening (not), I must tell you that I'm not going to make constant reference to exotic plants, just some. I did actually see a Brugmansia sanguinea at the Eden Project in Cornwall, though, and committed the name to memory, because in brackets it said 'Angel's Trumpet,' which I thought sounded amusing and saddish at the same time.

I don't mean to appear grand, by the way—'committed to memory'—but I sometimes think of weird ways of remembering words. For Brugmansia, I imagined a man who spent most of his time by the brook near his village (probably a bit of a loon: helps with the overall picture). He was known as 'Brook Man' and wore a trumpet-shaped hat (stay with me), and on the rare occasion that he ventured into the village, the people would whisper to each other, "Brook Man's here!" Et voilà—'Brugmansia'.

There definitely aren't enough words to describe what I felt when it all happened. I wish I *could* describe exactly what I felt...

I feel sorry for words sometimes, when they kind of don't properly explain things. 'Sad'—I mean, what's that about? Imagine an 'Emotion Library' where you could look up such things: thousands of different emotions labelled in jars on shelves. You could pick one from a shelf, unscrew the top to get a feel for it, and hover it over your heart and think, *Ah! So that's what she meant when she said 'suffocating anger'*. I mean, you can buy bottled air, so why not emotions? I wonder if they'd have to have a sell-by date? How long would the essence stay in the jar? Librarian: "When you've finished with that 'disastrous jealousy,' son, pass it to me, please. It'll need replacing. Goes off quickly, that one. But you there, don't worry about that jar—'paralysing loneliness'—lingers for years."

You can't buy this type of air, at least I don't think you can, but Nathan farted into an empty coffee jar once. He didn't leave the lid on long enough to discover if the smell seeped out over time, even when stored in a tightly sealed receptacle. When he opened it in my face, I was glad of the abiding coffee odour. I didn't point out that it was a rubbish choice of jar for his purpose.

My mam once left four Virgin Marys on a plane; we never heard the end of it. They were just Our Lady–shaped plastic bottles containing holy water to give to religious people. All I wondered was where they'd ended up and if 'stolen' holy water turns into cursed water. Or were they thrown away, and did the holiness gradually seep out?

I think that's probably what happens to our bodies—the trapping in and the seeping out, I mean. Something terrible happens to you, but the powerful feelings weaken over time. Seep out of your pores. The day it all began, it felt like lightning had hit our house.

What's Wrong With Lily?

"Stop! Please, somebody help me!"

"Mam! What's wrong?" I screamed as I left my key in the door, flung my school bag to the floor, and tore up the stairs.

"Hurry, Oliver! It's Lily! It won't stop!"

At the top of the brightly painted stairs, I spun to the left, grabbing the left side of the doorframe. I stood at the entrance of Mam and Dad's bedroom. I felt like I'd been struck with a stun gun. I froze to the spot, holding the frame of the door with both hands now. On top of a half-put-away pile of washing lay Lily, eyes rolling back in her head, her whole body jerking, her stripy legs going stiff then dropping down, like someone possessed. She'd had fits quite a few times and had even spent a few nights in hospital, but I'd never seen her like this.

Mam was shaking, trying to hold my sister still. "It's a really bad one. I don't know what to do. Make it stop. How do we make it stop? Help me, Oliver."

"I'll ring an ambulance," I said as I turned to bolt down the stairs.

"Come back. Use the phone here by the bed. And make them come now. They'll have to come right away."

The woman asked a load of pointless questions as the seconds ached on:

"Is there an adult with you?"

"Yes."

"How old is—?"

"Forty something."

"Not the adult."

"Fourteen, then. What? Oh, five."

"Is she still fitting?"

"Yes."

"How long?"

"I don't know. How long's she been like this, Mam?"

"God, I don't know… ages… a few minutes… I don't know."

"Are her airways restricted?" (Sounds stupid, but all I could think of was planes not being allowed to fly.)

"Yes."

"You're telling me she can't breathe?"

"No."

"Is she breathing?"

"Yes."

"You said her airways were restricted."

"No. She's breathing. She must be if she's having a fit, mustn't she?"

Mam shouted, "Just get them to come for pity's sake!"

"Please send some help as soon as possible; it's serious."

I positioned myself at the front gate, as Mam had asked me to go outside and wave to the ambulance in case it went past. She was losing it a bit because ours is the last house in a cul-de-sac, and if the ambulance had passed us, it would have crashed straight into a wall. Then Dad definitely would have gone ape because he'd just rebuilt it from Nathan destroying it with his skateboard ramps. After what seemed like ten hours, I heard the siren in the distance.

"It's here, Mam! It's coming!" I shouted to Mam upstairs as I jumped up the front step and ran back into the hallway. Once the ambulance was outside, a man sprang out and followed me up to Lily.

My heart stopped when we got to Mam's room: she was kneeling in front of Lily, her right hand clamped to her mouth. It was she who looked like a demon now, with desperate red eyes.

"It's stopped now," she said through sobs. "Everything's stopped." Lily was limp, lying on her back, her hair matted with sweat. "What's wrong? What's happened?"

The man took her pulse.

"She's okay. She's recovering," he said.

My jaw dropped open, and I fell sideways onto the doorframe, drunk with relief.

"But she's not moving," Mam said. "What's going on?"

"She's suffered a severe fit. She's exhausted."

I went down next to Mam and put my arm around her. "She'll be okay now, Mam. They'll probably take her in."

"Yes, we'll take her in," the man said. "They'll need to do tests and keep her under observation. Are you her mother? Can you come with us?"

"Yes. Of course I'm going with her."

"Mam, I'll come too."

"No, Oliver. You stay here, will you? Tell the others what's happening."

When turmoil hit our lives, Mam grasped at some semblance of order, and I became an item to be ticked on her 'normal-things-to-do' list. Life was upside down, but she had to keep some things the same, like telling me to do my homework and complaining about the stink in my room and the piles of glasses and crisp packets strewn about.

One particular day, about ten days after Lily was taken into hospital, I'd run all the way from school. I just wanted to clear my head, not talk with Kamal and not linger in the newsagents hoping Poppy Teasdale would turn up. I thought to catch Mam before she left for hospital, too, and find out exactly what was going on with Lily and have a bit of a chat, you know, see how she was coping.

When I arrived home, out of breath and clammy, Mam was at the front door, about to leave for hospital. I felt like barring her exit like some kind of bouncer, except, I suppose, bouncers usually stop you getting *in*, so… maybe like a guard in a prison or a mental institution or something.

"I'm in a rush," she said as she nudged past me like a stranger in a crowded street.

"Not got time for a cup of tea?"

"I have to meet the consultant. Cash on the table for chips [tick]. Get Dad to wash your shirts [tick]. And move those plants from the kitchen table [tick]."

"Hope he has good news then…" My words were drowned by the slam of the car door. I stepped back with the force of the explosion.

I wondered if she mostly forgot I existed. I know, I know—call me selfish, but there's some stuff you don't know yet. Anyway, I suppose Dad was at home a lot, in body that is, but his mind was in the hospital, too. The hospital's actual name is Newcastle Infirmary, by the way. Strange word, 'infirmary'; sounds like a factory. Patients in beds falling off the end of a conveyor belt into boxes to be sent to department stores and theatres and places where they need to buy people in beds.

I wanted Lily back home. The air in the house had grown stale over the long days empty of her. It didn't matter that I hated school when my welcome home was Lily and her cute stories about *her* school day: who'd been naughty, who was clever, that she'd got into trouble for hiding the whistle on family sports day, that Norman couldn't even fasten his own coat and always wanted to sit next to her on the carpet. She'd be home soon.

I had so many thoughts and spikey, cactus-type feelings. I know about plants, you see. I'm interested in the names and how they make me feel. You wouldn't know it looking at my patch in the garden. Put it this way: Dad says if I ever win a prize, it'll be for the tallest weed. Thing is, I like to put plants *into* the soil, not pull them out. I quite like weeds.

"Lily might have to stay in hospital for a *while* this time, they think," Dad told us late that evening at the kitchen table (not that this was the norm—the three of us having dinner with Mam and Dad. People did their own thing a lot in our house).

"You mean like a few more days?" Nathan asked.

"Could be anything, couldn't it… They don't know, do they?" Sam said.

"Could be weeks then," I said. "I wonder if she… She'll be out for Easter, surely. That's ages away, like three weeks or something."

"Oliver, we don't know. We'll find out more soon, but your mam's going to take some time off work so she can visit every day."

I wondered if Mam would've reacted the same had it been me in hospital. I'd overheard Auntie Colette talking to Mam once about the 'bad luck' of having three boys in a row. Said she'd never known anyone want a girl as much as Mam, and something like it was cruel, I think. Yeah, I'm pretty sure she actually used that word. Charming.

Mam had Sam, then after four years another boy, Nathan (their dad being a different dad from mine), then… wait for it, two years later, yet another son. Me. Anyway, took nine years, but Mam and Dad obviously got the daughter they longed for in the end. Everything felt properly balanced when she was born.

"With Mam being away, you'll have to do more round the house, you know," Dad said to us all.

"You think I'm gonna get Ollie to lift a finger in this place? He can't even lift his arse to bring his dirty plates and that down to the kitchen."

That's nothing new—Sam being on my case. You'd think he was a parent, except he doesn't want to live at home any more.

Nathan said, "I could cook more. I could make meal plans and take over Mam's cooking. They were amazing, those fajitas I made, remember? We could start getting the barbecue out as well."

"That was about two months ago," said Sam. "And the kitchen was like a bomb site."

"Well then, I'll do a rota for washing up as well. I'll do a cool sheet."

"We'll take it in turns, Nathan," said Dad. "That's a very helpful offer, though. We'll just all pull together, okay? Forget the barbecue, though. It *is* only March."

"I don't know what you're on about 'cooking plans' and 'rotas'—we don't really eat together anyway," said Sam. "We eat different meals at different times, don't we? Ollie's easy enough with his microwave burgers and all that rubbish."

Nathan said, "So could I make special simple meals for me and Ollie coz there's not much he eats?"

"He should sort his own grub out," said Sam. "Like I said, he doesn't eat like a normal person, so…"

"That's enough, Sam," Dad said.

"I'm just saying it doesn't make sense fussing over stupid people who are too lazy to—"

"Stop it!" Mam said. "D'you think I haven't got enough to worry about without you lot being vile to each other? And you two: I expect you to keep an eye on Oliver."

She seemed to think I was more likely to get into trouble looking up words, hanging out with Kamal, or planting seeds than Sam at The King's Head and Nathan skateboarding in Newcastle.

So we didn't know when Lily was coming home. And that meant Poppy Teasdale wouldn't be coming over to look after her either. My mam knows her mam; they live on our street. Poppy was in year ten, the year above me, and she loved Lily, and Mam seemed to love *her*. She worked in her mam's garden shop on Sundays, so I used to spend ages in there, choosing a plant or a packet of seeds. I always asked her advice, even though I knew she'd always say the same thing: "Look it up if you want." She'd plonk a huge plant encyclopaedia on the counter without even looking at me sometimes. Other times, she would be much more friendly and we'd joke on. We'd have a good laugh with daft plant-talk. She'd be perched behind the counter on a high stool, texting or reading an article in some girls' magazine. I'm not bad at reading upside down, so we'd sometimes read bits of her magazines together. Some of the stuff in there…! You get the normalish ones like 'Boy Problems Solved', and then you get the ones that someone must have made up like, 'My Best Friend's Massive Boobs Came Between Us'.

I wanted to talk to Poppy so much, but I never had much to say about her magazines and we usually ended up with little bursts of coded plant-speak. As communication goes, Poppy's and mine wasn't what you'd call smooth and flowing, so the shop wasn't exactly a hub of vibrant social intercourse, but at least it wasn't hospital.

Lily Laughing

We all went with Mam to the hospital twice a week during the first few weeks, but Dad usually came later, after work. I won't be calling it infirmary any more, by the way. I mean, you're not infirm if you're having a baby or donating blood or you're a rugby player who's broken his little toe or something. I think Mam considered me a pain in the rump when we were there. She thought I didn't care because I asked for snacks and drinks and stuff. I sat next to Lily's bed and found myself saying things like "How long are we staying?" Sam gave really useful responses like "We're here till we leave, okay?" and Nathan made daft suggestions like "I'll take you home on the train if you want."

It wasn't really boredom. It was something else. It's hard to explain, but it was something that felt a lot worse than being bored: looking at my sister lying in bed with tubes and machines and everything. A few weeks before, she'd been chasing me round the house with a hairbrush to hit me, laughing her head off, her tights halfway down her legs, her hair in pink ribbons. She'd shout my name… well, 'Oliber', which was near enough. I thought it sounded cute, except Dad had started calling me that and that just sounded annoying. Nowhere near as annoying as seeing Lily lying in bed hardly moving with a tube in her nose and one of those name label things round her wrist (as if she were going to run away?). I don't mean Lily—Lily wasn't annoying in any way. Nobody had made a diagnosis, so they were guessing at treatment. Watching my sister being ill and no one doing anything about it. She wasn't talking much at all, and we had to feed her as she was weak; but she didn't seem in pain or anything, and Nathan made her giggle a lot by tickling her and putting on funny voices. It brought colour to her face and a bit of hope to us. I was scared to touch her myself in case I hurt her.

But it was the place as well and the smell—a sickly mix of ill people, gravy, and bleach. And the noises: ten different TV programmes clashing, library voices, beeps, and rattling curtain hoops being pulled back and forth around beds. And just being in a room with so many sick children—trying not to stare but not being able to stop yourself. And the faded cartoon creeping around the walls with its laughing, clownish faces smashing into my mood.

On one visit, when I'd been sitting at Lily's bed so still for so long that somebody could have painted me, her whole body jerked, and her podgy face twitched into a smile. It made her cry, and Sam ran to get a nurse. Another fit.

"Is she okay, Mam? Does this happen a lot?" I asked, as Mam jumped up to put her hand on Lily's head and stroke it.

"I wish I could tell you. Someone'll tell us soon."

Nobody knew, you see—I mean, whether she was okay or not. Nobody even knew what was wrong with her, and we were all desperate to find out.

The fit passed quickly, which was such a relief because I'll tell you, you haven't a clue what to do when it's happening, apart from scream inside. When I kissed her goodbye, I felt sure she let out a sigh—very soft like a bird, but a faint sigh nevertheless, and I knew this meant she was okay for now.

She wasn't fat, by the way. I mean, I know I said before that Lily's face was podgy, but that was because of all the drugs she'd been taking. She wasn't a drug *addict*, of course, like someone on cocaine or heroine—let's face it, she was only five. No, I mean lots of medication. She didn't swallow tablets or anything; she had medicine injected into her body. I must say, her arms and legs *did look* like a drug addict's: covered in bruises where they'd pierced her skin with needles. They kept trying new things out because they really didn't know what was wrong with her. I couldn't stop my eyes burning every time I saw the bruises. I wanted to punch the person who'd given her them. "You touch her again and you're dead! Completely and totally dead, you bastard!" But I just stood there, pathetic, like a weeping fig.

Mam and Dad got so frustrated when the nurse said a consultant would speak to them before we left, but after ages, no one came.

Everything seemed to take so long, and arrangements changed all the time. The waiting-to-get-results hours went on forever. When I'd been there the week before, a nurse had said, "The consultant's coming to discuss the findings at five." Five o'clock passed, then quarter past, half past, and then finally, at six, a different nurse tapped up to us and said, "The consultant had an emergency, so he'll drop by tomorrow morning some time."

I say a nurse 'tapped' up to us because the floors were so smooth and hard that shoes, even with the softest soles, couldn't help producing a tapping or squelching sound. Come to think of it, hospitals would be quite good places for tap-dancing, though I don't imagine much of it goes on. If an old man were groaning in pain and a nurse were tap-dancing past his bed, it wouldn't seem right. Or if a nurse was collecting a full bedpan and she tap-danced out of the ward, she'd splash its contents all over the place, onto people's dinners and grapes and get-well cards. "I've brought ye a wee bunch o' grapes" would take on new meaning.

Dad said he'd take us all home while Mam waited to see the consultant, but I was allowed to stay with her. This was the first time Mam had left me alone with Lily. When the nurse said she'd have to wait another hour, Mam's head dropped backwards, and she throated air out of her mouth, like a deep-sea diver, and sat like that, staring at the ceiling for about twenty seconds. When she eventually dropped her head forwards a hundred and eighty degrees, so that now she looked at the floor, she said, "I'm going outside," in a croaky voice only just audible. She did that a lot, went outside. There was a bit of a garden to go to (a soothing distraction from illness) and different air—'fresh air' as Mam called it—to break the sameness of sitting in the hospital ward. There was nothing particularly fresh about the air. It was in Newcastle-upon-Tyne city centre, so 'you do the math,' as they say in America. What's more, the 'fresh air' she was taking included smoking loads of cigarettes.

It always surprised me how many people stood just outside the hospital doors, smoking. Just seemed messed up, you know—doing something that might make you ill or even die outside a place where people are ill or even die. The week before, when we were sitting in the car outside the hospital with Dad, waiting to take Mam home, Sam said, "Look at that idiot! He's wearing pyjamas, attached to a drip, and he's dragging on a rollie."

"Urgh, gross!" Nathan said, when the man spluttered out a cough. You know, that revolting, phlegmy sound people make when their bodies are full of gunge.

I wanted to tell the man he *wasn't* an idiot and it *wasn't* his fault, but instead, I imagined how his life had brought him to this state. He looked depressed, so I imagined him at his mother's funeral, pouring tears and smoke onto the flowers he'd bought for her. And now, not long before the earth would swallow him up, too, he looked frail and stooped, like a weeping birch, staring through the drizzle, attached to a drip, attached to a cigarette, wearing his pyjamas, outside Newcastle Hospital. I prayed to God Mam wouldn't end up like that.

Anyway, when Mam went out for some 'fresh air,' she left me alone with Lily, who had apparently had a good day, though it didn't seem like that to me because she still wasn't walking again or anything.

She was asleep anyway, so I sat on the chair next to the bed with my drink and got out a book Auntie Colette had just sent me called *Tree Wisdom*. At first glance, I had thought it was a general book about trees, but it turned out to be somewhat unusual and was subtitled *The Definitive guidebook to the myth, folklore and healing power of trees*. She probably just bought anything with the word 'tree' in the title. I'm lucky I didn't get something like, 'Researching your Family Tree' or 'How to make a Pair of Clogs out of a Tree.' I glanced through the book and it seemed on the weird side, but I did think there was probably something in the idea that plants and trees could heal since they have a positive effect on people. I glanced round the ward to see how many plants they had and just as I was thinking *Blimey! There aren't any at all, or even flowers!* Nurse Celia came over.

"What you thinking? You've got your thinking eyes in," she said.

"There are no plants in here. Not even flowers... I don't get it," I said, and to my amazement, she started singing, 'You Don't Bring me Flowers Anymore'!

"It's not funny though really, is it?" I said while smiling.

"They're not allowed these days; the idea's to stop infections spreading due to high counts of bacteria in the water et cetera. Load of tosh if you ask me. Ooh I shouldn't say that!"

"But plants and flowers are to lift the spirits. It's so obvious—"

"Well the patients have me. *I'll* have to be their flower."

And I'd say she was. Her middle name was even Dahlia—fact. She pushed me affectionately when I said that Celia Dahlia sounded ridiculous, but that the shorter version, CD, sounded worse, though it suited her as it was kind of old-fashioned like her.

I didn't usually feel comfortable speaking to strangers, but there was something about Celia that made it easy. Even though her hair was trying to be neat, up in a bun thing, there were always dark brown wispy bits sticking out all over the place. She had a sort of straggly poise, like a late-summer sweet white violet and a voice that could send you to sleep.

She told me I'd better not start calling her CD, which is like telling a kid not to eat the ice-cream while you leave the room. She asked how I was. I hadn't answered when Lily woke up. She told me I should play with my sister on the soft mat. 'Play?' What was I supposed to do?

She unhooked Lily from a machine and lifted her from the bed, placing her on a grubby-looking large foam cushion, just the right shape to support her. I stayed sitting on the chair, looking down at Lily. She wasn't moving, which was good because it meant at least she wasn't jerking with the fits. But even though she was still and quiet now, I didn't want to see her like that either. She did seem to be looking, though. Not at me, just up at the ceiling. I know it sounds weird, but I had a sudden urge to scream, "I want my money back! She doesn't work any more!" She used to cling onto my back when I lumped around the living room like an elephant, and now she hardly seemed to be clinging on at all.

I felt a strong pain in my throat.

"Go on. Go and sit with her. She's in a good mood, isn't she?" Nurse Celia said, taking my can from me. So I did. Once I was down there, I rested my hand on her messy hair as gently as I could. It was damp and sticky from little pads she'd had stuck on for a brain scan that morning.

"Her hair's growing a lot isn't it?" I said.

"So's yours! How d'you get it boofed up on top but somehow hiding those lovely blue eyes of yours? I don't know, you kids. I'll bring my hair kit in if you'd like. I'm a hairdresser on the side."

"It's okay, thanks."

"And look at the length of her eyelashes! You've got them, too, haven't you, Oliver?" she said, sweeping my hair up and back off my face. Very bodyish, nurses are. I suppose they're so used to touching people that it's all in a day's work for them, but I wished she wouldn't do it.

"Are all nurses a bit obsessed with bodies?"

I managed a smile when she laughed so loudly that she woke up the boy in the next bed and then bit her bottom lip and flung her hand to her mouth.

"You could say bodies are my bread and butter," she said through her fingers.

"You sound like a contract killer."

That time her laugh got *me* going, and we didn't stop till another, more-senior-looking nurse called her to the office.

I turned back to Lily and put out my fingers, sweeping her hair back now, just like Celia had done with me. Lily's cheeks used to be rosy, but today they were pale and puffed. I knew she would get better, but I wanted it to happen quickly. I wished miracles had been my thing. I would have said, "Take up thy bed and walk," and she'd have turned to me, all sweet, natural smiles, raised herself up, proud and strong, and tapped and twirled her way across the shiny floor in her pink clothes my mam loved to buy her. I felt a wave of anger, and for a moment, I just wanted to run, to get out of there, but instead I went to give her a hug and found myself rolling about with her and tickling her like mad, as I used to before she got ill. And then... she laughed a huge laugh, much louder than her giggles earlier on! My throat started hurting again, but in a different way. That was a new level of energy. A good sign.

I was looking forward to telling Mam about Lily laughing, but in the ten minutes she was away, she'd missed (you guessed it) the consultant's visit. She'd have to wait *again* to find out what was wrong with Lily. I thought she'd go crazy when I told her, but she just shrugged her shoulders saying, "Yep. That's how it works."

I had to look away because I didn't believe her, I mean, believe that she wasn't angry. She looked at me in an odd way with a weird, blank face. I didn't know what to say. She didn't even comment on Lily being on the mat till I pointed it out. She dropped her head into her hand and said it was time to leave. I wanted to give Mam a hug, but I couldn't spoil her efforts to be strong. I hugged Lily instead and kissed her puffy cheek before leaving.

The thought of sitting in school all the next day, waiting to hear what was wrong with Lily...

"It's so mental that they can't tell us, isn't it, Mam? So frustrating."

Mam must have been mega-tired because she just said, "You're making me depressed. Let's get out of here."

Celia-mail 1

Dear Mam,

Rushing this email as my ward shift starts at five and I've laddered my tights on the bike again, so I'll have to nip into Newcastle. I'll stick to my promise of writing every other day, but they might be boring or on the brief side! And yes, we're coming to your eightieth party, Mam, you sausage. It was me who suggested it—remember? They seem lovely there, so we'll have a nice time.

Sad day yesterday, as that little girl died. I think I told you she'd been ill a long time. A little darling she was. It's so heartbreaking every time, Mam. Like you say, though, at least I'm with kids all day, and well, it doesn't look like anything's happening with Joe and me. You had me so late though. Surely I might be the same.

Swings and roundabouts though, because that little treasure, Lily, with the prettiest curly mop and great long eyelashes, seems to be perking up. I can't say anything. Just a feeling, like I tend to get, Mam. I love that name, Lily. Do you?

Her mam's in all the time. She's got a lot of anger, like they usually do, but I wish she'd cry more because there's a lot pent up there. The dad and three big brothers come in a fair bit. It's hard to keep your eyes off them because they're all so handsome! The youngest boy's got something about him, but he seems depressed. Oliver. Funny, that's the name I was going to give to, well, you know. With any luck, the little one will get better, and the mam'll come round and catch him before he starts sinking. What am I like?! Notice everything, me, and can't help my earwigging! You used to tell me I could hear the grass growing, remember?

Next time I'm in, I'll have a word about that man in the room next door to you. Is he still watching Jerry Springer at full volume? At least it sounds like he's on his last legs.

Much love,

Celia x

Pratt and Prejudice

Not that I've ever liked school, but when Lily was in hospital, I so didn't want to be there. The Monday after the day Lily laughed, though, something extraordinary happened. Well, *two* extraordinary things, in fact.

I walked in with Kamal; we always went to school together.

"Do you even see the point of going to school at all, Kamal?"

"An outside chance one might learn something of benefit? Your sister okay?"

"Not really, but she's getting better."

"Did they find—"

"No."

"But I thought—?"

"No."

"Oh."

Kamal could talk, as in *talk*, but he somehow knew to restrain himself when it came to Lily.

"What's first on the menu, Ollibags?"

He had this knack of calling me something different more or less every day. I say 'knack,' but truth be told, it could be pretty annoying—sometimes felt funny, but mostly irritating. I had once told him that I liked the idea of a nickname, so he just kept trying loads out. I told him to drop it, but he's so stubborn.

I was his walking timetable. Despite his apparent genius in certain areas, he was a right div when it came to knowing where he was supposed to be from one minute to the next.

"PSHE," I told him. Personal, social, and health education. We mostly got nowhere during the lessons, just sat doing worksheets. The teacher ran hot and cold with it. Sometimes he was strict and keen to engage us in discussions; other times, he couldn't be bothered and even let us listen to music, like it wasn't a proper subject. So, in turn, a lot of the kids came to view it that way. *I* did, too, some of the time. Other times it seemed to be the most important subject of all. If it hit on a topic you wanted to shout about (not that *I* ever spoke up), it could be quite satisfying.

Kamal hated PSHE, but he *loved* acting. He wanted to be in a Shakespeare play. He read books all the time, and he did even actually read Shakespeare on his own as well! Maybe that's how he knew so many words. It's partly him who got me looking words up all the time. I don't know how he became so ambitious or how he has a clue about the future, but he says he's going to Oxford University to study 'History and Politics'. Big ideas for a skinny guy.

I wasn't surprised at Kamal's response to the news we were kicking off the day with PSHE.

"Waste of time. Mr. Wetherill. What a puttock! 'And what do you think about abortion?' 'Well, sir, I had quite a strong opinion about it till I met you!'"

"Ah, Kamal, that's mean... Anyway, what's a puttock?"

"Wonderful word, isn't it? From Shakespeare."

"It's just because he sent you out of class last week. What did you say again? 'I simply refuse to do this worksheet.' And that posh voice. Ha ha!"

"'*Worthless* worksheet,' Ollibags. Vital word, that. 'I refuse to do this *worthless* worksheet.' It was the 'worthless' that got his goat, don't you know?"

"So why didn't you just say 'worksheet,' you nutter?"

"Because I *wanted* to go out. Because it *was* a useless worksheet... And I wanted to make the *joke*. I mean, if he'd been in the right mood, he might've even cracked a smile."

"Why would he have smiled? You mucking up his lesson? Oh, and Matthew Murray falling off his chair, he was laughing that much!"

"Yes, but Matty Murray is wont to fall from his chair on a regular basis: sleep-induced tumbling by all accounts. And it's not a case of narcolepsy—snooker to blame. Plays till four in the morning, his brother informs me. Anyway, Wetherill *should* have smiled. I refused to do the sheet because it was entitled 'Using Assertiveness Skills.' I refuse to do...? Get it?"

"Oh, right."

"God, there's not much hope for you if it takes you a week to get a joke! When he came outside to do his, 'Well? I'm waiting?' routine, with his hands on his hips, I thought at least I'd be able to explain myself and he'd see the funny side of it, but he said, 'I've had just about enough of your pathetic little jokes. If you think you're so clever, why don't *you* take the lesson?'"

I thought to myself that Kamal would have *jumped* at the chance to take the class.

"I'd have jumped at the chance to take the class," he said. "I should've said, 'Ooh! Yes please, sir! I'll do 'Bullying' if that's okay? Would you mind being in my role-play, sir?' but of course, he didn't want an answer. I hate that power thing with the rhetorical questions when you're not supposed to answer, and the pregnant pauses. 'What if I kept the whole class in over break?' Pause. 'How would you feel if I cancelled the whole trip?' Pause. 'Why don't you tell the whole class what's so funny?' Pause. And they're not even meaty rhetorical questions like 'What is the world coming to?' or 'How much longer must they suffer this injustice?' just pathetic teacher ones."

"Yeah, I know. Pregnant? What d'you mean, pregnant?"

"Who?"

"You said 'pregnant pause' or something."

"Ah, from Shakespeare, my dear Ollibags. Heavy with meaning."

When I asked Kamal if Mr. Wetherill had given him a detention, he said, "Do the bears shit in the woods?"

Once registration was over, we made our way to Mr. Wetherill's room. A tap on my shoulder just outside the door. Poppy Teasdale. Apart from "hi," we didn't really speak to each other at school. I felt so embarrassed, like people were shielding their eyes from the intense glow from my body. I imagined her saying, "Do you know that you've had an extreme allergic reaction to something?" like that advert on TV when the guy's told he's been burgled when he hasn't and his house is just really messy.

"How's Lily? She coming out soon?"

Beads of sweat formed above my lip and I needed to take a deep breath. "Um… Yes… I mean, um, no, she… Sorry, what?"

"*Lily*. She okay? How's she doing?"

"Yes."

"How is she?"

"I'm seeing her Wednesday."

"Oh, okay."

"She was better last week, I think."

"Oh, great."

"Blooming."

"Ah, that's great news. Five-star."

"Yeah, blooming like a pink polyanthus." I felt like a right git saying that, but words seemed to be just coming out of my mouth.

"Sounds good. She talking?"

"She laughed actually."

"Five-star! You will let me know when she comes out, won't you? Cool. See you, Ollie."

She turned to go.

"See you, Poppy." In my mind, my arms grabbed her back and spun her round to face me. In real life, I stood watching her move further and further away in slow motion, her ponytail dancing on her rare head, like yellow whitlow grass spouting from limestone, bobbing in the wind. I imagined myself a bee, nestling there, pollinating.

Kamal could see I was in a trance and acting weird. I said, "The way she said, 'See you, Ollie'… "

"Mellifluous," Kamal said.

"Hmm?"

"Mellifluous. Never mind. Are you sure she wasn't saying, 'See you, wally'?"

Once in the classroom, PREJUDICE was written on the board in huge letters. This was a new method. He didn't normally go in for writing much on the board; he just sat at his desk, sipping caffeine and poking his nose. *This could be good*, I thought. But I realised that it would only be good if we had a different teacher, which made it all the more surprising when a woman I didn't recognise walked in. She had dishevelled, short red hair and wore smart red trousers and a purple blouse. She was like a walking fuchsia.

A sparkle in her eye, a spring in her step, she started with "Hi, guys. Your usual teacher's on a course, so I'm afraid you're stuck with me this morning—Miss Pratt."

She wrote her name on the board. Only Darren Cragley laughed. She even told us her first name—Patricia. I was amazed no one pointed out the cute notion of 'Pat Pratt.'

Pleasant enough introduction. She hadn't sat down, and she hadn't even called us 'Nine B'. It got better: instead of asking us loads of questions or passing round sheets or getting us to read or more or less ignoring us, she started telling us about herself.

Intrigued though I was as Miss Pratt began, my mind wandered. I hadn't told Poppy about Lily's tests that never seemed to prove anything. I was trying not to think about that. Thing is, I hadn't told anyone about Lily laughing, yet I'd just told Poppy. What was that about? And what the heck was happening with me? I'd been friends with Poppy since I was about six, but, I don't know, something was definitely changing. She had started making me feel weird— mushy and pathetic. And had I detected a smidgen of awkwardness in her? What did that mean? She'd come to find me. She'd found out what lesson I was going into and had chopped her way through the undergrowth to get to me… Well, actually, I suppose I was only next door to her form room, but still, she had made the effort to speak to me. I'd have to go and find *her* if Lily got out of hospital that week. How would I look cool? I could maybe gulp down a huge icy drink beforehand. Would that stop me blushing? Maybe I'd write her a note instead! No. That would be lame… I'd ask Kamal what to do.

I tuned back into the lesson.

"Yes, I'd always wanted to be a teacher, so I was excited before the interview. And it was my first choice of university."

After Miss Pratt's interview, which she told us had gone well, she explained that she'd left the room, but something made her stop at the door and listen to what they had to say. She told us that the room had been at the top of some steep stairs and that nobody was around. There had been three interviewers, and she heard one of them say, "Did you notice she was wearing trousers?" to which a woman responded, "And your point?" The man came back with, "Well it's not very ladylike; I much prefer women to wear skirts at interviews... and in schools, for that matter. She's obviously something of a rebel, probably a troublemaker—can spot them a mile off."

Miss Pratt stopped. The class were silent—a bit like one of those pauses Kamal had mentioned, only this was different. You could see she wasn't desperate for pity or for us to like her or think she was clever: she just wanted us to think and question.

"Wanker!" shouted Jade Hilton. No one laughed. There was another one of those pauses, but different again. She always had to spoil things, Jade. She'd just come off report for throwing a fish finger at a dinner lady, and now this. Actually, she wouldn't have been found out because the fish finger got skewered on a hairpin and wasn't even noticed, but Darren Cragley snitched on her.

"Me or the interviewer?" asked Miss Pratt.

Now, everyone *did* laugh, with relief as much as anything else.

"That loser, Miss, who dissed you just for wearing trousers. Ah, my God. Can't stand things like that!"

"Why?" Miss Pratt asked, by now sitting on the desk, leaning forward, head tilted to the left and eyes screwed up, like she really, really wanted to know.

"Coz he was so, like, judging you, Miss, and that is, like, so wrong."

"Maybe he had a point? Perhaps I should have worn a skirt."

"No way, Miss! He was bang out of order. End of. I mean, he's sitting there, right, and you're, like, all nervous, giving it your best, and he's, like, not even listening! He's not seeing you nor nowt. Is he seeing you for what you are? I don't think so! He's looking at your clothes, for God's sake! What was he on? He's judging you on your kit, and I bet you was right smart anyway, Miss, like you are now. Sexist pig. And the woman should have stuck up for you, daft cow!"

"What's your name?" Miss Pratt asked.

I thought, *She's going to put her on report again for bad language*—which would have been a shame because I'd never heard Jade Hilton say that much ever in any lesson—but she said:

"Jade, well done. Smashing that you used the word, 'judging,' because that's *exactly* what we're talking about—judging people before you know anything about them. Pre-judging. 'Prejudice.' Do you see?" (Jade's nodding madly.) "Just be careful of your language, Jade, especially negative words about women; there are too many of those about, but great ideas. I love your spirit."

Jade recognised this as a compliment and looked chuffed.

"Yes?" Miss said, pointing at Alex Beaumont.

"Did you get on the course, Miss?" Alex's hand had been up ever since Miss Pratt had finished her story.

He didn't usually say anything at *all* in lessons.

"No. They didn't accept me."

The class took in a collective breath. Naz Khan looked horrified and asked, "But what about the other two? They must have, like, liked you, Miss, didn't they? Didn't they say anything?"

Then I heard Kamal shuffle in his chair next to me. That always meant he was about to say something profound. I so admire his confidence. I can never work out how he became so sure of himself in spite of what has happened to him in his life.

"Sometimes the cruellest people get their own way," he started. "They use fear and manipulation. That's how bullies function. Psychopaths. Hitler, bully of the twentieth century, got ordinary people to hate Jews, even kill them. This is a small-scale example. People follow tyrants because at least it's not *them* being persecuted."

"Give it a rest, Kamal! We only on about trousers, man!" Jade said.

"What's *your* name?" asked Miss Pratt.

"Kamal, Miss."

"You think a lot, don't you?"

"Someone's got to."

Their interactions started to sound like an American detective show, but Miss seemed quite taken with him.

"Excellent. Excellent talk, Kamal. You read a lot, do you?"

Then it happened: the first time I've ever said anything much at all in class, never mind something like *this*. The words had stuck in my mind from before and I heard myself saying:

"Does Kamal read a lot? Do the bears shit in the woods?"

Everyone howled, and my eyes watered. I suppose I was proud of speaking out and excited, but quickly scared, too. I looked round at the contorted faces. Slow motion. Then my eyes panned back to Miss Pratt.

"What's *your* name?" she asked, with a straight face.

"Oliver, Miss… and…" I wasn't sure how to play it. I'd gone too far, and my eyes suddenly felt watery in an *embarrassed* way. "I'm sorry, Miss."

Yet another one of those pauses before Miss said, "Good use of rhetorical question, Oliver."

My jaw dropped open in double surprise. Kamal and I looked at each other, our open jaws turning into open-mouthed smiles. How did she know Kamal had—? I suppose it was just one of those days.

I felt so sort of included in that lesson, so part of the whole thing. It was brilliant to just not think about stuff for a while. We got on to all sorts of topics: goths, rap music, TV shows like *Family Guy*, *The Simpsons*, *The Inbetweeners*, *Waterloo Road*, and *Hannah Montana* (Kamal had to point out that the word "Hannah" was a palindrome—the same forwards as backwards—at which Miss Pratt practically wet herself), *Playboy* merchandise, accents, burkas, mini-skirts, women priests, and wearing trousers halfway down your arse. And we didn't write anything at all. Miss said we'd have to write something for homework to prove she'd taught us. She must have forgotten to give us any because I don't recall doing it. One of my most memorable lessons, and it was as if it didn't exist because there was no 'evidence' of it. It was the first time I remember feeling confident in class. Would people like me more if I weren't shy? Perhaps I *could* go out with Poppy. Maybe I *could* tell Mam how I felt. Was there a chance I could be in a band, perform on stage? Exciting prospects opened up like a packet of all-red-and-black Fruit Pastels.

At break time, I explained my Poppy dilemma to Kamal. He rubbed his chin for about two seconds then said, "She adores Lily, doesn't she? Invite her to go to the hospital with you. I'm surprised she hasn't been yet."

Genius.

Don't Blame Lily

Even though we'd had Games after Break, by lunch I was still buzzing from PSHE and thought to strike while the iron was hot. I'd go up to Poppy Teasdale, bold as brass, and come out with my invitation. I was just her friend anyway, so it would be a totally okay thing to do.

I told Kamal of my confident mood. He reminded me that it wasn't exactly a date, going to visit my sick sister in hospital, and to keep a lid on it. Trust him to dampen my spirits just when I was getting all revved up. I went up to Poppy, who was, much to my relief, on her own, playing tennis against a wall. Clutching onto the cool, confident mood, I tried to call her, but nothing came out of my mouth. Watching her floating about with her racket reminded me of how much I'd love to impress her. I wished I could be good at something.

I shouted, "You on a team or something? You're good."

Had I really come out with that? Not bad.

Kamal was hiding behind some greenery, and at hearing my attempt to get her attention, a Kamal-shaped bush gave me the thumbs up. But no response from Poppy.

"I just said, are you on—?" I tried again.

The Kamal-bush interrupted with a violent shake and a rapidly-waggling-side-to-side finger.

"What?" I loud-whispered.

"Music!" Kamal said.

"I'm not singing, you loon!"

"No, stupid, she's listening to music. You'll have to go and tap her on the shoulder. Go on! Make haste!"

I was starting to feel about as bold as a mouse at a cat's cheese-and-milk party. The heat and the sweat and the breathing returned.

"Look, *I'll* go and tap her and dart to the side, so that you'll be all she sees when she turns around, okay?" Kamal said.

Just as I was agreeing, from nowhere pounced a year eleven boy, Callum Gaskin, who clenched Poppy round the waist, knocking her to the ground. My ears stung, and I took in a sharp breath. I shouted, "Hey! Leave her alone!" I had to listen to him being foul to her:

"Come here! I'll give you better fun than you've ever had against a wall!"

"Get off, you creep!" she shouted.

He pulled her up by the wrist and slammed her against the wall. He flung her racket away, which snapped on a tree, and her ball went to find a new life.

I stood, frozen to the spot. Kamal to the rescue. He leapt from behind the bush.

"Thou bawdy beef-witted barnacle! Thou goatish rug-headed lout!"

Callum swung round. "What the—? Is that even English—?!"

While Callum was distracted by Kamal's insultathon, Poppy pushed him aside and ran for it.

Kamal said to him, "From Shakespeare. And no, that's not the name of a band. Well it probably is but—"

Kamal wasn't expecting the comeback:

"What? *The Paki of Venice*?!"

To say Callum Gaskin had surprised him is an understatement, but Kamal stood his ground and said, "No, nor *The Two Jerks of Verona*, *The Merry Twits of Windsor*, or *The Taming of the Schnook*."

"Weirdo! Go back to Pakiland, you revolting little orphan knob," Callum said as he looked to see where Poppy had got to and strutted away when he couldn't see her.

I stood in disgust at how Poppy had been treated and how Kamal had been treated. How did Callum even know about…? I felt completely useless that I hadn't stopped it. It was hard to believe just how badly wrong a romantic venture could go. But all that came out of my mouth was "Schnook?"

Kamal, apparently unfazed by the clash with Callum, said, "Plan B, methinks."

"Sorry, mate, I should've… I'm useless. I wish—"

"Plan B, my man. Good name for a band, that."

We didn't get round to plan B.

When I got home after school, Poppy was in the kitchen with Mam; Poppy was admiring a design my mam had just finished drawing. I tried to regain the confidence I'd felt that morning, but I was beginning to hate myself for my wimpy reactions to seeing her.

"Ah, there you are, Oliver. I've asked Poppy to come to visit Lily tomorrow. The others are going to see a film," said Mam.

"That looks great," I said, tilting my head to get a proper look at Mam's art work. "So intricate. Would be cool on the front of a card… What? What film?"

"It's just a doodle; I find it relaxing. You're too young for the film. And I've told you: chocolate makes your zits worse. Where did you get that huge black hoodie? That's not a heavy metal band is it, Volcom? Anyway, you'll show her round, won't you, at the hospital?"

"Skating," I said.

"It's a make of skateboard clothing, Mrs. Campbell," said Poppy.

Just then the phone rang. As Mam answered it and took the receiver outside with a cigarette, I put my bag down and went to the fridge for some juice. *Show her round*, I repeated in my head; what a tour that would be. It was just the wrong expression, you know? "Come on, I'll *show you round* my prison cell. I'll *show you round* the torture chamber."

"Want some juice?" I asked Poppy.

"Got some, ta."

I went to the biscuit tin. "D'you want a biscuit?"

She pointed to a crumb-speckled plate in front of her. I decided to go upstairs. I really wanted to be in the room with her, but I was starting to feel awkward and stupid.

I was walking out of the kitchen with my drink when Poppy said, "You're always messing with your hair."

"What?"

"You've always got a hand in your hair, haven't you?"

"Dunno. Have I? Suppose so."

"I saw you today."

"I know."

Just as I was considering the horrible possibility that she not only hardly ever noticed me, but hadn't even remembered talking to me that morning, she added, "You and Kamal said something to Callum."

"Oh, that. Yeah. Were you okay? He hurt you, didn't he?"

"He was so annoyed. Really angry. He's such a creep. It was well funny."

"Funny? Oh. Did he tell you what Kamal said?"

"Neh. Saw him ranting with his mates and kicking someone's bag, the idiot."

"*Dangerous* idiot. Poisonous. Like Atropa belladonna."

"What? Oh, isn't that Deadly—?"

"Deadly nightshade. Yeah. Causes nausea, you know, makes you sick."

It felt powerful, making her laugh.

"Especially the young plants," I said.

"Can it be fatal, then? I mean because of *deadly*?" she asked.

"Yeah it can be… for sure. Did he say sorry, by the way?"

Poppy laughed and asked if I was joking. Needless to say, I felt like a prize dork once more and felt my blood, as an enemy, rushing to attack my face.

"No, Ollie. I just mean Callum's always like that. He's always messing on."

"So you don't mind?"

"Well, I do but, I dunno. It's kind of like attention, isn't it?"

"You don't want attention like that, though, do you? Anyway you must get plenty of attention."

"I don't really know what you mean. No, I don't. I mean, you know, I don't like that, and no, I don't really think… Anyway, I dunno what you mean."

I felt the confidence I'd felt in PSHE that morning resurging. I started to slip into a fresh mode: 'feeling almost normal talking to Poppy Teasdale.' I walked up to the table and put my drink on it.

"You must get loads of attention because, well, you're so confident, and you're good at everything and—"

Enter Mama.

"Could you go to the shops for me please, Oliver? Sorry, Poppy, I had to take that. And I meant to say please take those bits of dead plants or whatever they are off the kitchen table!"

Of course they weren't dead anythings. I swear she took some perverse pleasure in winding me up. Maybe it took away from the pain of Lily. With that thought, I decided to say nothing. Mam asked me to get some bread and milk, and Poppy said she'd walk with me on the way back home. She only lived four doors away so we would have had time for about three sentences, but she said she'd come with me to the shops. It was so much easier talking while walking: being outside, going the same way, the movement, and not looking at each other. Kamal told me philosophers used to teach like that—walking along. Poppy said,

"I'm not, you know. I'm not as confident as I seem. I am in a way, but well, people don't like it necessarily... girls."

"And boys?"

"I don't care about boys."

Now it was my turn to laugh. Boys swarmed around her at school. And the way she looked: her hair, make-up, clothes. Her whole way of acting really. You could just tell. It was obvious she wanted that attention from boys, and she got it. She did admit that she did sort of care about boys, but said she seemed to attract the wrong sort. *Charming*, I thought. At that, my enemy-blood returned to my face, but she couldn't see me, so it didn't matter. It occurred to me then how great it would be to write to her, like via email or something, or even letters—not having to let her see me.

On the way back from the shop I said, "Sorry I was useless, you know, with Callum today."

"You did shout at him. Most people are threatened by him, and they don't usually say *anything*, so at least you said something. He's a dickweed, anyway."

"A stinking willy!"

"Shut up! That's not a plant!"

"Yeah, honestly, it really is. I'll show you in the book on Sunday."

"Five-star! Amazing, Ollie."

When I said goodbye at her door, it felt wrong, like we should have hung out and talked for hours. "Amazing," she'd said. Is that really what she'd said? I knew it was "Amazing" comma "Ollie," but it played over and over in my head as "Amazing Ollie" without a comma in sight. During our ten minutes together, I took every glance, half-smile, flick of the hair, touch of the face to mean she must like me. At least a bit. Well, I knew she liked me, but I mean, you know, I hoped she *liked* me. You know what I mean.

So, this particular grey Wednesday evening, Dad had taken Nathan and Sam to see a film, and it was hospital for Mam, Poppy, and me.

It's funny, I was so used to the taste of the hospital, I didn't notice it any more; but this time with Poppy, everything about the place shouted itself. The swearing began before we'd even parked. We rarely found a parking spot easily.

"Piss off. You're not welcome here!" the hospital mocked.

Mam added to the general feeling of agitation: "Jesus! Is it not bad enough without this? No spaces again! Sorry, Poppy. It's just so maddening. Every time…! Oliver, jump out and take Poppy in, will you? I'll have to try round the other side. God almighty. Every time. Why? Uuuuh!"

I saw the hospital through Poppy's eyes now. Concrete. Grey. It spoke to us:

"Forget about smiling now. Be smothered with my greyness. Be serious. Be spaced out."

"It's not an art gallery or a flower shop," I said to Poppy as I led her on the road to the brain ward.

"You like art galleries?"

"I didn't say I *liked* art galleries; I'm just saying it won't be perfume or pretty pictures that overwhelm you in this place."

It took me by surprise when she laughed. "*I* like art galleries. I'm going on that London trip with your year coz I missed it last year."

"Oh good. Yeah, the art trip in May. We're looking forward to that, Kamal and me… I do, too."

"Do what?"

"Like art."

"I thought you said—"

"Not *all* of it. Look! What's with that, for instance?" I pointed to a new row of paintings. Kids' paintings. Desperate attempt to jolly the place up, like a clown's last trick for an unmoved audience.

"They're bright enough, aren't they? Who likes all of anything, anyway?" Poppy said.

"I like nothing about this," I said, sweeping my right arm out in an arc.

"It's not that bad, Ollie. And think of the five-star doctors and nurses here. "

"Yeah, imagine being so clever and caring and working in a place like *this*? It even smells grey. D'you know what I mean?"

Having swung open the head-injury saloon doors, I pointed to where Lily was. My heart did its usual messed-up beating, and I took my usual sharp breath in. I didn't want to stretch Poppy's space, so as she approached the bed, I explained to the nurse who she was and that my mam was on her way. I was glad it was Nurse Celia—Viola alba (Latin name for sweet violet). She was a glug of water on a twenty-mile jog, an opened window in a summer-exam room, a ping on a microwave oven. She sort of read my mind, too:

"Let her have a few moments, eh, sweetheart?" then immediately hugged me into her, touching my head and scraping her over-washed fingers through my hair. She held my gaze, and for a split second I thought of tucking an unruly straggle of her hair back into her bun, but only a mad second like when you think of things you wouldn't do in a million years, like throwing a baby out of a window.

"I'd love to get my scissors to your mop! Have you got taller since last week? I don't know, you young boys. Hey, listen to this, Oliver: Lily spoke today. How 'bout that?"

"You're kidding! What did she say?"

"You're not going to believe this. She said, 'Where's Mammy and Daddy?' and I told her they'd be visiting soon, then when I was doing her hair a few minutes later, she said, 'Where's Oliver?'"

"Oh my God. And she said 'Oliver' did she, not 'Oliber'?"

"You've got me there. She did. She did actually say 'Oliber.' You're like me, you are—listen to everything."

I did an odd thing. I hugged Celia back. Then I felt awkward and pulled away before focusing on Poppy. Both of her hands were covering her face. I ran over, and she put her arms around me and started to cry. It was hug city. I didn't feel embarrassed or anything because being near Lily in her borrowed bed made me feel kind of steady.

"I thought you said she was better. She looks so... She doesn't look... I can't believe it. She's so brave, Ollie."

She was. And she was beautiful too, I thought as I gazed upon her. I didn't 'think' that word very often, but what a word it was. If words could win awards, it would boast a gold rosette. My beautiful sister who was getting better. Who had spoken. My heart was about to burst through my clothes and dance around the ward. And Poppy being sad was somehow beautiful too. I imagined scooping her and Lily up, flying out of the window to a soft, warm, safe place and looking after them both for eternity.

When Mam arrived on the ward, she kissed Lily, patted Poppy and me on the back, and chatted to Celia. She handed Celia the picture she had made to put on the wall behind Lily's bed. I was dying to see Mam's face when I told her the news, but apart from smiling, she didn't go over the top or anything or carry on the hug-fest. She was probably a bit shocked.

"She's getting better, Mam. We can bring her home soon."

"Don't make things up. I'm not sure about that. What makes you think you can decide anything anyway?"

"What? I just thought—"

"Well, you thought wrong, Oliver. It's small steps here, and if she does come home she'll need a lot of care and a quiet, peaceful house. I'm going outside again."

Poppy said, "Don't be embarrassed. She's just really worried, Ollie. I can't imagine what it's like for her."

I could imagine very well because I was worried, too. Worried about Lily. Worried about Mam. But Lily was obviously getting better. I'd thought Mam would be ecstatic.

While she was away, I tickled Lily and spoke to her a lot. Like I said, I'd been afraid of hurting her when she first got ill, but now I knew her speech was coming back, I was desperate to get some sort of reaction from her. It's peculiar, but I talked more to Lily when Poppy was there. She spoke to her, too, asked questions, and even sang a little song. This from someone who professed not to be that confident! At the end of her song, she nuzzled into Lily, and I was mega cheered up when Lily laughed and said, "Oliber's here. Poppy's here."

I didn't tell Mam about Lily laughing and talking because as soon as she came back in, she went to see a boy in another bed. This kid,

Lewis, I think he was called, had a head injury from being beaten up, but the nurse had told us he was rarely visited, so Mam used to see him quite a bit. She's kind like that. She talked to him more than she talked to me. He was very rough. He swore a lot and came from London. I think Mam liked that (both things). His mam did eventually show up once, but she brought nothing for him, and when she left, he had a massive outburst and was taken to a secure ward. Mam still visited him in there—she made a big effort for him. And now he was back. I thought it was cool that she was trying to cheer up this boy, and she did seem to come alive when she spoke with him.

Come to think of it, it wasn't just Lewis she made friends with; there was Joaney as well, and her mam, Wendy. Joaney had a brain disease and was in and out of hospital a lot. The sight of Joaney back in her sick bed, and her mam next to her, brought a bigger smile to Mam's face than I could or actually anything else could at that time. Everything about Wendy was big: hair, shoes, bag, voice, hugs. I dreaded her spotting me on the ward. She'd give me a sloppy kiss on the cheek and gush all this shouty stuff to me—"My little darling! You okay, Oliver? Ah! Must be so hard, you little beauty! Come here!"

For Mam, it was different; she felt twinned with Wendy. They regularly left the ward, involving a coffee or a walk or a cigarette or a combination of the three, and always involving tears. They'd tramp back in as if from a sauna: sweaty, red, wet-faced, and relieved. And often riled about something. I'd hear one or other of them saying stuff like "I'll kill that doctor if he doesn't bring that medication tomorrow!"

When she'd finished with Lewis, Mam came over to Lily's bed and snuggled into her, whispering. She jangled a toy in front of her face, but I think Lily was tired from Poppy and me, so she wasn't responding. Mam put her hand slowly to her own face, almost covering it entirely apart from one eye. Nurse Celia approached the bed and put her arm around Mam.

"Shall we give her a nice bath, sweetheart?"

"Yeah. Okay then."

The nurses always managed to distract her.

Poppy and I helped a bit, but I left the bathroom when Mam started singing. Not because I didn't like her singing—I just... I don't know. I stood in the corridor in front of the window near the bathroom, watching the grey and the rain and trying hard to think of nothing. I failed. Mam seemed hyper anxious; maybe Lily was *not* recovering? Mam was not happy. At all. Did she know something I didn't? Was I adding to her unhappiness? Surely not, since I felt invisible around her. Did she wish it were me in that bed? She wished it were me in that bed. My eyes and throat stung and everything went blurry. "Dizygotheca elegantissima, Dizygotheca elegantissima, Dizygotheca elegantissima..."

The drive home took about half an hour, and it was, at first, heavy with the usual unspoken words. Poppy sat in the back. I had wanted to sit next to her, but it seemed too pushy, so I took the front seat. I enjoyed the sting of the glass on my cheek as I leaned against the rain-battered window. I felt my mouth going into a half-smile as I remembered Lily's laughing and talking. My smile widened as I visualised Poppy's face reacting to it. I broke the silence:

"While you were outside, Lily laughed and spoke again, you know? She really did, Mam. You've got to believe me."

"Did she?"

"Yeah. She did, didn't she, Poppy?"

"Yeah."

"Oh no. Celia was right then."

"Did you not believe her, Mam?"

"It's all so confusing, that's all. I'm so sorry I missed that. You kids are great at getting her to respond. And I'm sorry if... It's just been—"

"I know, Mam."

"I do still notice things, you see? And you moved those bits of plants off the table like I asked. Where did you put them?... Dad spent a long time repairing a step in the garden last night and said you hadn't been out as much recently."

It was so unusual for Mam to speak to me in whole long sentences that I hardly knew how to answer. I just said I kept meaning to go out to the garden but didn't seem to have much energy of late. And I added, "When Lily gets home, I'll get back into it."

As we neared home, Mam switched into the more usual tick-list mode, churning out the usual questions:

"Have you got any homework? What day do you have Games again?"

When I told her Games was the next day, one word came to her head: "Bugger!"

This didn't mean she had an aversion to all things sporty (well, actually, she *did* a bit); it just meant that she hadn't washed my sports kit. At this point I should have said, "Thing is, all I did last week was sit on a bench, watching everyone *else* play football, so it wouldn't be the most unhygienic thing in the world for me to wear the whole lot again." But I didn't want to disappoint her or for her to be any *more* disappointed than she already was, so I said nothing.

Thing is, I had been quite into football, but I'd gone off it. At one point I thought I was going to be really good at it; then I realised I was rubbish. I wasn't good at sports, not like Nathan. I did think there must be something I was good at. It was just a question of experimenting. I had started to play the drums. Not that good or anything. Not like Sam. My dad and Sam both played guitar, so at any given moment, there'd be a chance that some corner of the house would be filled with mellow plucking and strumming of strings.

Once out of the car, Poppy hugged me goodbye. This hugging was exquisitely new and welcome. Mam and I trekked down the dark side alley of the house; we hardly ever went up the steps to the front door. On approaching the already-open back door, the sounds coming from the kitchen were *not* mellow. Dad's voice was raised, in fact, shoutier than I'd heard him in ages. He sat opposite Nathan, interview style, leaning forward all tortoise-necked, in the midst of some sort of showdown.

Celia-mail 2

Dear Mam,

Shouldn't be writing this at work, so I'll be quick. Sorry to hear about Mr. Granger passing away. And to think his daughter said it was a blessing, his heart attack being brought on by a *Jerry Springer* programme. Mind you, she's on the odd side at the best of times. Did you see what she had on at his ninetieth last month? You won't remember, but it was a tight short gold dress and her hair crimped, and she's what, seventy or so? Have you got a new neighbour? Hope it's a nice quiet one!

Yes, I *have* got good news to report on the ward. The sweet girl, Lily, with the lovely name, the eyelashes, and the three brothers, is on the mend, only it'll be slow, and Anna, the mam, is desperate to take her home but scared stiff. She was saying she'd probably send the fourteen-year-old (called Oliver, I think I told you) to the grandparents for a while so she can have a quiet house and focus on the little one. I don't know, I think she'd be best off leaving him be. He seems troubled enough as it is. She even asked my advice, but I can't have a say in that, can I, Mam?

Oliver looks like Lily and the other two look different, so I think they don't all have the same dad. I did hear the oldest boy calling the dad Ben, too, and not "Dad." Oliver seems very close to Lily is all I'm saying, and I wouldn't send him away like that. Not a chance. They don't even live in the same place, the grandparents. I mean, don't these people know how lucky they are having two, three, ruddy four children? One gets ill and they have the barmy idea of splitting them up! It's not right, Mam. I'll shut up now. Got to go into town, as I forgot my hair clips.

I know you always tell me to keep it to myself, but I get so excited to tell someone—I'm late again this month! Might be more good news to report soon!

Much love, Celia x

What's Wrong With Nathan?

Nathan's head was hung low, and he was rubbing his blond, spiky hair, and I was glad at least that Dad obviously hadn't said, "Look at me when I'm talking to you!" I never get that. It's such an unnatural thing to do when someone's telling you off. In fact, he hadn't even told him to stop fiddling with his mini-skateboard. Sam leaned back against the sink, legs crossed, arms folded, like a third parent, glaring at Nathan.

"What the hell's this?!" Mam always had a subtle approach to delicate situations. "What's he done now?"

I didn't know what she meant by 'now.' Nathan didn't get into trouble much. He didn't like Mam's attitude, though, and he turned to her with a look of disgust.

"I've had enough of this," he said, as he ran straight past us both and out the back door.

I didn't know exactly what Nathan's 'this' was, but I was starting to feel a 'this' that I didn't like either. Dad was livid. He jumped up, followed by a string of unfinished sentences:

"Just you...! Get back here, you...! If you don't...!"

"Leave him, Ben." Mam had changed her tune.

"What d'you mean, leave him? That's the trouble—we've been *leaving* him too much. Sam, go after him!"

"No!" Mam kind of screeched. Dad, Sam, and I did one of those double takes that you see in comedies, only it wasn't funny.

"He needs some time. For God's sake... we all need some time. Just... just..." and then as she opened the fridge door, "Give me strength! Ben, give Oliver money for a burger and Oliver, just don't go to Games or something tomorrow. I don't c—I can't be bothered."

"No, he can eat what's in the pan," Dad said.

"He doesn't like stir-fry."

"He can eat what's in the pan or go hungry! I'm not doing this 'special treatment' any more."

"Don't be stupid! The boy's got to eat!"

"Anna, you should have fed him at the hospital. I tell you, I'm not doing this any more!"

So what was *Dad's* 'this'? Was it me?

"Oh, so you think I haven't got other things on my mind at the hospital?"

"I know, I know, but it's not all about Lily, Anna!"

Mam sat down with her wine. "It is. Of course it is," she said.

"So all this is Lily's fault? Is she the cause of all this?" Dad said.

"Yes."

'This' again. I wasn't sure if it was a different 'this' or the same one, but I couldn't see the point of Mam and Dad's argument. And I didn't like her blaming Lily. I went up to my room.

"What was all that about?" I texted Nathan as I walked up the stairs. By the time I'd got into my room and sat on the bed, he'd texted back:

"No homework for a month. Skipped all detentions. M&D been called to school."

My initial reaction was that it was no big deal, but I wanted to be on his side. Another text came through:

"On way to Luke's. Don't tell. Not comin back. Delete this." I had just deleted it when Sam walked in.

"Where's he gone, Ollie? I heard your phone."

Before I could even answer, he grabbed my phone.

"Hey! Give it back! I don't know where he's gone. Sam! Give it here now!"

He ignored my response.

"Little git!"

He flung my phone onto the bed and slammed the door on his way out.

I was glad that I couldn't tell if the insult was meant for me or for Nathan.

I sat on my bed and looked around my room. I was lucky to have so much stuff. My little TV and a computer sat on my desk, but I had no inclination to switch either of them on. I thought of closing the curtains, but decided against. I *never* shut them, so I don't know what I was thinking. I was lucky to have the valley view. I looked up at the shelves in the corner; I was lucky to have Sam, who was so artistic and had helped me arrange the fifty-eight Coke cans on them.

"Little git!" repeated in my head. Of *course* it was me he was talking about. Who was I trying to kid? I noticed the rapidly increasing collection of dirty glasses and plates and bowls scattered round the room. And trousers and T-shirts weren't being put away. Even my shirts weren't hung back on my clothes rail.

I was lucky to have all this stuff, but there seemed no order to anything any more.

"Useless git," I changed it to when I scanned my posters of accomplished skateboarders and drummers and guitarists on the wall behind my bed.

I reached up to the bookshelf above my desk for my dictionary and lay on the bed with it. I looked up 'mellifluous' that Kamal had said at school and 'bugger' that Mam said a lot, but was haunted by images of Lily and Nathan. I fell into a sort of half-dream, fully clothed, slumped over my Chambers dictionary. Strong images battered my mind. Nathan took Lily from her bed and climbed onto the roof of the hospital. He had a megaphone and a machine gun and was shouting, "Nobody moves till you give us the diagnosis for Lily!" He swore a lot and started shooting into the crowd that had gathered below. "If you try any stunts with helicopters, I'll gun you down!"

When I came to with a stiff neck, it was one o'clock in the morning.

I saw lights on downstairs, so I crept out of my room and went down. I passed the living room and stood at the top of the second set of stairs leading down to the kitchen. I could hear Mam. She was crying.

Nathan had stuck to his plan and hadn't come back. I don't think any of us could sleep because he'd never done anything like that before.

I made my way downstairs and hovered at the entrance to the kitchen, still not sure what to do. Mam was on the phone:

"I'll have to go back on them. I'm just not managing too well... I don't really know what you could do to help apart from maybe have the boys for a bit... Well, just Oliver then... I know, but there's only so much I can take!... Well it may seem that way, but I assure you it's all a front... I know, and I am on the case! Sam hasn't heard from him and nor has Oliver... Yes well, he hasn't coz Sam checked his phone!... I'm *going* to call the police if he's not back by two. He is seventeen... I know, I'll get off the line now... Yes, yes I'll let you know."

"Just Oliver then." What was she on about? Split loyalties. I wanted to support my brother and keep his whereabouts a secret, but Mam was in such a state.

Mam said, "What you doing up? It's—"

"I know. Who was that?"

"Are you eavesdropping? How long have you been there?"

"Who *was* it?"

"Grandma. She's worried... like *I* am."

"You shouldn't worry," I said.

"I realise you're trying to say the right thing, but that's stupid."

"I mean you don't have to worry because Nathan's at Luke's. He just texted me."

"Oh, Thank God. Tell your dad—he's outside. Bloody gardening in the middle of the night. We're all going insane."

"Are you sending me away? You'd better not. I won't go."

"Just tell your dad!"

"You trying to get rid of me?"

"Stop being selfish for once and tell your dad your big brother's not bloody dead! Now!" She started crying again.

Dad was out the back, a small cigar in his gloved hand. He only smoked them on special and, I realised now, unusual occasions.

"Nathan's at Luke's."

"For God's sake. Why did you wait so long to tell us?"

"I only just found out."

"Right, we're going to get him. You'll have to come with me," he said, resting the cigar in an ashtray and peeling off his gardening gloves. "I don't know where he lives."

When we got back inside, Dad ran to grab his coat, but Mam said to him, "I'm so tired now. Look, we know where he is. He's safe. Just let him sleep it out, eh? You can talk to him after school tomorrow."

"*I* can talk to him? What happened to 'we'?"

Dad was so on edge and Mam looked like she was going to break down, so I interrupted:

"She'll be at hospital, Dad. She has to be with Lily. And we think Lily might be getting better anyway; did you tell him, Mam? We can all be a proper family again and I can help when she comes home. Why don't we all get some rest? I'll text you both as soon as I see him at school tomorrow, so you know he's okay. Okay?"

For the first time in ages, they both looked at me like they were really listening. In the midst of the mayhem, I felt suddenly important.

Back in my bed, I thought of Poppy and Lily. I thought of school. The first seemed life sustaining, and the other, well, something like life sapping. I looked forward to Lily coming home. We could make a banner and buy her favourite sweets and stuff. I thought ahead to what planting we could do together. April—perfect. If Dad wouldn't let me have any more garden, I'd pull out most of the alliums and give them to Mam; there were too many of them anyway, and they ran all the way across the front. I fancied something exotic, but for Lily, delicate blooms would be in order. She could choose, anyway. We'd go to The Fuchsia's Bright and have a look round the nursery garden. Poppy would love that; she could help us plant as well. I'd ask her at school.

But I didn't know if I'd make it into school; it wouldn't have been the first time, to be honest. Sometimes Dad tried to force me by giving me a lift in, but I'd refuse to get out of the car. It wasn't just Lily, you see, I mean, the reason I hated school. I felt like a ghost sometimes, floating round school, like I wasn't actually present. I might have been invisible except I couldn't have been because Darren

Cragley, Callum Gaskin, and the other ones always seemed to know where to find me. I would try to get out of the car, but it was like I'd been hypnotised and my bum was stuck to the car seat (you know the sort of thing—"When I count to three, your buttocks will cleave to the seat and you will be unable to wrench them upwards").

In fact, shortly after Nathan ran away, I missed a whole *week* of school... and all I'll say at this point is that it wasn't because I was ill.

Saved by Lily

It took me two minutes of the twenty-minute walk to school to start telling Kamal about Nathan running off, and the possibility of me being banished. I'd already covered the Poppy hugs and the I-reckon-there-might-be something-there speculation.

He just said, "That's dodgy." (He was referring to Nathan, being more interested in him going missing than Poppy.)

"Yeah. It's mental. He'll be at school, though. Tell me if you see him."

As we approached the school gates, I started scanning the playground for Nathan, like I was in the 'Find Wally' championships. I imagined a searchlight, panning across the crowd until it darted back as it spotted something. There was Luke, laughing, looking at his phone, with a boy who definitely wasn't Nathan.

"There's Luke. I'm going over," I said.

Kamal wanted to come with me, so we rushed over to him.

"All right, mate? You seen Nathan?"

"Neh. Int seen 'im."

I waited for him to tell me that he meant he hadn't seen him because Nathan had left his house before him or something. Nothing. Then I thought, *Aha, he's probably covering for him.*

"I know he kipped at yours last night," I said.

"Neh, mate. He never."

I waited again before Kamal said, "His mother's beside herself with worry because Nathan stayed out last night."

"Well, he never come to mine. I haven't even heard from him."

Kamal and I had the same response at the same time:

"Shit!"

I texted Nathan during registration, but this time the message wasn't delivered. Kamal said we should miss assembly and go to the office to check whether Nathan had registered or not.

We were told, "Nathan Campbell... let me... see. No—no mark. Not here today."

'Dead Man Walking' (our nickname for one of the teachers), appeared from nowhere looking grey and severe, his murky fish eyes trained on us.

"You're late for assembly. *Thought* I'd scoop up some deadwood out here. Always some dozy floaters lurking round reception."

He managed to say all this without moving his mouth. He was an experiment gone horribly wrong: a ventriloquist's dummy crossed with a serial killer.

"Hop it!" he shrieked.

We ran to the hall, which was only about ten seconds away. We were just taking our seats on the 'late row' at the back of the hall, when assembly began. It was exciting in a way, going to the latecomers' row. I would say it's actually the best place to sit. You had to sneak in through a door at the top of the slopey seat section—raked seating, it's called—so you were at the back, higher up than anyone else. It was definitely a top spot for spying. Once sitting down, I was completely distracted by this sea of fidgeting in front of me. I went to a play with school once where they had binoculars behind every chair. Well, that wouldn't be a bad idea in schools, for when you're not interested in the assembly, which is about 99.9 per cent of the time. I had just spotted Bill Owusu rolling a cigarette two rows in front of me, when the proceedings kicked off. Usually all the teachers sat on chairs on the stage, but Thursday was 'performance assembly', so we had some sort of show or short play or something to look forward to (not).

Kamal nudged me and pointed out Poppy. The boy to her right whispered something, and she turned, slow motion, towards him, her hair snaking round. Her fringe was in her eyes, brushing her eyelashes that were caked up with thick black gunge; and it sounds rude but her upturned nose reminded me of a pig just then, or I suppose a piglet. Not that she wasn't pretty, by the way. I wanted her to continue turning her head so that her gaze would fall on me and she'd wave, as if she somehow knew where I was, but all that happened was she shoved the boy's shoulder and turned back to the front.

My attention shifted to Dead Man Walking, who had spookily materialised on the stage, even though we'd just seen him in reception. His real name was Dr. Spark, deputy head and chemistry teacher, nickname chosen because he never changed his facial expression from one of gloom. My dad told me he wasn't a medical doctor (thank God—he'd probably end up poisoning his patients), but one with a PhD. To become one, I think you've got to learn a heap of stuff about one massively particular area, like 'How an Ant Carries a Crumb' or 'The Use of the Word 'the' in the Works of Shakespeare' and write a humongously long essay-type thing about it.

He stood in front of the microphone stand and started:

"Notices first: "Tonight's year nine girls' hockey match cancelled."

[I hadn't rung Mam! She was going to be sick with worry.]

"First Eleven Football Team lost thirteen-nil."

[Should I pretend I'd seen Nathan? No, stupid. Bonkers idea.]

"Says here, 'Danielle Bell who left last year has given birth to triplets—Chanelle, Sherelle, and Rochelle. There's a card to sign in the sixth-form common room. Only sixth-formers to sign.' I don't want to see anyone else hanging about over there. You've been warned."

[Should I go looking for Nathan? *He* would have come looking for *me*.]

"From now on, anyone caught smoking behind the bike shed will report immediately to the head teacher, Mr. Hickey."

[Yes, I would bunk off school and go looking for Nathan. He couldn't have gone far, but he did have that naïve side to him. What if some weirdo had lured him off somewhere?]

"Now all eyes to the front to watch a number from year ten's new show, *Killer*. I said all eyes to the front!"

[Oh my God, he could be dead. My mam and dad would lose it completely!]

"What an inspiration this man is!" said Kamal. "I wonder what his *second* choice of job would have been? Someone high up in chemical warfare maybe?"

I just wanted to leave immediately, but I had to sit through this wacky show that I didn't get whatsoever. I would ring Sam. He was always ultra sensible in panic situations.

I wasn't in the mood for Kamal's banter: "Lucy Pool's got socks down her bra! It's a dead cert. Look at—"

"Shush for once, will you?"

"Ooh! What's up with you today? Sorry, I know. Look, he won't have gone far. Probably at Newcastle skate park."

He was right. Kamal always sussed things out really quickly.

When Mr. Hickey got up afterwards, praising year ten's efforts and gushing how proud he was of them, I wondered if he'd seen a different show. At least he was a positive kind of person, I suppose.

I had to text Mam and Dad. That way, one of *them* could go looking for Nathan, too. As we walked out of assembly, I told Kamal what I thought.

He said, "Yes of course we'll leave school together. Better that more of us are looking, Olvo."

Instead of texting Mam to tell her Nathan hadn't turned up at school, I rang her, as she'd already tried to ring me twice. She sounded like it might send her crazy and said she was contacting the police. I was more determined than ever to help now.

Kamal and I sauntered out of school and back to the school gates in a we're-walking-really-slowly-because-we've-so-got-permission-to-leave type manner. We made our way to the metro station feeling conspicuous; neither of us had played truant before (well, not as blatantly as this). I must admit that it was coupled with a sense of freedom. I'd got out of school. I'd escaped from jail, escaped from my jailers.

To come clean, I was kind of bullied at school... well bullied, not 'kind of.' That's the thing, you see, people always play it down because it's embarrassing somehow. Kamal knew about it: he was bullied, too. It sounds weird, but I think it was because people thought we were from a privileged background or something. There was a lot of that went on there. I probably did get new trainers and stuff more than some of the others. I don't know.

They used to take my lunch money. They said they'd beat me up if I told anyone, so I started bringing packed lunches, which ended up being even worse. They stole my lunch every day and threw it on the ground or at me. I didn't eat anything in the end and told no one about it. Why didn't I just stop taking any money *or* lunch to school? Or eat it really early? Well, I tried all that. They threw stolen food at me, and I don't mean bread or biscuits—it was mostly yoghurt. It was great for them because I'd not only stink for the rest of the day, but they'd find me at afternoon break and follow me round chanting, "Sloppy Ollie!" over and over in an exaggerated whisper or chase me home, chanting the same. They made me scared. It was pathetic. Mam would have been straight into school, but thing is, I didn't tell her. She called me greedy for eating loads of crisps and yoghurts when I got home after school, but it wasn't her fault.

I'd left school that day before anyone could take my lunch. There'd be one less person to harass, it occurred to me. I even started feeling quite excited about eating it, though I only had beef-paste sandwiches to look forward to. My dad always made my lunch for me. I'd pretended to him that I'd started liking beef-paste (which Kamal really *did* like, as it happens), because I didn't want to waste proper stuff like ham or cheese.

"What you got for lunch, Kamal?" (You know where this is going.)

"Banana, two samosas—"

"Fancy swapping a samosa for a beef-paste sandwich?"

I hadn't even tried one before, but I figured they couldn't be worse than beef-paste sarnies. Kamal was excited by the idea:

"How about *two* samosas for *two* beef-paste sandwiches! Anyway beef-paste sandwiches are the British equivalent to samosas!"

"Sam would say that's depressing," I said and we laughed.

Deal done. Things were already feeling positive.

Once on the train, it was getting on for ten o'clock, which seemed more or less lunchtime. We sat eating samosas and beef-paste sarnies (they were tasty, by the way, the samosas. I imagined eating one in front of Sam and watching his reaction because I never normally ate curry or anything when they did).

I asked Kamal, "They still take your lunch?"

"What?"

"You know. Are they still stealing your lunch and throwing it away?"

"I don't know what you mean."

Even my best friend couldn't talk to me about the bullying. It made me feel lonely, and I think Kamal saw that.

"Yeah. Okay. Yes. Yes they do… but they don't get their grubby hands on my cash any more. I hide it. I fashioned a compartment in the base of my shoe. I know what you're thinking—James Bond."

"You're kidding! Genius!"

"Yeah, I have my secret stash, safe from thieving hands. They're too thick to think of it."

"D'you really think they're thick, then? They're clever in a way. I mean, *we're* not daft, and they have one up on *us*."

"Olvo, they'd take chocolate from a baby! And that's because they're nasty not clever—nothing to do with clever. They're A1 puttocks! They only pick on us because we're decent. You don't think they'd pick on someone who'd fight back, do you? Anyway, look."

He swivelled his right ankle sideways onto his left knee, and after surreptitiously glancing around the carriage à la James Bond, as he would have it, he opened the heel of his black polished shoe to reveal a tenner, sitting proudly underneath. My jaw dutifully fell open.

"That's a lot of dosh, Kamal."

"Always a note. No coinage, dear boy. Can't risk the danger of the jingle factor."

"What about the falling-on-your-face factor when your heel drops open?"

He pushed me and we both laughed.

"Babies don't eat chocolate, by the way. You wouldn't know," I said.

He's an only child, you see. He's *very* only, actually. His mam and dad died in a car accident in India when he was a baby, and he moved here to live with his aunt and uncle. I puzzled over how together and confident he was, because he very much knew of the tragedy. I found out snippets when Nathan asked him stuff; I found it too awkward to ask anything myself.

He hated to be wrong about any single thing, so he said (lamely in my opinion), "But *you* eat chocolate!"

We both laughed again. I laughed only because I'd felt a fleeting pang of pity for him, to be honest. With this laugh came a guilty surge of pleasure at how smoothly our mission was going.

Things continued to go well when the ticket machine was broken at the metro, and the barriers were open at Newcastle. That tenner had 'table for two' written all over it.

We made our way to the skate park, trying to look like school boys with a perfectly good reason for not being in school but soon realising that we were not exactly in a huge field or woods or anything but in a big city with lots of police officers and social workers. We were both quite tall for our age, so we put up our hoods in an attempt to foil suspicious onlookers. We wore a uniform with stripy tie and blazer (plus black polished shoes in Kamal's case), but wore casual tops over them.

Once at the skating area, my heart sank—no sign of Nathan.

"Is it okay if we hang around for a while, Kamal?"

"Yeah, mate. He's bound to turn up at some point. Have you checked your phone?"

Still no word and my last text not delivered. I wrote again: "Luke said u didn't go to his. Txt back." There were eight or so hooded 'dudes' skating and a few sitting round, so we blended in. Some of the skaters looked as old as twenty-five, and I wondered what they did with the rest of their lives. We sat on a broken bench. Sam, who'd been into BMX when he was younger, had told Nathan that skating was a waste of time and not to fool himself that he'd be able to make a living out of it.

"Did I tell you Nathan won another competition on Saturday?"

"Yeah? He's always winning. What an achievement. Must be cool, winning something. *You* ever win anything?"

"It's not about the winning, it's about the taking part," I said.

"You ever taken part in anything?"

I shoved him and said, "You're such a blinkin' stinkhorn."

"Ah! One of those beloved botanical insults! I'd prefer the Latin though, Olvo."

"Phallus impudicus to you!"

"Oh my God! Divine! For real?!"

"Yeah, it really is."

"You absolute loon of loveliness!" And he grappled me to the ground, in raptures.

Once settled back on the bench, I said, "By the way, Nathan's mate filmed it on his phone—the competition. It's on Facebook. Pretty cool."

"He's ace, your brother. I wish—"

"Sam thinks he's wasting his time."

"How can doing something harmless that you're good at and is *healthy* be a waste of time?! He's probably just jealous. Older people are always warning you about life's little mantraps that have to be negotiated."

I knew he had a point, but I also knew that Sam cared a lot about Nathan and that his intentions were probably well meaning. I said, "Maybe it's his way of trying to cushion his fall, you know? It won't stop him or anything anyway. He loves it too much. It's like when you said to me that Lisa Comrie would break my heart. It didn't stop *me*, did it?"

"Mate, you didn't exactly sweep her off her feet! Not like me when I cooked pot noodles for Rebecca Bailey and even lit a candle."

"Hang on a minute!" I said. "You weren't exactly Mr. Smooth, from what I remember. I thought that went horribly wrong."

"Yeah, well. I had the candle going—Auntie had fancy lemon ones for outside."

"The ones that keep pesky flies away, you mean?" I said.

"Eh? Anyway, I had on new hair gel and Lynx body spray. It was all in the bag, so to speak. I said, 'Guess what's for dessert?' and she said, 'Butterscotch Angel Delight?' I thought, *Do you think I'm made of money?* I had second thoughts about serving up what I'd prepared and decided *she* was, in fact, dessert, so I lunged in for the big kiss, but things went slightly awry."

"Doesn't sound like you had quite enough *in the bag*, so to speak!"

"Ha ha."

"It must be tough getting a date right, I suppose," I said. "It might have been a bit adventurous, you know, for a fourteen-year-old? What went wrong, anyway?"

"She threw the noodles over my new Arsenal top! Curry ones as well."

"Ha ha! Timing, Kamal, timing! You should've let the lady finish her main course. At least the candle worked for her—kept annoying little creatures away. And you wore your Arsenal top; trying to get her all fired up I suppose because, of course, she supports Newcastle United." Mental that he supports The Gunners, but his family is from London.

Kamal hit me, saying, "Come on then, tell me the secret of seduction, you smug git! And, in fact, she supports Manchester United; she was born there. 'The Red Devils', they call them. Adore that."

"You knew that? So why didn't you wear a Man United shirt? Mentola! Did the noodles spell out 'loser' on your Arsenal shirt?"

"You kill me, you really do. So what was your amazing move on Lisa, then?" Kamal asked.

"I gave her one of my drumsticks... and she threw it into the field."

"Ha ha ha! I rest my case. Only one stick as well. Mean."

"So what exactly was it you were going to serve Ms Bailey for dessert? Ben and Jerry's ice cream, was it? Or chocolate gateau? No, don't tell me, strawberries and cream?"

"I had taken it upon myself to create my own masterpiece if truth be told. Impressed or what?"

"Ah God, I've got to hear this."

"I googled what girls like in a dessert, took note, and incorporated as many ingredients as I could get my hands on. The result was out of this world—a layered delight."

"Yeah...?"

"Well, girls are partial to sensual sweetness, so one layer was dark and lovely—"

"Chocolate!"

"No, prunes."

"What! You've got to be kidding?"

"I chanced upon them in the cupboard. Just as sweet, and cut down the costs no end."

"Great start. Mmmm. Go on," I said.

"All these interruptions. Am I divulging here, or am I taking this recipe to the grave?"

"Or is *it* taking *you*? Sorry, sorry, go on. End of interruptions. I'm all ears. Can't wait."

"So after my special prune-mushing technique using a remote control for the second layer ("Ha!"), the bottom layer was stamped-on biscuits. I know what you're thinking, but the aforementioned cookies were placed in a plastic bag ahead of the crushing. Rather romantic, I found—felt like I was treading on grapes to make wine. ("Unbelievable!") And amidst the plethora of ingredients, the biscuits' verging-on-staleness would have gone quite unnoticed, I assure you. Layer three was custard—"

"At last! Something normal!"

"Well, I *say* custard, but we had none in and I wasn't shelling out for the real deal. Looked it up and it was a cinch to make—eggs, flour, cream, sugar, and vanilla."

"Now this *is* starting to sound impressive."

"I picked up swiftly that you have to be flexible with ingredients. I crushed up some sweeteners instead of sugar. And who has cream lying about in the fridge, I ask you? I used milk. Oh, and hands up who can't get moved for vanilla pods in their pantry? 'A store cupboard essential' it was described as on one website, I mean come ahhhn. The image showed little black dots from the vanilla, so I used kalonji: an inspired move, I thought, to involve onion seeds. The whole thing was pleasingly yellowy white with the requisite black specks... not that it looked much like the picture. But, let's face it, everything's airbrushed these days."

"How's your dessert, madam? Very yellowy white in an oniony way, thank you!"

"It's the consistency that's tricky to master—it'll come with time. Couldn't find a whisk, so I used my aunt's head-scratcher, which is similarly prongy. I gauged it to be just as suitable an implement to achieve frothy smoothness."

"And what did you get? No cream? Don't tell me, frog spawn?"

"Hmmm. An accurate comparison, I must admit. We had tons of flour, so I used that as a thickener. Not entirely sure what happened there."

Kamal went on to describe more layers, which included rhubarb yoghurt and mouldy gooseberry jam (does gooseberry jam even exist?), the top of which he'd scraped off. I was feeling sick by the end of it. Unable to find a pastry brush, he had used his toothbrush to apply a coating of egg white on the top layer, which was his version of flaky pastry—don't ask. Even though it had taken him a whole afternoon to make, I was surprised to hear that it was completely polished off. But then he confessed that the neighbours, Maria and Henry, who had wolfed it down, were actually Pugapoos (dogs which are a cross between a pug and a poodle, also known as Puddles, Kamal told me). We were both in hysterics, and Kamal actually laughed himself off the bench. When I said not only did the pudding truly sound 'out of this world', but that he should enter it into a competition, he was about to get up, but when I added, 'Coolest Canine Cuisine,' he started rolling about, holding his stomach like he'd been shot.

Things took on a serious tone when we started discussing improved girl tactics, particularly Poppy tactics.

"Now that's a tricky one," Kamal said. "Treat her like a lady instead of a girl; then she will become a lady. Do you see? Power of suggestion, my man! Next time she comes to the hospital, buy her a cappuccino and go for a wander. Wrap your coat around her shoulders without asking if she's cold, that sort of caper. Recite a Shakespeare sonnet, without asking her if she wants to hear one. Take control!"

"Recite poetry? Are you mental? I'd rather throw myself at her naked in the middle of assembly."

"Not a bad idea!"

"Anyway, I wish we could hang out more, but not at the hospital. I wish it didn't have to be the hospital."

"It doesn't have to be anything. Listen to yourself. You're so negative. Ask her to a film."

"I don't know. It's only when *she* talks, I mean, speaks quite a bit to me, that I start to feel confident."

Kamal said, "Nail on head! Girls like to tell you lots and lots. The trick is to really listen."

"Well, you can't talk in a cinema, can you? Anyway, I had the idea of writing to her—texts and email and that. At least I'll have time to think and she won't be looking at me."

"Can backfire badly though, Olvo. *Really* badly!"

"What d'you mean?"

"After the noodle night, I fell even deeper for Becky Bailey. Call me a mug, but I like a challenge. And there's something about feisty girls... I took the bull by the horns and the next day, texted, 'I love you,' without a full stop or anything—more poetic, I thought."

"And?"

"The thrill when a return text flashed up seconds later! Hard to put into words."

"That's a first for you. So, what did she write?"

"'Bog off!'"

"Ha ha! Class! How romantic. That is bad, man. See what you mean, though, about the backfiring. So what did you write back?"

"What did I write back? Are you mad? Nothing, of course. What was I supposed to put? 'How long for?'"

He saw everything so clearly, Kamal did. He said, "So, speaking to Poppy's actual face, no matter how avant-garde that sounds, is the best policy, Olvo."

"And really listen, you say?"

"Exactly."

"I would say I do... I *do* listen, I think."

"Well, that's true. You hang on her every word. Yes, I'd say good listening skills."

"Might not be able to hear her at all soon. Think Mam's going to send me away."

"You said something about that. What do you mean?"

"I'm not going. If she doesn't want me, I'll go away myself. Maybe I'll stay in London when we go on that art trip. It depends if Lily comes out of hospital."

"Don't be mad. I wish you would just have a good talk with her."

"I don't know when, but I think she wants to get rid of me. For a while anyway. I just think it'd be better if it were me in hospital, so she can't bear to look at me. She's sending me to my grandparents."

"Hey, mate, don't think that rubbish. And she's probably not thinking straight. I mean, they live in miles away! You can't go all the way down there."

"She wouldn't listen. She never does these days."

A voice interrupted, "*I'm* listening!"

It was a policewoman, and we both froze, even though she hadn't actually said, "Freeze!"

"How old are you two?"

We both said, "Fourteen." We were getting skilled at the speaking-at-the-same-time trick, which was a good start in the avoiding-being-arrested regard. Then, before she could say any more, Kamal went on in an urgent voice:

"We're going to visit his sister in Newcastle Infirmary. She's very ill, and we have permission to see her today because we were busy with sports at the weekend and couldn't get to see her. Her name's Lily and she's on the paediatric neurology ward and we have to go there now because she'll be expec—"

"Okay, okay, okay!"

She really did say it three times. We would definitely be in serious trouble now after Kamal's stupid lies.

"I shall accompany you to the infirmary then, gentlemen."

Panic set in now and I felt like shouting, "No! Lily's got nothing to do with this!" I didn't want to go to the hospital. Oh God, I thought, Mam was going to go absolutely crazy.

As we all set off towards the hospital, I went into daze mode but kept seeing Kamal staring at me, his big brown eyes growing even bigger behind his glasses, like a hypnotist, as if to say, "Come on. Stay with me, stay with me." I bet 'PC Whoever' was sure we were lying and was probably already imagining all eyes on her, back at the station, as she related the amusing case of the lying boys and their humiliation when faced with sick children in a hospital ward. She actually said, "This should be fun!" under her breath, and I instructed my voice to stay silent as I moved into hospital mode and started to experience the exact opposite of fun.

She somehow knew the way to the children's brain ward, and just before she pressed the bell, she said, "This better be good!"

The nurse who came to open the door was Celia.

Lunch for Lily

"What's all this? Hello Oliver! Come in, sweetheart."

The policewoman looked curious, like there was a mystery she needed to solve. "You know these boys? Found them loitering in the skate park."

"Loitering." They speak in such a funny way sometimes, police people—kind of clever in a sense, but comical as well somehow. As Celia and the policewoman were talking, Kamal whispered his impersonation:

"I did apprehend these suspicious individuals in an urban facility. On enquiring as to the nature of their misdemeanour, I was forthwith witness to their claims of an alleged intention to proceed to the Newcastle Infirmary. I subsequently accompanied them to the aforementioned edifice. On arrival at the cited location, it became immediately apparent that I looked like a right tit."

We both creased up, trying hard to suppress our laughter, which must have looked pretty grotesque in the circumstances.

Celia said, "Oh, all right, Officer. I see. Yes, their mam's let them visit today. They didn't get much time with her this weekend."

"Is that so?" PC replied.

I couldn't believe she was still talking like that. But mostly I thought it was cool we'd got away with it. I couldn't understand why Nurse Celia had made something up to help us, though. She couldn't lie in a job like that, could she? The PC followed us into the ward to check I had a very ill little sister. The nurse called out to Lily's bed, "Nathan, your brother's here."

What a relief! I closed my eyes, and my left hand pressed to my forehead for a few seconds before I gathered myself together. Kamal and I went up to Nathan, who was leaning over Lily. I patted his back and said, "You're here, thank God... Don't ask."

I heard the policewoman say, "Everything seems in order."

Then, just as I was thinking, *No, things are desperately* out *of order*, Kamal said, "She's just doing her job."

As she was leaving the ward, I swear I heard her say, "Poor mites." I think she meant the children in the ward, but I'll never know. Then she called over: "Take care when you're out of school. Essential to carry a note, boys, you understand? It's for your own safety. I wouldn't want *my* fourteen-year-old wandering round the city centre on a school day."

"Yes indeed, Officer," said Kamal. "Thank you for your diligence and advice."

"Thanks," I said.

"Who's this?" Celia asked me.

"My best mate, Kamal."

"I'm not happy with you turning up on a school day with no note, Oliver, not happy at all."

"Oh." Felt weird being told off. She was usually so amazingly upbeat and smiley. Thing is, and this sounds terrible, I didn't want to see Lily. I wasn't prepared. It hadn't been planned. As soon as the policewoman left, I wanted to leave, too.

After Nathan realised that telling me off for skipping school didn't make sense in the context of him being officially *missing*, he explained that he had texted Luke, got no reply, stayed at a different friend's, and when he woke up, knew he wasn't going to school; he'd gone straight to the skate park, and when a friend asked how his sister was, he'd felt the urge to be with her.

Kamal seemed shocked. "She looks different."

"I know," I said.

"What you supposed to do? Can she hear?"

I said, "Yes," at the same time as Nathan said, "No." Then Nathan added, "We're not sure, but yeah, I'm sure she can."

"Is she getting better?"

Kamal was asking all the right questions, but hearing them reminded us of how little we understood about Lily's illness. I said, "We think she is; she started talking again, but it's slow."

Nathan then slipped into his hyper mode, which tended to occur when he felt choked. "'Course she'll get better, won't you, Lil, eh, won't you?"

He started tickling her, and she giggled and said, "Make me laugh."

"Ah! She *is* speaking!" Nathan said. "There, see? She's gonna be fine, aren't you, cutie? You'll be coming home soon, won't you, eh?"

Saying really positive stuff was normal for Nathan, but his talk was getting on my nerves. He looked scruffy and slightly demented, too—hair matted, grubby khaki T-shirt, hands grazed, and face smeared with dirt. For a moment I imagined him as a soldier who'd rescued a child and brought it to hospital.

"Anyone hungry?" I interrupted.

"God, Ollie, don't be rude in front of Lily!"

"I'm just hungry."

"And selfish!"

Obviously not always positive with *me*.

"Leave him, eh, Nathan?" Kamal said.

"He's thinking about eating and Lily can't even eat anything, man."

"Nathan..." Kamal said.

"You wouldn't want to be lying there, would you?" Nathan said to me.

"I would. I *would* lie there."

"What?"

Kamal put a hand on each of our shoulders and said, "Come on. If Lily *can* hear, do you think she wants to hear you two bickering? I think Ols is right."

"Who the h—?" said Nathan.

"Ols here is right. We should all go somewhere and grab a bite and relax for a bit. What say you?"

Nathan said, "Suppose so. It's this place, man. I've been here ages now anyway. Read the same story to Lily about ten times. If you want to go and eat, my mate lent me ten pounds, so we could get burgers or something."

"I've got the same," Kamal told him, "so we could go to Mozzarella Cellar! We'll have enough to share two pizzas and still have enough for the train back. You can owe me."

Now they were talking. Things were looking up again. Well, not everything. I found myself standing at the end of Lily's bed like a ghost hovering in another world, staring at the space she occupied. Nathan needed the loo, so we waited in the ward for him, which left Kamal full of questions; but something told him to refrain from asking them.

Instead he said, "Mozzarella Cellar! Result, eh? Ols?"

I didn't respond so he changed his tack.

"It makes sense now, why you don't like coming here."

His eyes fell on Lily's bed just as mine looked away.

"You've never seen her here, have you?" I said.

"You've never asked me."

"It's not exactly something you invite people to do, is it? Sit and watch. Just sit here and feel useless."

Kamal started describing his memories of Lily at home, which I didn't want to hear.

"Remember that time in your kitchen a few years ago when we all cried laughing? Your Mam had cooked curry—"

"Mam actually cooked, did she? I can't remember that."

"She made this vegetarian curry and Lily was having pasta, but she kept pinching our poppadoms!"

"Lily could eat poppadoms?"

"Yeah, don't you remember? She was about two or three."

I think Kamal was nervous, and he launched into one of his endless narratives:

"Your mam thought Lily would choke, but your dad assured her she'd be fine and she was. She sat in her high chair saying, 'Yummy! Yummy!' She was perched between you and Sam, I think. Kept saying, 'More pease, Oliber' to you every time she'd finished her miniscule mouthful. You were having a burger with your poppadoms. I even fed her some of my curry; she loved that, too. She and her tray were speckled with rice; looked like she'd been caught in a hailstorm! Then she started feeding the rice to Sam! Remember, he was pretending to be a dog, and her face was scrunched with chuckles. And that started us all off. We were all crying laughing, weren't we? Ah, then your mam was drying her eyes with her napkin. That was classic—got curry in her eye from the napkin and started jumping all over the place like a crazy thing, and that was it! We were rolling about!"

I did remember it, but it seemed like a different lifetime, a different sister, a different mam, a different me. His words made my eyes sting as I looked back at my sister, motionless in her bed cage.

"Can you really not remember that?! Ols? Can you not?"

"Yes. Yeah, I can. Mam jumped up to go to the sink, and Lily got a shock," I said.

"But your mam made a funny face, and Lily started laughing again," said Kamal.

"I know... She still laughs."

"You said."

"Look, Nathan's here. Let's go," I said.

I went to kiss Lily. Although she was talking a bit again, when I took her hand, it was limp. I watched it drop back onto the bed. I'd have loved Lily to get a shock then like she did when Mam jumped up to go to the sink. To look. To react. I couldn't bear to stay. I couldn't bear to leave. I just massively longed for her to come home, you know. I should have picked her up and said, "Right. I'm not doing this any more. This is all wrong. I'm taking her home. She should be at ours instead of in this grey, squelchy, beeping prison." I bashed the wall with the side of my fist, so hard that it made a nearby machine rattle, and clenched my teeth. I dropped my head and let it hang until I could move again. As we left the ward, Nurse Celia put her right arm round my shoulder and squeezed me into her (tightly). With her left hand, she grasped my chin and pulled my head up.

"I know. It's okay to feel angry, Oliver."

I used all my strength to not make a fool of myself. I said I was fine and pushed my mouth into a smile.

"Your mam'll be glad you came in."

I wanted to say, "No, she won't," but Celia wouldn't have understood. I was nearly at the door when she called my name and approached me. When I turned, she faced me full on and put her hands on my shoulders.

"Everything... all right at home? You all managing?"

I looked at her straggly hair, her bright eyes, her scarlet zinnia-lips bleeding leftover lipstick into her kind face, the black ink mark on her cheek, and I wanted to cry really badly. I forced another smile and said, "Sort of," and held her gaze just a tad longer than felt normal.

"See you soon, then, you and your brother. Bye, Nathan and Camel."

As we wandered away up the corridor, I turned back and she was standing with the ward door open. I shouted, "Bye, CD," and she ran towards me with mock strangling hands, then stopped and put her hands in her pockets, eye-lazering me with a look of assurance. We held each other's gaze again as I walked backwards, slightly lagging behind the boys and she was still standing there when we turned the corner. As I spun round to walk forwards, I felt a sort of double-stab leaving Lily and Celia Dahlia.

Once outside the hospital, I took a deep breath and slowly expelled all the remaining hospital from my lungs. It was wrong, feeling so relieved to be leaving, knowing that Lily was still in there. Seconds after walking away, I felt a jolt. Like that frozen moment when you think you've left your phone in a shop or something. But in this weird world we were trapped in, we *meant* to leave it. And it wasn't just a phone we'd left.

On the way to eat, I texted Mam to say Nathan was okay but didn't say we weren't in school.

The clatter and bustle and jazz music and sweet smells at Mozzarella Cellar had never been more welcome. Our minds were soon off the hospital and onto food.

So, here's the deal—we could afford two pizzas. Nathan and I wanted pepperoni and Kamal wanted... wait for it... mushroom and pineapple! I thought he was messing about, but he was serious. He did often choose to eat vegetarian food. He was good at maths, and he worked out the percentage of mushroom and pineapple section he'd be entitled to on the 'sectioned pizza,' as he named it. Nathan and I would have half of one pepperoni pizza each, plus a sixth of the sectioned pizza. I know, I know, he's a nutter. Can you believe this—Kamal drew a diagram of the peculiar pizza on his napkin for the chef! It looked like a dial showing eight o'clock, and he'd written 'pepperoni' on the small section on the left and 'mushroom and pineapple' on his big bit. Then at the bottom he'd written, *Dear Chef, Add a bit o' spice to your life with this outrageous concoction. Cheers mate.*

We couldn't afford a drink, but Kamal said, "Aha! Our unviolated lunch boxes!"

"Un-what?" said Nathan.

"He means no one's tampered with our lunches today," I said.

"Hadaway. Someone messes with your packed lunches?"

"No, just happened a few times, you know. No big deal."

"Straight up? Only I'd have something to say if someone was messing with your things."

We shared the carton of apple juice and the can of lemonade between the three of us. Yes, you guessed it—Kamal poured the two drinks into three glasses, making fizzy apple drinks.

Over our mocktails, we considered possible punishments for skiving school. I guessed we'd get detention every day for a week.

"I've never even had detention ever, never mind for a whole week," I said.

"Two life sentences without parole," sniggered Nathan, and Kamal joined in:

"Solitary confinement, no visiting rights!"

They both thought it was incredibly amusing.

"It's actually not that funny at all, you guys."

"Well," Kamal said, "I do believe that the punishment should fit the crime, so let's think about this. Nathan, you did a runner, overnight no less, so you're in it up to your neck. You should be sent off alone to sleep in a field for the night and experience something of the fear your parents must have felt when you were missing. This would be a lesson to you."

"You sound like a judge, man, or a priest! I could handle that, anyway, no probs, Kamal!"

"But we would have to throw in some unpleasant elements," Kamal added. "You should wear a flimsy girl's dress, be blindfolded, so you can't dodge the cowpats, and have nothing but sour milk to drink."

Nathan and I laughed, bemused by the whacky scenario Kamal had conjured up.

"What!" Nathan said. "What's all that about, you dipstick?"

"Ah, you see, the dress represents humiliation, which will mirror that of your parents and family when your misdeeds are announced at school, the milk, the nasty taste this whole saga has left in everyone's mouths, and the blindfold, the agony of the unknown."

"Kamal, you're well odd, man. So, come on then, what'll happen to you and Ollie? What would be a good punishment for you two?"

"Well, we broke out and escaped on a train, so we should be blindfolded and sent on an unknown train journey."

"What's with this blindfolding? You're obsessed! I know what— you and Ollie could be told you're being sent to London on a train, but end up in Edinburgh! How's that?!"

"I'd love to go to Edinburgh," I said.

Kamal agreed: "That wouldn't be a punishment. That's seriously flawed."

"Yeah, but you would *think* you were in London, don't you get it? The mess you'd be in! You think you're in London, and you end up in a different *country*!"

"Hardly Alcatraz," I said. "And will we be provided with ear plugs, too?"

"What you on about?"

Kamal got where I was going with this. He said, "Edinburgh's in Scotland, Nathan. Scottish people live in Scotland and they sound... Scottish. It would take all of one second to work out you weren't in London."

"One pepperoni and one 'mixed,'" the waiter said.

Kamal's diagram and note had worked, so we dug into our thirds of pizza and enjoyed not thinking of anything while we devoured it... at least *I* wasn't thinking of anything, well maybe just about the pizza, you know, but not worrying.

It was all a bit low-key, travelling back home on the metro. That is, till I started feeling queasy. I couldn't stop myself dwelling on the trouble we might be in when we got back and whether a car would be waiting to take me away. And having seen Lily, I felt guilty eating the pizza and started to feel sick with it all. I didn't say anything, but I suddenly had to rush to the loo and everything came up—the pizza, the mocktail, Lily. My throat burned and my eyes watered. I looked at myself in a piece of not-quite-flat metally plastic that was supposed to be a mirror. I imagined this tiny room was my prison. I wondered if they'd chosen not to install real mirrors in case they broke and somebody hurt themselves. Thoughts came into my head like how people seem to think of absolutely everything these days, but they couldn't think of what was wrong with Lily. I struggled over that ridiculous reality. It was like the sound and movement of the train became part of me. Chugged along, without any influence on life. I was losing myself in these thoughts and was in some sort of trance, when there was a *thump-thump-thump* at the door.

"Ollie? Ollie! What you doing? Are you okay?"

Nathan's voice sounded comforting.

"Yeah."

Kamal said, "You sound like an old man. You haven't been time-travelling in there, have you?"

"We're nearly here, you know," said Nathan. "You coming out? You'll have to come out now!"

Something peculiar inside me wanted him to smash down the door, shouting, "Don't worry! You're safe! You won't be trapped much longer! I'm getting you out of here! I'm letting you out!"

Instead I heard, "Hey, you bonehead! Get your ass out of there now, man!"

I slid the lock open just as we were pulling into the station, now brimming with anxiety over what punishment lay in wait for us. I could think of nothing else on the long walk home.

Celia-mail 3

Dear Mam,

Sounds great that your new neighbour's deaf and uses subtitles. What a pleasant change for you to have such quiet, and how nice you can practise your sign language with her. You were right to go ahead and take your level-two British Sign Language all those years ago, weren't you, even when Dad said it was a waste of time because you were 'only' a classroom assistant. He said you'd make a fool of yourself. His face when you showed him your certificate! And a stroke of luck that this new neighbour, Emily, used to organise parties for high-society folk in London and is going to help with yours! Hope her ideas aren't too fancy. You know how you get led into things!

It should have been me planning it all with you really—I still wish you'd let me give up work to look after you at home.

About the Campbells, the family with Lily and the boys. Yes, I'm not shy to speak my mind, but you have to be careful with what you say, and Anna, the mam, is trying her best, so she doesn't need people interfering.

Had the young one, Oliver, and his brother, Nathan in today. They'd both played truant from school, so I was in a panic about what to do. There was even a policewoman here. It was my duty to tell the ward sister about it, and she phoned the parents. She said Mam had cried and said, "That's it now." I think she meant about sending Oliver away. I'm still worried about him. Call me a daft sausage, but I'm really extremely fond of the lad. He was very out of sorts today. You can tell he's feeling neglected just the way he holds himself, and he looked so unhappy when I asked him how things were at home. I wish I could take him home myself! Anyway, I think little Lily, the girl with my favourite name, will be out within a week, so Mam will surely change her mind about sending the boy to his grandparents. I can't imagine what it would do to him if his sister goes home and they still send him away. I know you'll tell me not to get so embroiled, but I can't help it.

Nothing to report with you-know-what. I shouldn't have said anything. It was a big upset this time, Mam, as it's been six years to the month since I lost my baby boy and not much less since we've been trying again. I'm afraid I got myself into a right state. And no, I won't take your money for an IVF cycle because that money is for your cruise, Mam, so I know you're trying to be kind, but please don't mention that again because we won't take it.

Must dash, as I have to pop into Newcastle. It's Cheryl's leaving do, and I was supposed to bring a quiche.

Much love,
Celia x

A Homely Prison

By some stroke of luck, Kamal escaped punishment for our truancy. He had this idea that it was 'fate,' but in my opinion, that is slightly fanciful, since I found out Kamal had asked Alex Beaumont to say, "Here," when his name was called during lesson roll calls and afternoon register. He'd even arranged for Becky Bailey to say, "Here," in English in a deep voice, as Alex was in a different set from him; he'd convinced Becky that she owed him one since Noodle-Gate.

Nathan and I were suspended from school for a week, which seemed an odd punishment because for me, that was a reward. Being grounded for a week, however, was not so sweet. I could build up some motivation and get stuck into a gardening project at least.

Dad had gone crazy when he got back from work. We didn't even know Mam was in, but she had gone to bed feeling ill, apparently, and had been crying about it a lot, Dad said. I felt terrible. In fact, the only thing I was glad about was Sam being there because he was the sort of grounded person who didn't go ape.

Dad seemed more on edge than I'd seen him for ages. Sitting with lunatic eyes, he had pushed away Mam's candles into a clump and was tearing mint leaves he'd picked from the garden which were in a mound on the kitchen table—and when I say mound, I mean more like a mountain; looked like he'd scoured not only our garden, but a five mile radius. When he saw my expression, "Tea," was all he said. I wanted to say 'Who for? A herd of elephants,' but that would have been about as appropriate as saying 'Ooh a mint mountain! Nice one, Pops! Let's make heaps of mojito cocktails and get wasted!" Then Dad's loony eyes turned on us.

"For Nathan to go off was stupid enough, but for Oliver to then go on walkabout as well!" he said. "I ask you! What on earth were you thinking? Yes, yes, I know it's a difficult time for everyone, but you're putting your poor mam through pure hell with all this! Do you realise?"

"They're back now, aren't they, so let's just chill," said Sam.

"That is so amazingly helpful," Dad said, getting up, "but we'll have less of your advice, thanks! Oliver, what made you think it was sensible to sneak out of school when we were already worried sick about *Nathan* going missing?"

Sam had an answer to that too: "It's obvious. He was trying to help."

"I've asked you to stop, Sam, so please... Oliver? I'm waiting."

"I just thought that, I thought if more of us were looking—"

"See? Makes perfect sense," said Sam.

"Well, you're all out of order, and you two will not cross these doors the entire week. Do you hear me?"

"What? But I've got my competition, Dad. I can't miss that," said Nathan.

"You should have thought about that when you—"

"How predictable. 'You should have thought about that'! Why don't you find out *why* Nathan ran off?" said Sam. "Do you think this whole thing is about you and Mam? You need to look at the big picture, Ben."

"You and your bloody psychology! You haven't got a clue, you smug—!"

"Hey, come on. Losing it's not going to help. Can't you see?" said Sam.

"Oh, I can see perfectly well, Sam. You're trying to turn the boys against me! You're trying to cause rifts in your clever little cunning way!" Dad stood up.

"What are you talking about, Dad? Cunning?" said Nathan. "My head was exploding, and I wanted to get away, that's all."

"*Your* head was exploding? Brilliant! Try being your mam and me for an hour! Anyway, keep out of this—"

Sam said, "Why should Nathan keep out of something that he's completely the centre of? You're being crazy now."

"Because you should be supporting us, you... I'm sick of this. I'm the bloody father here and you're the sons! Learn some respect!"

"You're not though, are you, and maybe we're all coming at this from different angles."

"You nasty little... after everything I've... I've always tried my best with *all* of you. You should know that. You ungrateful—"

"Let's just calm down and talk about how to move forward," said Sam. Dad started waving his finger manically at Sam.

"Don't you dare tell me to... Do you know what we're going through? Every day... we don't know what's wrong and we can't... "

Dad fell heavily into the chair at the kitchen table, his forehead thudding onto his folded arms. I'd never seen him cry before except when Lily was born. Sam and I looked at each other and he moved his hands from his hips to face his palms up to the ceiling, and contorted his face into a sympathetic but unwavering scrunch. When I saw Dad so helpless, and risking being smothered by mint, I wanted to go to him and put my arm round him, but I seemed glued to the spot.

It was Nathan who made a move. He sat in the chair next to Dad and said, "Come on, Dad. I'm sorry. I'm sorry to cause you trouble. I didn't think. We'll stay in the house all week like you told us, won't we, Ollie?" I nodded. Nathan put his hand on his back and said, "I can make you some dinners for when you get back from work. I'll make you that, what is it you love, saggy loo."

"Sag aloo," Dad said with a wobbly voice, his mouth still a few inches from the table, now spluttering leaves.

"Spinach and potatoes," I said.

I can't believe that was the extent of my involvement in the argument. I could imagine Poppy asking me what my contribution had been to this intense clash, and I'd have to say, "Spinach and potatoes."

Sam spoke next: "Nice idea Nathan. Shall we all try to move on here? Sorry if I got carried away but what's said is said. We'll have to try and pick up now. Ben, you've got your book club this evening, haven't you?"

At this, Dad lifted himself to a sitting position and flopped his hands into his lap, head drooped forward, saying, "Don't feel up to that."

"I think it'll be good for you. And you've been reading the book for a month. Why don't you just get ready to go out, and I'll have a talk with these two? There's absolutely no point in missing it."

Dad put his hand through his greying hair and made a flappy mouth pant, like a horse.

Sam seemed to have calmed him down. Dad's more or less last words on the whole thing were "Maybe. I'm going upstairs." But then he added, as he made for the door, "Your mother wants... It might be best for everyone if the two of you went over to your grandma's for a while. Sorry, it's not the right time to tell you, but I was supposed to... I promised I'd mention it."

As my and Nathan's jaws dropped, Sam said, "I'm not sure what that would solve, but let's discuss it tomorrow when everybody's calmed down."

Mam and Dad argued about if the two of us should go away or just me or if we should just stay at home for now and if so, which one of them should stay in to supervise us:

DAD: I've got very important meetings this week, Anna.

MAM: What about? Microchips? That's interesting, but I've got a child protection case tomorrow. I'm only back at work these few days because it's so vital that I'm there. They need me.

DAD: Can't someone fill in for you? I'm sure you all discuss each other's cases.

MAM: ...

I can't actually say what Mam said next, but Sam convinced them that we should absolutely stay at home and would be fine on our own and that they should both go to work.

The question was, were we really not going to cross the door for seven days and nights?

Needless to say, Kamal was at the door at four thirty on the dot every day, to give me the latest from school. Poppy had apparently asked Kamal to send me her love. I knew it was a cliché, but I was convinced it meant she actually loved me, which Kamal laughed off. I made him describe her facial expression and how she was standing when she said it, so he scribbled three drawings depicting exactly that, in various degrees of close-up. He gave lengthy accounts of events, re-enacted scenes, drew diagrams, and even produced a cartoon! The cartoon, presented on the Monday, was particularly impressive. It was entitled, 'Miss McGinty's Groodies.' The setting was the stage in the main hall, seconds before assembly was due to begin. The teachers often held cups of reviving liquid in an attempt to muster enthusiasm.

Mrs. Ireson had fainted while holding a cup of coffee, which had subsequently sprung out of the cup directly onto the front of Miss McGinty's white blouse, who, rumour had it, was not wearing a bra. On realising that the blouse had become suddenly see-through, Mr. Berks, head of PE, had dramatically untied a sweatshirt from his waist and flung it across the stage, in Miss McGinty's direction. The sweatshirt had missed, and knocked music teacher Mr. Osman's glasses off. He was groping for them on his lap as Miss McGinty scuttled off stage, or rather was scuttled off by Mrs. Marshall, one of the deputy heads.

The last drawing showed Mrs. Ireson being carried off by Mr. Wetherill with a think bubble from his head saying, "I've waited five years for this!" Mr. Hickey, the head teacher, was in every drawing, looking aghast with a hand to his head. One of the pictures of him included a think-bubble that read, "God forgive me, but why can't I just fire them all and start again?!"

"Epic! Can't believe I missed that!"

"Yeah, Olivo, but there's more. Get this, when the assembly started, Mr. Hickey switched on his power point and it said 'The Domino Effect' with the subheading, 'Careless Actions Make Ripples.' The room erupted. I don't know how many people weren't optically tricked into reading 'Nipples,' but I wasn't one of them."

We both laughed and couldn't stop for a good few minutes.

"What did Mr. Hickey say?" I was trying to picture the scene.

"He waited, looking at his feet for a while until things died down. Then I think the irony of his assembly topic suddenly twigged; you could see his shoulders start to shake. It was vintage! The school erupted again! A few teachers couldn't hold it together and had to get off the stage. So, Dead Man Walking goes over to Mr. Hickey's laptop, and, typically unmoved, turns off the display and whispers something into Mr. Hickey's ear. Mr. Hickey gathers himself together, lifts his head, and makes this super-human effort to put on a serious expression. We all laugh again, and he has to cover his face before finally composing himself. Then he says, 'We're going to look at what can happen if you don't take responsibility for your actions,' and then this film about Newcastle Prison comes from nowhere onto the screen!"

"You're kidding!" I said, not wanting the story to finish.

"'Her Majesty's Prison, Newcastle-upon-Tyne, has five hundred and fifty-one inmates spread across six residential units...'"

"Urgh! How d'you remember all that?"

"Just the stark contrast from what came before. He had everyone's attention, you see. We were lapping it all up, and then these subtitles got lapped up as well."

"Mental. He could have flashed something up that was remotely worth learning!"

"Indeed. The words of Shakespeare or Martin Luther King Jr or Noam Chomsky or Tony Benn or Sylvia Pankhurst or Margaret Ashton or Betty Bumpers... Yes it is a real person."

I was intrigued. I was also not only disappointed to have missed this dramatic assembly, but was gutted, too, to hear that not only was the supply teacher, Miss Pratt, back in school, but she had taken them for English as well as PSHE since Mrs. Ireson was now off with a nervous breakdown. What's more, she had started up a Shakespeare drama club.

"Inspired teaching, but her casting skills are severely lacking," Kamal moaned. " She's got Jade Hilton playing Ophelia, I ask you! "

"Have you got a part?"

"Does the name *Hamlet* mean anything to you...?"

I knew he was talking about a Shakespeare play, so I said, "At last, your great role!"

Turned out *Hamlet* is the name of one of William Shakespeare's most famous plays. Kamal told me Shakespeare wrote thirty-seven plays in total! I'd only heard of three, well four: *Romeo and Juliet*, *Macbeth*, *Midsummer Night's Dream*, and now *Hamlet*.

"And what a role! I must be careful not to be dragged in too deeply, you know, struggling with those great questions. Who would choose to endure the pain of life if he were not afraid of what may come after death?"

"Is that a rhetorical question?"

"Aha! You learn well, Olivo! You learn well!"

"Are you going to speak like that all the time now?"

"What meanst thou?"

"You're so annoying. Hey well, this could be the beginning of a glittering career."

I found myself feeling eager to get back to school. Perhaps Miss Patricia Pratt would find a little part for me if she hadn't cast everyone. Even if she had finished casting, I wondered if she could maybe create a new role for me: nothing great, just a tree or a crow or something.

As well as getting the lowdown from Kamal on significant events at school, I spent a lot of time with Nathan during our week of shame. He taught me some skateboard tricks in the garden (which we decided to count as part of the house), and I taught him some drumbeats and forced him to help me tend to some plants in the greenhouse. "What? You actually have gardening clothes?" he had said when I suggested he make do with an old smock I kept in a drawer in a little cabinet in there. He put it on, but wouldn't shut up with his, "If my mates saw me now!"

I had Nathan cut up plastic bottles to make covers to protect some pots of seedlings from the cold, but it was when we were pinching out shoot tips on my fuchsias to encourage bushier plants that The Fuschia's Bright came up, and so Poppy Teasdale. I told him about my feelings about her, which, to be totally honest, was something of a gigantic mistake as he wouldn't stop taking the mickey out of me all week. I told him I was getting agitated about Mam sending me away; he said he would go with me whatever Mam and Dad said.

We decided we shouldn't go out at all, as Mam and Dad had been so upset about our behaviour. That's why we were shocked when Sam suggested a trip: not just a walk into the village, but a train trip to Durham! He said that if we got found out, he would take all the flack—more or less say he forced us to go. He said he wanted us three to have an adventure together.

Thing is, Nathan and Sam's dad lived in Durham. Nathan had never lived with him, so he wasn't massively close to him, but Sam had lived with him on and off since he was thirteen. He was an architect and an artist, and they now saw him regularly. He had designed parts of railway stations around England, and as a result, Sam and Nathan had free metro and first-class train travel. I think that's why Nathan got the train into Newcastle so often—plus, it wasn't just a train pass; it was almost like a pass into another life. And that's how Sam could flit between Newcastle and Durham so easily.

John, their dad, had an exhibition stand at an art show in Durham, and he needed someone to cover for him on the Thursday, from eleven in the morning till three in the afternoon.

"I thought we could just hang out there, you know, have a laugh, help Dad if you're up for it," Sam said.

Mam had been ringing about three times a day to check on us.

"What if Mam rings? She'll kill us," I said.

Sam was unfazed by this: "Suit yourself. She knows you never answer the landline. What's the big deal? You just answer and speak really loudly and make it short—say you're dying for the loo."

"Ollie's right. What if there's background like music playing? She'll suss it out, man; she's no bonehead. And Dad needs us to do the right thing now."

In his usual matter of fact way, Sam said, "Don't come if you're that worried. *I'm* going anyway coz I don't go into college on a Thursday, so I'm just saying, it could be good. And like I said, I'll take all the blame if something goes wrong."

"Ah, how kind of you to lower yourselves to sit with me in a standard carriage!" I said to my brothers, even though I knew they weren't actually bothered about using their first-class option. In fact, I think Sam didn't usually go in first class at all because he thought it was embarrassing and he said a true socialist would not travel first class. I wasn't sure about that.

We had a laugh on the way to Durham. Although Sam sometimes seemed like a third parent and used to tell us off a fair bit, today we were all the same. He had brought his MacBook Pro, which he never seemed to be without, and a dongle to get the Internet.

We showed each other hilarious clips from YouTube like that fake of the man going down a huge waterslide and flying 115 feet into a plastic kid's pool.

We played daft games like 'first one to see a red car slap your hand on the table.' I won that game—reckon my drumming skills helped, you know, quick reactions.

We were fascinated by a man who was dressed as a woman. He had a blond wig and hadn't even bothered to shave. He kept talking about nail varnish and shoes and things. At one point, he said to his friend, "Don't buy ruddy tights from Primark! They might have a decent pot-squeezing panel, but you only have to look at them and they ladder!"

It wouldn't have been that funny if his friend hadn't been a big, rough-looking bloke. I said that could be us one day, which made Sam and Nathan crack up even more.

We played the staring-out game, which we were all rubbish at.

We gave points out of ten for four girls a bit younger than Sam, who looked about eighteen or nineteen, sitting near us. Nathan insisted we should give points over four categories: face, body, voice, and overall impression. The one with a croaky voice and jet-black shiny hair won. It was her scores for 'overall impression' that clinched it—she had a certain grace about her and a sincere smile. Or I suppose it could have been because she was the only one without a pierced lip, which none of us seemed to massively like.

What we didn't talk about was a mother, similar age to our mam, with a little girl of about five. I think we watched their every move and heard their every word without even realising it. The little girl was in pink and had fair, curly hair. She was sitting next to her mam, and every time she laughed—a teeny, cute, unfeasibly-high-pitched giggle—I couldn't help the sound spiking my throat.

After marvelling at the view of the castle and cathedral perched above a loop in the river, we pulled into Durham station. Nathan and I were first to the door. Sam, behind us, noticed the woman struggling with two bags. As he asked, "Can I help you there?" and reached for the bags, the mother held onto them and pointed with her head down to the little girl.

"D'you mind, flower?"

There was a still moment where Sam looked like someone had asked him to blow up his MacBook; then he tightened the straps on his backpack and reached down for the pink girl. He held her securely in his arms. I don't think he actually said anything, but they smiled at each other.

"You lookin' after me?" the girl said in her tiny voice.

Sam just nodded, still smiling, but sort of a pained smile.

Once off the train, the mam was very grateful. "Thanks, pet. She doesn't always go to strangers."

There was a slightly awkward moment when Sam seemed to be holding onto the little girl too long. Then he very carefully put her on the ground, moving down with her, so that he was on his haunches, on her level, by the time she was standing. They were still smiling at each other and he said, "It's a pleasure," all the while looking at the pink girl. He said it in a way that people don't normally say it, you know, in other words not like 'whatever' but like 'that really meant something to me'.

Sam walked in front of us and didn't say anything all the way to the exhibition hall, even when Nathan asked where it was. We were just arriving when Nathan's phone rang. It was Mam, but luckily she was in a rush; she was about to go into a meeting and couldn't talk. I heard Nathan saying, "Yes, fine, Mam"; then Sam snatched his phone and said, "They're working on some music, so ring *me* if they don't hear their phones later. I'm here all day."

She said she'd phone about three o'clock. Seemed to defeat the purpose of checking on us—telling us exactly what time she was going to ring—but I guess it was just how things were then. Anyway, I was glad Sam had made up something clever.

As we approached the exhibition hall, I worried over whether we'd get away with it and wondered what John's pictures would be like and if we'd sell any and if we'd get any wages. I was hoping they wouldn't be rubbish or rude.

The Great Exhibition

John was waiting for us at his stand. I'll tell you, he's the most laid-back person I've ever met—you know those cool people who nod their way through life. Sam is a bit like that, too, but he gets in moods or he can get passionate. John wouldn't even see the point in wasting energy doing that, I don't think. He didn't even question why we were all there. I liked him, but I hardly ever saw him. I think he was only interested in my two brothers, for obvious reasons. He told us there were some beers and crisps if we wanted. He didn't even say, "But not you two, of course."

"Nice one. Cheers, Dad." Sam was always kind to his dad. Come to think of it, most older people seem to be really kind to their parents all of the time. I wonder what age that starts to happen?

"Ollie's made a packed lunch anyway," said Sam.

"No, I haven't."

"Oh. I thought... ah well, no sweat. Never mind."

He's good like that, Sam. He can be narky for the slightest thing, then when you expect he might go mad with you, he's all calm and forgiving.

Sam had asked me to make some sandwiches, but it had all felt too underhand and even when I pulled myself together to make them, I automatically made beef-paste ones (duh), and I knew none of us liked them. As I threw them into the bin, I felt like a bully who'd just stolen someone's lunch. I sat down at the kitchen table and tried to fathom out what possible joy a person could get from chucking someone else's grub away since I was even feeling guilty just for throwing my *own* sandwiches in the bin. I was just pondering the question of whether Lily would ever eat a beef-paste sandwich and what I wouldn't give to see her at the table eating anything or not eating anything for that matter, when Sam shouted down, "You ready Ollie? We're leaving."

I suppose you might be guessing that we all dossed around and got sloshed at the art exhibition; sorry to disappoint you, but that would be quite wrong. We didn't touch any of the beer. What we did touch were two bags of crisps each (me, cheese and onion, Sam and Nathan, pickled onion Monster Munch) plus coffee, tea, hot chocolate, and some freaky vegetable cake from the woman on the next stall. I think she said it had carrot and beetroot in it. She seemed to be constantly brewing up some drink or other. She obviously had a lot of time on her hands; Sam said he couldn't imagine she was seeing much till action. She was selling what looked like manure thrown onto toilet seats with glitter stuck on, like nightmare doughnuts. The glitter was shaped into words like LIGHT, SEARCH, PEACE (I'd have been tempted to spell it PEESS), and HOPE.

"She must be overdosing on hope," Sam said, "to entertain the thought that she has a cat's chance in hell of selling a single piece."

"Harsh, man. They're unusual, you know, so someone might 'get' them," Nathan said.

"We're immersed in the cut-throat world of art sales, Nathaniel," said Sam.

"Was I christened Nathaniel?"

"I don't think you were christened at all," said Sam. "Doomed! You'll go straight to hell!"

"What! Do you really believe that?" Nathan said.

I was still laughing at them both when I took a gander round the hall. It was ice-cold even though it was April, and fingerless gloves seemed to be the order of the day. The air was filled with muffled jazz music, and you could hear the scrapes and knocks of stands and chairs and stuff being readjusted. The gentle hum of hopeful voices was somehow soothing; no hard selling in this market you could tell, for sure.

In fact, you may be interested (or not) to hear that we had quite a cultured and enterprising time at the exhibition! Any whiff of mischief or hard selling came from Nathan, who turned out to be a talented salesman, as it happens; we sold three of John's abstract works, which was two more than the day before, apparently. He made lots of eye contact and actually said things like "You look like someone who can spot a masterpiece!" and "Let me guess. You've got a flash pad that could do with a stunning work of well-cool art!" Nathan was great at the flattery part, but he even made some stuff up. One time, this man was checking out a particular painting, looking really like he might buy it, you know, mouth open, rubbing chin, eyes slitty and all that. Nathan looked at Sam and said, "Aren't that couple coming back in half an hour for that one? Didn't they say they wanted it for their new trendy bar or something?"

And the man actually bought it!

His cheesiest line, though, was to a female student who was staring at a blue canvas:

"That one's so you. It matches your eyes!"

Sick bucket, please. Sam made a fingers-in-throat gesture, and I chuckled. She didn't buy it (in both senses), but she did take a photo. We didn't know if that was allowed, but Sam said, "Can't do any harm. Exposure and all."

Sam showed himself to have commendable marketing skills, too. Turned out Doughnut Deirdre (that *was* her real name—the Deirdre bit, that is) had a bag of glitter going begging, so Sam got hold of some boxes, which he deconstructed, and made signs using slogans like Hang the Cost, You'll Get the Hang of It, Do I Need to Paint You a Picture? and a big one saying Art Is Long and Life Is Short. When I suggested that this last one might actually put people *off* buying it, Sam said I was being a pain and sent me off on a wander around the other stalls, you know, check out the competition. We only had a short time left before we'd have to leave, so I had a good look around.

It wasn't like a competition, though. Everyone was so friendly and upbeat. Lots of the artists looked interesting and individual with mental hair and unconventional clothes. It was like a commune or something, you know, where loads of arty people live together, light fires, and dance naked and that. I came upon a stand showing glasswork. I thought the panels were brilliant the way the light shone through them and cast coloured flashes across the room.

"How do you do that?" I heard myself asking the lady. She was very pretty with black spiky hair, a short yellow vest with flowers stuck on (not real ones), and, I couldn't help noticing, tight jeans that were not doing a fantastically good job of covering up her whole rump! There was a sign—Sophie Sunstone. Couldn't have been her real name, surely. I loved drawing, but I imagined making something like those glass panels would be amazing. I visualised Mam's face opening one I'd made on her birthday—a glass star or heart maybe. I could make a guitar for Sam, too, and probably a skateboard for Nathan and a lawn for Dad... No, that would just be a green square... maybe a totally stunning plant like a Heliconia rostrata. It means lobster claw because of the shape. Interesting fact of the day: this plant is related to the banana.

The lady explained a bit about the process: "You lay the artwork on the glass, and you fire it in the kiln."

I thought to myself, *It can't be that simple. Does she take me for a fool?*

"Maybe I'll ask for a kiln for my birthday," I said. This could be my thing...

She laughed like I'd made a joke, so I forced a grin like I hadn't been serious, and changed the subject: "They'd make great presents," I said.

"Yeah, cheers. Gave one to my best friend for her wedding. Flowers on it."

"Did she carry it down the aisle?"

She dropped her head back and laughed hard and I noticed she had her tongue pierced. I honestly wasn't even trying to be funny; I just kept saying stupid things.

"Dead lily, she carried."

I stopped breathing for a moment. She twizzled the ends of her black spikes with her left hand, her right hooking the back of her neck.

"What?" I said.

"Poor thing thought she'd look sophisticated with a single flower, trying to be poetic, but it was so hot. We were *all* wilting that day," said Sophie Sunstone, with a sarcastic smile.

"Oh... I'd better get back to my stand."

"Which one's that?" Her fingers were now miraculously squeezing into her front pockets.

"John Webster's. Over there." As I pointed, she nodded, which made me feel all sort of part of it and important.

"I dig his work."

Do people really say 'dig'? Then she added, "It's so enigmatic, don't you think?"

She was surely trying to show me up now, and I didn't even have a dictionary with me.

"Enigmatic [whatever that meant], yes. I was just saying that before. I must get back anyway, and thanks, you know, for the information. Nice glass."

As I walked back, I felt a sudden surge of panic. Had I just said, "Nice ass"?!

By the time I'd got back, John was there: all smiles and cracking open a beer.

"Sure you won't join me, Sam?"

"Nah, Dad, we've really got to get back."

"Four pieces! I can't believe it!" John said.

"What, you sold another while I was away?" I said.

It turned out that just after Mam had phoned, in a hurry again and suspecting nothing, Sam's glitter sign, Art Is Long and Life Is Short, had gone for fifty quid! Some guy had offered twenty pounds, but Nathan said they were keeping it for an American Art collector who'd left a deposit of sixty pounds, which Nathan grabbed from the tin and waved about. He had apparently convinced the man that he had a steal at fifty quid! Unbelievable!

"Yes, not a bad day's work, Ollie." Sam was chuffed, but there was unease in his voice. "There may just be a burger in it for you, if we get to the station early enough. We're catching the 16.32, Dad, so we'll really have to shoot."

"There've been some cancellations this afternoon, so feel free to stay at mine, all of you, if you get stuck."

It was jaw-drop city.

"Hey! I didn't say the station's been taken over by terrorists! Just some cancelled trains, that's all."

Our train was due in at 16:45 and we absolutely had to be back by then, because Mam got in between half past five and six o'clock.

"I promised to get them back that's all. Sorry, but we'll really have to go. See you soon, Dad." Sam gave John a hug, as did Nathan, but I didn't. Well, I hardly knew him.

"Geez. This is all very sudden. Well, hey, thanks boys. Great job." He pressed bank notes into Sam's then Nathan's hand, and we walked off at a very brisk pace.

"Hey! Ollie!"

I turned round to see John beckoning me.

"Go on then, Ollie, but hurry up!" Sam said.

John gave me a fiver, saying, "I haven't got much but thanks, Ollie, you know. Cheers. Take care."

He patted me on the back. I mean, it wasn't like I didn't have my *own* dad or anything, but I appreciated the thought. And I hadn't even done any work.

"And you must do this again! Good team!" John shouted after us.

Once at Durham station, "Shit!" was Sam's reaction to the departure board. The next three trains were cancelled. We'd have to get the 17:51, which would get us in at 18:10, then there was the long walk home… Half past six! Mam was due home by six. Ouch.

The return journey home couldn't have been in more contrast to the outward journey. We all sat with our music on. The only words I remember being spoken were Nathan's to me: "Stop shaking your leg. It's getting on my nerves." I imagined Lily sitting on my knee, pointing out the animals in the fields and us all laughing at the cute way she said "sheep."

The train got in five minutes late. We had just started our walk home, and I was hoping Sam was making up some clever story to explain our absence when Nathan's phone rang. Mam.

"Hello? Oh, okay. No worries... Yeah that'll be nice... Yeah he's fine... Okay. Bye."

Mam had apologised for running late. She'd be home at half past six. Then it was a scene from a cop show—we all stopped dead, looked at each other, looked at our watches, Sam said, "Run!" and we started legging it home. Only, I couldn't keep up with them.

"For God's sake, hurry up Ollie! We're gonna get caught!" shouted Nathan.

"Just go ahead! If Mam's back, you can distract her or something."

"We're going through the vicarage! It's quicker!" he said.

"No, Ollie, go the long way," Sam said. "The vicarage way is dangerous. We'll cover for you if we get back in time."

As I panted along, I saw them both bound over the high vicarage wall and disappear. I'd never even been that way, but if it really was quicker, I'd have to trust Nathan and give it my best shot. My heart was thumping in my throat, but I was glad of the rain when it started: it cooled my sweaty head.

How the hell did they get over this? I thought. The limestone structure loomed in front of me, not remotely wanting to be got over, like a prison wall. Barbed wire wouldn't have seemed out of place. An imposing blockade for a religious wall. I thought Jesus was supposed to be arms open—"suffer little children to come unto me" and all that. I had to do it. I found a nook in which to slot the tip of my right foot and hoiked myself up so that the wall came to the top of my nose. I flung my arms over the top to pull myself up, grazing my chin on the damp roughness, so that I was sort of hanging over the other side. When I got myself in a horse-riding position over the wall, "You've got to be joking!" The drop on the other side! It must have been three feet more then the roadside. *I should get back onto the road*, I thought, but I felt fired up. I'd take the risk. Maybe we'd all get back before Mam that way. She was always late anyway. I had got both my legs on the vicarage side of the wall. I desperately fumbled my feet against the wall to find a crevice. I looked down and saw a piece of wood jutting from the wall. I put my foot on it. Crack! It gave way immediately, and I went crashing to the ground. I fell on my back, and it took the wind out of me. My right arm had scraped past a severely pruned rose bush, and my hand was scratched to hell.

When my breathing came back to normal, well, I say normal, but more precisely, normal as in halfway-through-a-marathon normal, I sat myself up. As I sat, gasping for air, I realised I didn't even know the way out the other side. I thought, *He must mean just go through the gate. Yeah, that's over the other side. I'll just run around the house to the other side.* As I leant on my hands to push myself up, I took a sudden breath through clenched teeth—my hand stung and looked like it had got in the way of Edward Scissorhands, with blood oozing out by now.

I stood up, wiped the soil off my left hand with the back of my right, and started sprinting again. I ran up a slopey lawn. Once on the gravel path—the unmistakable noise of a mad dog barking. The path, which ran up the side of the house, led to another lawn, so I picked up my step and scrambled across the lawn. The grass was slippy, and just as I was nearing the last section of the 'shortcut', kind of sliding towards the tarmac path, like I was surfing, I lost my balance and was thrown onto it, knees and hands first. By some weird miracle (maybe because I was near a vicar's house), I only put my left hand out, which I got scraped to smithereens on the path. I looked back over my left shoulder to see the dog bounding towards me. If I could just make it to the gate! I clambered onto my feet and raced to the gate. I couldn't climb over it, as there was a stone arch around it, so I had to grapple with the agonisingly fiddly latch. "Jesus!"

An excruciating pain in my right ankle, then a voice: "Elijah! Here, Elijah, here! Leave him! Here! Elijah!" The dog let go of my ankle and ran to the front door of the vicarage. "Inside! Inside now!" the man said, as he started walking away from the door, towards me. I thought, *Open the gate and run, you fool!* But my mind wouldn't talk to my legs as I stood on the spot, shaking and watching the dog sneaking out of the house again.

"Ooh, dear!" the man said, as he saw my hands. "You'd better come in. I'm the vicar. Michael. I live here. Catherine!" he shouted to a woman who'd appeared at the door.

"Elijah's out again—get him! He's caused enough trouble to last a lifetime!"

"Elijah was your bloody idea, remember!"

"Catherine, please, not now. Anyway, he was from poor Simon Armstrong who lost his sight—thought he'd be docile like his owner. Right, young lad, take my hand and I'll lead you along the path."

"No! I mean, no. I have to get home."

"Do you think Elijah's bitten you?"

I twisted my right knee leftwards and pulled up the leg of my trousers, to look at my ankle. Now *he* did one of those quick breaths in through clenched teeth and said, taking my arm, "Ah, the evil hound. Just the excuse I needed to see the back of him. You need someone to look at that now. Come this way."

"Mr. Armstrong was a police officer, Michael," Catherine said, still not moved from the doorway. "I thought you knew it was an ex–police dog when you insisted on taking him on."

"What in the name of...? This boy needs help. Get Elijah, Catherine, or I'll have to shoot him! Come along, lad."

"But I have to get home! I'm late! Do vicars have guns? My mam will be... my mam'll—"

"Catapult, silly. I'm telling you, young man, that you need to come inside. We have to help you."

"... kill me!"

Celia-mail 4

Dear Mam,

That Oliver I've been mentioning, well, she's sending him away to his grandma and grandpa. She was in tonight on her own and told me Oliver and the older boy, Nathan, had been getting into trouble and it was all too much to cope with. I told her Matilda, the ward sister, had mentioned they were going to send Lily home in a few days to stop her worrying about the boys and to see she didn't have to go to those lengths. She knew it must be true because she's seen that the senior nurse doesn't give much away. Can you believe it—she stuck to her plan and said that if Lily was going to be home, she'd need a very calm and quiet environment? And the grandparents live miles away! Like I said, I feel like taking him home myself. Should I offer? I know, I'm being crazy. You know what I get like. I just can't imagine how the poor boy will take all this. He's longed for his sister to be home. I get the impression he and Lily had a very close relationship before she got ill, too. Anna said she'd let him see Lily for a day or two before getting him picked up by the grandpa. Hopefully he'll only be away a short time like a week, while the little one recuperates. Seems daft though, doesn't it? I think Oliver would *speed* her recovery. I know, I get too involved.

So you're going with Emily's idea and having the party on July 27th, your actual birthday? Don't let her take over, Mam! I'm not sure about the theme either, *The Wizard of Oz*, I mean you don't even like musicals, and it doesn't seem fair that she's saying she wants to be the only Dorothy. The canapé ideas might be tricky too because tiny little burgers, hotdogs, and kebabs don't seem posh to me and don't match very well with shaky hands.

And is she serious about thimbles of baked beans with a cocktail stick? OK, she said it worked well at her cowboy party for Lady, what was it, Shufflebottom-Smythe (are you sure that's right?) in Kensington twenty years ago, but I don't know that it would work with a crowd your age. And the mini ice creams—why has everything got to be mini, for pity's sake? You don't want people breaking their necks slipping on mini fast food that's spurted out of everyone's hands and being blinded with flying beans. I can see it now. It would be carnage. Last time I was there, that Denis dropped his lunchtime cheese bap, and that's huge food in comparison! Just make sure you think carefully about it all, Mam. I'll be in soon and will have a chat with Emily about a few of my ideas.

Had to dash out earlier because Matilda gave me an Easter card and I had to go and buy her one plus we were supposed to bring in Easter eggs or chocolate for the children who can eat it on the ward, and I didn't bring any. I didn't forget, I just thought it wasn't fair for the kids who can't eat chocolate, but Matilda said I was being over-sensitive, so I popped into Newcastle.

Have to run. Spilt carrot soup down my top and I must wash it off properly. It looks like I've been sick!

Much love,

Celia x

Lily's Plants

Talk about heavy silences! In the car on the way home from 'minor injuries,' I couldn't even look at Dad. I did think if I glanced to the right without moving my head, and squinted, I'd see steam coming from his ears. I could feel him looking at me from time to time ('looking daggers,' as Kamal described it when I told him—think it's from Shakespeare), but I continued looking blankly through the windscreen or leaning on my left hand to look out the side window, then flinching with the pain as a result.

Once home, Dad got out of the car without saying anything, slammed his door, and walked down the side alley to get to the kitchen. I stepped out and did the opposite. I mean, if there'd been a competition in closing car doors unbelievably quietly, I'd have definitely won. Or maybe it wasn't actually closed properly.

I didn't want to be there. I didn't want to be noticed. I climbed the two front steps of the house, knowing that the door was probably locked, and I was right. My head dropped back on my shoulders, and I took a deep, slow breath in. It was dark by now, and the rain had stopped. I looked deep into the sky and thought that I'd much rather be up there right now, floating away from everything.

At that moment, Sam appeared from the alleyway, round the corner of the house.

"Are you okay?"

"No."

"I told you to... no point now. You'll have to face the music."

"Dad didn't speak to me. The whole time."

"You messed up. He's upset. It's to be expected."

"What about Mam?"

"Same. She's not here though. She's at the hospital."

"I thought she'd been today."

"They wanted to discuss something, so she went back at half seven.'

"Lily's coming home?!"

"Not sure."

"It will be, I bet!"

"My lie didn't go to plan, by the way, just so you're in the picture," Sam said. "Mam's car was here when we got home; she was in the house. Nathan managed to scale the wall and get into the tiny bathroom window up there. Couldn't talk him out of it; he'd made up his mind."

"So did he get caught?"

"No. Far from it. For all they know, he's been in the house all day."

"Wasn't he all sweaty and puffing and that?"

"Sweaty? Get this—I told him to stay in the bathroom till I came to the door. I managed to keep Mam talking for as long as I could in the kitchen, and when we both got up there, he was in the bath! Yes, he got into trouble, but only for using a load of Mam's really expensive bubble bath! He smelt like a perfume shop."

"What did you say to Mam anyway?"

"We'd have been fine if you hadn't... You're so annoying at times. I had a front-door key, didn't I? She was at the back in the kitchen. I did leave the door open for you, but Dad locked it and was waiting for you when that priest phoned.'

"Vicar."

"Whatever. I talked to Mam about Lily. Then I said you two were in the middle of some music upstairs. Obviously I thought when Nathan opened the bathroom door to us, he would pretend he'd just gone to the loo."

"What?!"

"I thought you were just behind us!"

"So what about me, then? You said you'd—"

"I told Mam I'd shouted at you earlier. I said I'd upset you, and it hadn't surprised me that you'd gone off."

"So you told her I wasn't in the house, then?!"

"She has eyes, Ollie."

"Nathan didn't put his foot in it then?"

"He did suggest you might be at a play rehearsal at school."

"At school? I'm suspended! And I'm not even in the play!"

"Then, when we heard you were at the vicarage, he said you wanted to start going to that church."

"Oh my God!"

"Exactly. I know. Come on, you need to rest. You've had a shock. I'll get you something to eat."

"Am I in trouble, though?"

"Look, stop feeling sorry for yourself and just come inside. It's done now. I spoke to Dad; he's agreed to leave it till tomorrow."

"Leave what? I thought you said—?"

"You've got a good imagination, Ollie. Think of a vicarage alibi."

If Everyone Knew Every Plant and Tree

After Dad ignoring me, Nathan saying I looked like a zombie (because of the bandages on my hands), and Sam making me a sandwich and a hot chocolate before seeing me into my room, I sat heavily on my bed. I asked Sam to pass me my dictionary so I could look up 'vicar' for some ideas and 'enigmatic' that Sophie Sunstone had said, but it was too hard to turn the pages. I looked up Kamal's Betty Bumpers on Wikipedia instead. She was real: an American art teacher and a world peace person who pushed for desegregation and vaccines for little kids. I wished there'd been a vaccine to prevent Lily's illness, whatever it was.

I lay back and ran through the day in my head. I smiled when I remembered the journey to Durham: how we'd laughed and how together and samey we'd been. I wished Lily had been there. Maybe she would be back soon. It wouldn't be long before we really were on a train together. She'd be sitting on my knee. "Look at the horse, Lily. Can you see the lovely horse in the field? It's learning to gallop." And she'd be learning all those words, wonderful words. I could teach her: gallop, canter, trot, scamper, scurry. "Look at that beautiful oak tree! Lonely looking, but it's strong and bold, isn't it?" Hazel, hawthorn, holly. "Shall we buy an ice cream when we get off the train?" Peach? Pistachio? Pomegranate?

Would Mam let her come with Dad and me to Kew Gardens in August (if they really were going to take me all the way to London)? We could start teaching her some Latin flower names. Lilies.

Lilium pyrophilum

Lilium albanicum

Lilium longiflorum

I dreamt that I held a huge exhibition of my stained-glass work, and every piece was of Lily: Lily eating curry, Lily dancing, Lily on an elephant, Lily laughing. There was a massive glass window called 'Lily Swimming' and Dr. Spark said he wanted to buy the one called, 'Lily Drowning'. I screamed at him to go away and told him there was no such title. He pointed to the stained-glass window, and it did say 'Lily Drowning' underneath. I dived into my backpack to grab my gun, but there was nothing but beef-paste sandwiches. I started cramming them into Dr. Spark's mouth. He struggled and his muffled voice pleaded, "I'm drowning! I'm drowning!" Then Sam was running up the aisle of a church carrying Lily who wore a pink dress. He shrieked, "You've killed him! You'll go to jail for life! You'll never see us again! You'll never see Lily again!" I picked up a stone and threw it at the huge stained-glass window, which shattered into millions of pieces in slow motion. The sparkling jags and shards turned into stars, and everything went black.

I woke up aching, anxious and eager to see Lily. I knew I couldn't: I was grounded.

Dad stopped my pocket money for a month and took my phone and drumsticks off me, even though I had come up with the great idea that I had gone to the vicarage to arrange to get Lily christened. Mam hardly ever spoke to me those days, and when she did, it was usually shouting, and for only the slightest reason. So it was weird the morning after she came back from the hospital smiling and talking non-stop. But it wasn't that weird... because anyone would be happy to know:

LILY WAS COMING HOME!

I couldn't believe it. I was dying to tell Poppy and Kamal... No, I wouldn't tell Poppy unless Mam had already told her. That way, it would be a great surprise when she saw her. And I wouldn't be going away now! Things were looking up big time.

We were told to expect a slow recovery, but once Lily was home, it was like a miracle. She seemed to be practically back to normal after a few days. The mystery illness had disappeared, although one of her arms had gone quite floppy because the fits had damaged it. Mam was obsessed with not getting her excited, but I loved to see her bouncing around and shouting and laughing, and I couldn't help myself encouraging it. I suppose she wasn't quite as bouncy as she had been, and she got tired a lot, but her talking seemed totally back to normal. I would be back at school next week, so *everything* was moving towards normaldom. Then after a week, it would be the Easter hols. Perhaps we'd be going away—all of us... the whole family.

The weekend before going back to school was brill. Lily was walking pretty well, so Mam said I could take her for a short stroll. I knew exactly where I would take her. I found Lily sitting on the sofa reading a book with Nathan.

"Guess what I thought we could do today!" I said to Lily.

"Go to the park... and the Nature Centre and, and... buy me a new dress with a lot of skirts in it with bits under coming down like a princess?"

"Uh, no. I thought let's go to Poppy's shop and pick out some new plants."

"What, and put them in the soil in the garden?!"

"And plant them out in the soil in the garden."

"Yaaaaay!" She jumped up and started spinning round and round then sprang right up onto me, wrapping her limbs around my body, like a pet monkey. She tucked her head onto my shoulder for a moment before pulling back, her good right arm wrapped around my neck and her face now inches from mine.

Nathan laughed. "She's like you, man—she's well into plants."

She said, "How many? Shall we get loads and loads so we nearly can't carry them all and we topple over and get soil all over the place and in our hair and in our mouths and we'll be nearly sick getting all the black soil inside us? And, and... then we might get trees growing out of our belly buttons and, and flowers growing out of our bottoms!"

While Nathan flopped sideways onto the sofa holding his stomach, laughing, I spun her round as fast as I could saying, "You're mad, do you know that?"

"I'm mad! I'm mad! Oh Gad, I'm mad!" she screamed as her head dropped back and her arm flung off my neck. She dangled backwards as I whirled her around till I got dizzy and stumbled onto the sofa, crushing Nathan.

"Come on then, slow coach! Let's go to Fushy Bright!" Lily shouted as she bounced up and ran (a bit slower than normal) to the door of the living room.

You couldn't not feel bright walking into Poppy's shop: the delicious sweet smell of earth and petals, Poppy posing with a magazine behind the counter, leaning low on the left hand of her bent arm, rows and rows of seeds and seedlings ready to be nurtured. Everything waiting to happen.

"Hey!" she said, sliding into a sitting position, to an upright pose, hands on hips, head tilted to the left. Then she saw Lily and leant forward onto the counter to get down from her stool:

"Lily!"

Lily got spun around again.

"Wow! You look so well! And you're so pretty in that coat!"

"It's new. I got it for coming out of the hopsital."

"Has Mammy been spoiling you?"

"Oliber buyed it for me, didn't you, Oliber?" She tugged on my hand that she was holding. I didn't answer and sort of grinned inanely at Poppy.

"You did, didn't you, Oliber?"

"Yes."

"That was nice of you. You don't buy *me* coats."

"Oh, Oliber, don't you ever, ever get presents for Poppy? Not even on her birthday? You should because girls like getting those things, like diamond rings and… and bicycles."

I stifled a blush as I remembered getting Poppy a necklace for her birthday and being too embarrassed to give it to her.

"Maybe I'll buy her a plant," I said.

Lily said, "Yeah, a plant… one with a lot of flowers. And you got to be careful because it can die. Oliber teached me you have to look after it. We're going to get lots of plants Oliber said, didn't you, Oliber?"

"That's right."

"I can help you choose," Poppy said, with her so-pretty smile.

"I was thinking a foxtail lily to start with, but I think it should be Lily who chooses everything. You have to choose everything, okay, Lily?"

We were ages in the shop and the nursery garden. Poppy came round with us, keeping an eye out for customers. The first pot Lily picked was an anemone. We all howled every time she tried to say it: a memony, a mememy, an emena, an enema. She jumped up and down when she saw a huge poster of an agapanthus and couldn't stop giggling when I told her its other name was African lily. We got some bulbs and she kept saying, "I want to be called African Lily!" She insisted on adding Antirrhinum seedlings to our trolley, too, and laughed again when I told her they were known as snapdragons. Actually she wanted two types: pale pink and dark pink. I'd have to put plastic bags over them to protect them from the cold. But I had to draw the line at a Zantedeschia.

Poppy said, "Honestly, don't bother telling her the Latin names, Ollie. They're too difficult... and anyway there's no point. This is called a calla lily."

"*I* want to be called Calla Lily! My name is Silly Silly Calla Lily now."

"Sorry, we can't get that one," I said.

"No, Oliber, it's the most bestest one that I've ever seen."

"It's just not going to work, that one."

"Well, you said I could choose, and now you're being mean because that's my favouritist and you're being horrible telling me now we can't get it."

"We won't be able to grow it, Lily."

"Why not?"

"It needs a hot country. It's not hot enough here. It'll die."

"It won't die. Don't say that. Poppy, will it die?"

"I think so, Lily. It needs hot weather like in Africa or Australia."

"I don't care. It must of got the train a long way so it must be strong. I still want it, and anyway, we can try to look after it and it might get very hot weather. And if it dies, we can bury it, can't we, Oliber, can't we? Like we did with Hector."

"You had a plant called Hector?" Poppy said.

"Rabbit," I said.

"We can set the 'larm and get up in the middle of the night and give it extra water and some food, and a bag, then it could really grow, couldn't it? But if it died well... well, we could bury it, couldn't we, Oliber?"

"Couldn't you put it in the greenhouse?" said Poppy.

"It's just that... it's very expensive and I can't afford it," I said to Poppy, then turned to Lily and said, "It's very poisonous, Lily. It's a dangerous flower, and if we get it... someone could get very ill."

By now Lily was crying. It was the first time she had done that since she'd been out of hospital, and I felt myself starting to well up, too, just seeing her like that. And probably I shouldn't have talked about getting ill. Poppy looked embarrassed and said it was only a flower and that why didn't we come back next month and maybe think about it again. She told me I'd nearly reached my budget limit, too. I hugged Lily into me and said sorry before suggesting that we buy a packet of seeds. She chose a packet of forget-me-nots. Poppy said they were weeds, at which I pulled a face and said:

"Don't say that, you phantom cactus."

"Hey watch it, Ilex vomitoria!"

"Aha, well remembered!" I said.

"You're supposed to be insulted."

"It doesn't sound insulting coming from your mouth."

A lingering look before Lily shouted, "A tree! We have to buy a tree, Oliber! Just a little one. Oh, pleeeese. I just really, really, really, really want a lovely little tree."

Poppy screwed her face up at me with smiling eyes then said, "I forgot to tell you: if you buy more than three items, you get a free tree."

"But they're so expen—"

"I'm giving you a free tree, Ollie," she said with eyes massively open. Lily chose a rose bush. I didn't make the point that it wasn't really a tree.

I phoned Dad from the shop, and he came to take us home with our spoils. But not before I had suggested in Lily's ear that Poppy help us do some planting. So it was arranged that Poppy would come round the next afternoon—Sunday.

Lily fell asleep in the car, leaning on me. It was only a short journey, but I could have stayed like that forever, and my face was paralysed into a smile as I looked at her soily face and stroked her hair. Back where she should be. Back to normal.

"Looks like you've had a lovely time, son," Dad said.

I nodded with my smile.

"Some nice-looking bits you've bought there, too, and is that a seed-packet you're holding? Mam's worried that you've been out too long, though. She said you were going for a very quick walk to the shops."

I said nothing.

"She's still anxious, you see, and she's petrified you'll trigger another episode if you overexcite her."

I said nothing.

"Are you okay about going to Grandma's?"

My back jolted me upright. Seatbelt, throat and heart tightened violently. "What?"

Dad said nothing.

"What, Dad?"

I slowly leant my lower back into the car seat, and my head dropped forward. I felt Dad's eyes watching me in the rear-view mirror. We pulled up outside the house and sat quietly for ages before Dad said, "Give me that packet of seeds, love, you're getting it wet."

I said nothing, but passed him the packet.

"Forget-me-nots. Myosotis. Won't flower till next year, you know? Weeds," he said.

Poppy had said that earlier. She was coming the next day. I was dying to see her again. Our time with Lily.

"Not tomorrow, Dad?"

"Next week. Then it'll be the holidays so you won't have the long journey to school. We'll just see how it goes. Your mam thinks... "

I dropped further forwards and put both my hands over my face. Dad got out of the car, closed the door softly, and walked into the house, leaving the front door open.

My moving woke Lily up, but I hadn't realised till she said, "Did someone hurt you?"

I couldn't look at her. I didn't want her to see me upset.

"I'll look after you, Oliber. I can look after you now, can't I?"

She put her arm round my back, but that made me worse.

Mam's voice broke the quiet. "Why on earth are you two still in the car? She'll catch a chill sitting out here."

I got out of my door so Mam couldn't see my face. I collected the plants from the boot while Mam carried Lily inside. She flopped onto Mam's shoulder.

"She's exhausted, poor thing. That was very irresponsible, taking her all the way over there and getting her all dirty."

I said nothing.

Flowers in Still Life

If I was on my best behaviour, Mam might change her mind about me going away, I thought. I pretended one of the plants was for her, to get in her good books, and asked very calmly if Poppy could come round to help with some planting and if Lily could watch for a little while, wrapped in a blanket. She not only agreed but said the forecast was for sun and that she'd make us some refreshments. Result.

"Do I look like an old lady?" Lily said, sitting on a camping chair with a blanket over her knees. Poppy and I looked at each other, smiling, both saying, "No," and both winking at each other. I'd told Poppy about Grandma's; the way she said, "You're joking," and touched my shoulder made me think there was a chance she really cared about me. And the way my heart skipped a beat when she touched me made me think *I* definitely cared massively about *her*.

The sun was out, as Mam had predicted, and everything felt bright again, the three of us sitting in my section of garden on level three. My dad is an expert gardener, you see, who's slowly landscaped our four-tiered garden over the years. It was the main thing we did together. He threw himself into it when Lily was ill. Sam said it was because he felt like it was something he *could* fix. But, probably like me, it's more like just being outdoors and being close to nature—how things look and feel and smell... and the stillness. I remember growing my first plant, a tomato plant; I was only seven, and it was magic to me. Dad wasn't trying to be fancy or anything, 'tiers' and all that: the garden was on a slope, so it *had* to be in tiers, like olive trees and vineyards have to be when they're on mountains.

The top level is a patio in front of the kitchen picture window, at the back of the house. Dad laid Italian stones in concentric circles. Mam thought he'd gone a bit mad—Italian stones!—but he'd researched it for ages, and that's what he chose. This level, outside the kitchen, was bordered by railings and a gate leading to steps to the left as you looked out. Mam loves to sit out there on the bench, with a coffee or a glass of wine, looking straight out onto the valley.

Dad spent months building the stone steps that wind down from the iron gate to the next three layers. He even fixed lights into the sides of the steps. The patio looks down onto the second tier, which is largely a pond with a decked sitting area and some grass and trees. On the third level, he constructed a shed and laid out rows and clumps of herbs and vegetables (that's where my section is). The bottom tier is laid to lawn where we have a trampoline and play ball games... correction—it's where you *could* play ball games.

"Can't I help with the digging? I really want to put in my special plants and flowers," said Lily.

I very much wanted us to do it together. That was the whole point, but Mam had insisted Lily rest.

"She could sprinkle the first bit of soil over each one," said Poppy. "That wouldn't take much effort."

"Like a celebrity. Imperative to avoid strenuous activity for a VIP planter," a voice said coming from the steps at the side.

"Kamal!" Lily shouted as she jumped out of her chair, tripping over the blanket. Kamal just managed to run forward to catch her before she hit the ground and put his hand on her head as she hugged into him. I noticed her left arm dangling down and thought Mam had been right saying she needed time to recover properly.

"Look at you!" Kamal said, getting down to her level and holding her face. "You look splendiferous."

"How did you know I was here?"

"It's all over the papers: Lily Ethel Campbell's Back in Town!"

"Is it? Is it really, Oliber?" she said turning to me.

"Don't tease her, Kamal. We have to be very gentle with her; she's still weak."

"I'm not weak. Look!" She held up the camp chair above her head. "And I can even do this!" She put the chair back and started jumping up and down. Kamal joined in.

"Their mam will go mad if she sees Lily being too active, Kamal. And she'll send Ollie away," said Poppy.

"What? What do you mean?" said Kamal.

"Shh. Let's not talk about that," I said.

"Why is Poppy telling fibs, Oliber? You not going to go away, are you? Are you going to leave me, Oliber?"

"No."

"What say we get on with some gardening?" Kamal said. "I'll procure another one of those chairs and sit with Lily, and we can proffer advice from the sidelines."

"You do speak funny, Kamal!" said Lily.

"Watch it, you, or I'll never make up another poem for you!" and he started tickling her. She giggled her way back into the chair, and I put the blanket on her just as Mam appeared. She'd brought a jug of orange squash and a platter of sandwiches.

"Hello, Poppy... Kamal. I've brought you these," she said, placing them on the grass. "You all have a great time now, but keep it low-key, remember?"

"Absolutely, Mrs. C," said Kamal. "Actually, could I trouble you to take a snap or two, please? I brought my camera to mark Lily's return home."

"Oh, that's very sweet of you. Yes, I'd be happy to."

Once Mam had gone back in and Kamal had fetched another chair, we got down to business. I had the idea of mixing the anemones with the forget-me-nots. With Kamal looking out for Mam, I let Lily sprinkle all the forget-me-not seeds over the entire patch we were working on. We had a mixture of white and purple Agapanthus (Agapanthi, should probably be), which would flower in the summer, and I'd thought to plant them in a woggly line at the back, but Lily said she liked them clumped together, so we put them in the corner. It was all going to look a bit mental now anyway so it didn't matter where the snapdragons went. Funny ones, snapdragons—they love the sun, but wilt if they get too much. A bit like people and wine. I wanted to try to protect them as much as I could.

I tried to get Lily's ideas on it, but she and Kamal seemed to have lost interest and were making up poems about the flowers. She loved Kamal. He always seemed to illuminate her whole face, sending mushy sparkles into her eyes. As I discussed where to plant the antirrhinums with Poppy, I could hear Lily crying with laughter at the rhymes they were both coming up with: Lily/willy, Poppy cheers/floppy ears, snapdragon/milkwagon, and even Kamal's anemone/

hegemony. Every time Lily tried to say 'hegemony' (don't ask me what it means, as I forgot to look it up), Kamal rolled about, blocking his ears and saying, "No! No! You're sending me insane, mispronouncing it!" and she would dutifully crack up.

I could only find one pair of gardening gloves, so Poppy had put on the right and me the left. As we were kneeling in front of the bed, digging a hole in which to put the seedlings, I was explaining how the Latin name for snapdragons, Antirrhinum, meant "like a snout," at which Poppy laughed, called me a geek, and squeezed my hand. Her touch sent buzzing all the way up my body and stung my ears. I turned my head to the left and caught her looking at me in a very sort of enchanting way, if that makes any sense. I kept my eyes on her for an embarrassing length of time until she pushed me over. The dirt on my trowel flicked backwards onto Kamal and Lily.

"Hey, you soily sods!" said Kamal.

Lily, of course, laughed and stood up to wipe the earth from her pink T-shirt dress.

"We're only messing, K," said Poppy.

"Indeed—messing is the operative word. And I'm off to the lavatory now before I mess my pants." He always had a way of pandering to Lily's humour. She practically fell off her chair.

While Kamal was in the loo, Lily had the idea of putting a worm in his drink. Poppy said she couldn't stand worms, so I set about trying to find one. I located one in no time. On Kamal's return, Lily immediately told him he should have a drink, slightly giving the game away. He actually let the worm hang from his lips; Poppy and Lily reacted by screaming. The screams turned to laughs and for Lily turned to a coughing fit, which couldn't have been timed worse as Mam appeared again:

"What's wrong? What's happened? What's happening to Lily?!"

Kamal said, "We were just having a laugh, Mrs. C. She'll be fine."

"With all respect, Kamal, you haven't the faintest idea if she'll be fine or not." Mam ran up to Lily and started patting her back. "Why's she crying? What have you done?"

"It's from laughing, Mam," I said "We've been having fun."

"So you've been over-exciting her again? I told you categorically to have a nice, calm time with Lily, and I can't believe you've... " Lily stopped coughing. "Look, I'm glad you're all here with Lily, but I'm so... I need her to have a restful time."

"Sorry, Mrs. C."

"Shall we leave now?" said Poppy.

"It's probably best. Thanks, Poppy."

Lily said, "But, Mam, my rose tree! Oliber, my rose tree! I want to plant my rose tree!"

"Quieten down, darling. How long will that take, Oliver?"

"Ten minutes maybe?"

"Back inside in ten minutes then." She kissed Lily's forehead and made her way back up to the house, saying, "See you soon, Poppy and Kamal."

"Bye, and thanks for having us, Mrs. C," said Kamal.

"And thanks for the sandwiches," Poppy added.

"Why's she still so anxious? I mean, Lily's home now," I said.

"This bush is not going to plant itself," said Kamal.

I brought out the rose bush and suggested putting it right at the front, but Lily wanted it against the wall.

"Doesn't exactly dance on the nose," said Kamal.

"What?" said Poppy.

"It's a bit dead, smell-wise."

"You can forgive it that: it's such a sweet-looking rose," I said. "Look how lush and dense the foliage is. Very thorny though."

"Yeah, they're five-star flowers, gorgeous pale pink."

"A type of polyanthus," I told them. "Fairy rose. Weird really because it shouldn't be blooming this early in theory. Magic. Poppy must have been giving it special treatment."

After my sister ceremoniously threw some soil to start planting it in, Poppy took her hand, sat on the chair, and pulled her onto her knee. Kamal tucked the blanket over them both and sat on the grass leaning on the arm of the chair. When I turned to see them there, all fixed on my performance planting, they looked like a still-life painting. I grabbed the camera and took a quick shot. Not one of them changed their positions or facial expressions for the photo; it was like time was standing still.

"Polyanthus," Lily said perfectly. No one clapped or laughed or patted her head or anything. We all just smiled. "You will look after that tree ever so carefully, won't you, Oliber? Don't let it die, will you?"

"Hey, we'll be looking after it together, sis... forever. And it's a tough rose; it doesn't catch diseases."

"But you have to be really in charge of it, Oliber."

"Shall we keep pruning it so it stays neat and small?" I said.

"What's pooning?"

"Cutting it back."

"No. Let it grow big and strong to be the biggest and bestest pol... polyanthus in the whole wild world!"

Then everyone did clap. A thought darted through my head—that Nurse Celia would have loved to see Lily now, and she would have clapped, too. Or maybe she didn't really notice individual 'cases': so many children passing through her doors.

Bang on cue, Mam called for us to go in. Poppy slipped Lily off her knee and said, "Is that watering can full? I'll just water the rose bush in before I go."

"Yeah, but I think Lily should water it in; it's her fairy rose bush after all."

I half regretted suggesting it when Lily seemed to struggle, her left arm unable to help her steady the right one, but Poppy helped and she managed it and we all clapped again, in relief as much as celebration.

I took Lily's hand to walk back up to the house. Poppy kissed Lily, then me on the cheek before leaving, which left me like jelly. As she and Kamal left together, I prayed that Mam would be pleased with me and that I would be allowed to stay at home. I suppose I'd find out that night or the next day.

Grandma and Grandpa's

Double-disaster Monday.

Disaster number one (slightly prepared for)—Grandpa was to pick me up after school to take me away. Nathan was definitely not going with me.

Disaster number two (*not* prepared for in any remote way whatsoever)—Poppy was not at school and was not coming back for ages.

I nearly had a heart attack when Nathan told me she was absent.

"She did want to say goodbye," he said when I saw him at break.

My face stung all over with prickles. I took a huge breath in and couldn't speak.

"Hey, calm down, Ollie. You trying to pull your hair out or what?"

"Goodbye?"

"She's gone to Australia, hasn't she?"

"What? Don't lie. She's supposed to be going in the summer."

"She has. She has, honestly. She's gone to the Land of Oz. I thought you knew anyway."

"Why didn't she tell *me*? I saw her yesterday."

"Her friend Daisy told me it was a sudden thing. Her gran, who she stays with, got seriously ill last night, so they took the next available flight. Maybe she's going to die."

"Oh no. Poor Poppy. I can't believe it. I wonder how long... I should text her. I don't know what to write."

"Aren't you used to texting her?"

"No."

"No? I thought you were really into her! You just don't follow the normal rules, man, do you?"

"I am, I do, I don't know what to write, okay."

"Oh my God! I don't get you. What are you like, you dipstick? Ask me!"

"What d'you mean?"

"When you don't know what to write, ask me."

"You haven't got a girlfriend, anyway. What would *you* know?"

"Hey! A lot more than you! Remember, I do actually have loads of friends who are girls!"

"What about now then?" I said.

"Now what?"

"Will you help me now? I have to write a text."

"Her phone's not going to work now, Ollie, is it? She's on a plane."

"And then she'll be in—"

"Australia. Yeah, really, Ollie. Bummer."

"She's supposed to be going on the art trip to London."

"When's that?"

"First of May."

"Well she might just be back by then. You're really gutted, aren't you? It's not the end of the world."

"Well, it's certainly the beginning of an ultra-*weird* world. One day everything's normal—well, not *that* normal, but at least Poppy and I are living at home—then, the very next day we're both living at our grandparents' houses! Does that make sense to you?"

"Oh yeah, that's true, isn't it! That's cool in a freaky way."

"No, Nathan. No, it's not cool in any shape or form. Do you think I *want* to leave home? Do you think I *want* to leave my sister who's finally home?"

"You know I would have come with you. Grandma said only one."

"So why not you?"

"I don't know. Because you've been in trouble a lot?"

"I'm not so sure about that. I was going to ask her to sit next to me on the coach as well."

"Grandma?"

"Nathan! The art trip."

"Oh, Poppy."

I had my outfit all planned. Even spent my savings from my plant-sales money on Etnies trainers because she told Nathan she liked them. And now I'd missed my big chance, well, probably a lot more than one chance, actually, because I didn't even notice chances, Kamal told me often enough.

"Mam'll have an address or something, I bet. Or ask to be a friend on Facebook."

"Mam won't be bothered about where they've gone."

Mam didn't seem bothered about anything except Lily—and I really don't think I'm being like a spoilt brat saying that because I did understand why, but I just definitely noticed it loads. Even though Lily was home, Mam spoke less than she used to and was still, I don't know, separate. I couldn't help thinking of her like a Fritillaria meleagris; it's like this droopy, sad-looking purple plant. I think my face had been screwed up in puzzlement in the car all the way to school that morning—apart from feelings about Poppy and Lily and why I was leaving home, why had Mam pressed my cheeks and stared into my eyes before I left for school like I was being sent away from the Warsaw ghetto to escape from the Nazis or something, when it was her who had actually decided to send me away?

I climbed into the front of my grandpa's orange VW camper van after school. I got a shock as we pulled away when Bill Owusu bashed the side of the van shouting, "Cool set of wheels, man!" but Grandpa didn't flinch.

I thought he probably hadn't heard it, but he said, "I'm used to that. Always been popular. You had a good day? What you in now, form three is it?"

"No, year nine."

"When I was a teacher it was form three."

"Oh, I didn't know you were a teacher."

"Didn't you? What did you think I was?"

"Dunno. Never thought about it. Maybe an organist."

"Well yes, you know I play the organ, but it's tough to earn a living from that. You still playing the guitar?"

"No, I never did. Drums a bit. I'd like to maybe learn the saxophone actually, but I think it might be too hard, and it'll take ages to save up for one."

"You'll be fine—just have to knuckle down. Practise makes perfect. Marvellous instrument. You can be a famous jazz musician. I'll come and see you and smoke a cigar—one of those big fat ones."

"Dad likes them sometimes."

"Oh? Your mam still smoke, too?"

"Yeah."

"You been looking after her?"

I didn't know what to say. Is that what I was supposed to do? Had I failed? Is that why... ?

"Grandma's always talking about her, worried, you know? Newcastle match tonight on the box!"

"Oh right." They were born in Newcastle-upon-Tyne and still had a bit of a Geordie accent.

"And Grandma's made beef stew... and she's put you in the back room, where your mam used to sleep."

"Oh right."

I usually looked forward to going to Grandma's house, but this was different. It was the first time I'd ever been on my own, for a start. The swollen golden hedge above the front garden wall didn't look as funny as it normally looked; instead of a bouncing clowny thing, it was drooping and misshapen. The squeaky gate wasn't giggling this time but squealing. The bright pink front door—painted that colour as it was the cheapest pot of paint Grandpa had come across that day, he had been proud to tell us—normally cheered you, but today it looked threatening. It was open, so we stepped up into the porch, and when I opened the glass door, Grandma's smiling face greeted me, her arms outstretched. I couldn't believe how pleased she looked to see me.

She gave me a big (long) hug and told me to change out of my school things. She gave me a VW van mug of tea with three ginger biscuits that she'd made and kept in an ancient tin, mostly stripped of its pattern; made me do my homework at the kitchen table with classical music blasting out of the radio; served me dinner and ice cream with apple crumble; and let me watch telly (football match that I didn't want to watch) and eat mint chocolates before bed.

Grandma told me Grandpa had put my electric blanket on. I love electric blankets—they're a cross between dangerous and cool—and showed me that she'd tidied the old desk in my bedroom, so I could work there from now on.

"There are still a few things in the drawers, but just you spread your things out how you want, pet. There's a brand-new bulb in the angle-poise, and I've sharpened those pencils for you." She pointed to a pot made out of the bottom of a drink bottle.

"What are those stickers on the pencil pot, Grandma?"

"I put those on myself to decorate it. Found them in a box of old teaching stuff. You know I taught in a special school?"

"No."

"Haven't got my glasses on, so I don't know what's on them, probably 'Well Done.' They're nice and colourful anyway."

The stickers said, 'I stayed dry all day!' When I told her, she did one of her funny throaty laughs and got me going. I stepped back, laughing, and fell onto one of the beds.

Grandma said, "Hey, don't mess that one up. You're in the other one. It's a newer mattress."

"How many decades old is it?" I said, and she burst out laughing again. Then, when she opened the wardrobe and showed me the motley array of dressing gowns to choose from, I had to slap my hand over my mouth to stop laughing again, and she suppressed another throat laugh.

When Grandpa stuck his head over the top of the bedroom door and said, "Goodnight, Olbol!" in a funny voice and Grandma brought me up a cup of Horlicks and told me she'd put some old albums called *Beano, Dandy,* and *Oor Wullie* on the table in between the two beds, I thought, *Maybe it'll be all right here.*

I lay in bed, surveying the cracks in the wall. I noticed how the heavy velvet curtains and the carpet and the duvet covers were all different patterns. I liked that nothing matched. I suppose there was a greeny-yellowness to the colour scheme with specks of red and blue; reminded me of flowers flourishing in a summer field—a meadow of buttercups, cornflowers, and poppies. I wondered if Poppy was in Australia yet and how I could contact her. I wondered what Nathan was doing at home and whether he was thrashing away at my drums with his mates. I wondered what Mam was doing and whether she missed me. I wondered if she loved Lily more than me. Lily probably missed me. She was much better now, but Mam was still obsessed with her having a relapse.

The loud ringing of the telephone interrupted my thoughts. I jumped out of bed and opened the door to listen. I could hear Grandma on the phone in the hallway downstairs:

"Oh hello, love... Yes, they got here in good time, and Dad says it's easily doable in the week. It's a bit of a way, mind, Anna; are you sure you want him to do that journey every day?... .. I know, I know, oh, but he shouldn't use Nathan's train pass. What if the poor lad gets caught?... They do I suppose... Yes, but Dad could take him; it's only about an hour and a half... We know that, but he'll insist on taking him... Okay, I'll suggest he takes him once a week. How long do you want us to have him?... Well, we're happy to have him as long as you need, but he won't want to be here, Anna, especially over the Easter holidays; he has no friends apart from Peter next door, but Peter's sixteen now, so he might not want to... Oh he'll like that. Camel did you say he's called?... Kam*al*, yes, of course, and he can sleep in the back room with Oliver. How's Lily?... Oh darling, I know... Oh that's good, sounds like she's improved tremendously... Yes, we could visit one day next week, perhaps the day Grandpa... Yes that's what I thought... I know we haven't, love, but your dad and I, we found it terribly hard to... I know, I know... Don't get upset, love... I know, now come on, Oliver's safe here and we'll come and see you and Lily next week and… It's okay, Anna… Yes… Yes. You have to take care of yourself and stop worrying about a relapse. OK, have a good night's sleep, pet, and at least you don't need to worry about Oliver… I will. Bye now, bye."

Then there was quiet, and I heard something I'd never heard before: Grandma crying. Grandmas weren't supposed to cry, and it was so powerful it was like she sent her sadness straight into my eyes and I went back to bed and lay face-down in the pillow.

I was not to go to school on the Tuesday—had to 'settle in' at Grandma's, whatever that meant. Grandma let me have a long lie-in before she poked her head round the door:

"Wakey-wakey! It's eleven o'clock. Careful with this tray: one of the ends drops off."

"Ah, cheers, Grandma."

She put the tray on my lap as I pulled myself up in the bed, and I smiled at its contents: smiley-face mug of tea, small glass of orange juice, two pieces of white toast with marmite, cereal in a bowl, a little jug of milk, and a few primroses in a tiny crystal vase.

"*Primula vulgaris*. Sound, Grandma," I said.

"I taught Latin for a while. You're like me. Your mam loved language, too; she was always writing a diary or a poem."

"Oh? I don't know anything, do I? Mam wrote a lot, did she?"

"I think she had a lot of secret thoughts and maybe worries and problems she wanted to pour out."

"Didn't she talk to you about those things?"

"We weren't really… She never seemed to trust me. She used to say nasty things to me a fair bit; she was quite an angry girl. She'd get upset easily and say *she* would be a good mother when she had a little girl."

"She thought you were unfair to her?"

"Mmm. I think she did, pet, yes. But she's forgotten about that now. We're fine now. Everyone goes through patches. She phoned last night—"

"I kn—"

"She said your friend Kamal wants to come and stay the night here. That'll be nice."

"Yes, but how long am I staying? And how come Nathan didn't come?"

"He's got his skating competition soon, and your mam says he needs to practise in Newcastle every night."

"And how long am I...? Oh it doesn't matter."

"Grandpa and I are singing tonight in a concert, and we're rehearsing this afternoon. Will you be all right on your own? I've made some soup, and there's a number for a pizza on the table with a ten pound note. There are drinks and crisps and that in the garage. We've only got certain channels, but there are DVDs if you like, and use the phone as much as you want; it's free up to an hour."

"Oh okay."

"We didn't want to leave you, but—"

"I'll be fine, Grandma. Honestly. Thanks."

She opened the curtains and, on her way out, gave me a kiss on the side of my head.

"Text my mobile if you need anything," she said.

By the time they left at 12:30, I was still in the bedroom. I stood for a while staring out of the window onto the back garden. What was that evergreen tree called? Certainly looked very old and overgrown. I didn't have my tree book. I couldn't even look it up. Perhaps Grandma had something; they seemed to have loads of reading material falling out of bookcases and covering surfaces in every room.

I walked over to the desk and opened the top drawer—a pile of old notebooks and papers. 'Private poems by Anna Olivia Campbell,' was written on the front of one of them. I sat on the chair and opened it, at the same time as calculating from the date that she must have been seventeen when she wrote it. Each page was filled with doodles, well, more like designs really, along with the writing. I flicked through the book. I laughed at a poem about a boy called Martin Mam must have fancied, though it wasn't supposed to be funny. Then, the title 'My Little Girl' caught my eye. It read:

> When I have my little girl,
> We'll watch the world, its fronds unfurl.
> We'll hang on branches high, and sway
> And drink the drama of the day.
>
> When I whirl her through the years,
> And save my girl from fears and slurs,
> I'll heave the hurdles from her trail,
> Then safe in love she will prevail.
>
> When I feel my colours fade,
> And cannot life's cruel fall evade
> She'll watch and wait and with me curl,
> When I shall have my little girl.

I walked back to the window and watched the garden again. It had started to rain. It rained in me, too. Salty pools brimmed and spilt from my eyes. A chaffinch and a wren flitted on the apple tree—happy and free. *My poor Mam*, I thought. *She had so longed for Lily all those years. No wonder...*

I decided not to read any more poems; after all, they were private. And I decided I would try my absolute hardest to be kind and delicate with Mam. It wasn't just Lily who was like a little bird.

I took the scissors from the same drawer and cut the page out of the notebook. I would put it in my special box, or perhaps I would give it to Mam when Lily got 100 per cent better… *if* she was going to get 100 per cent better. It was obvious she couldn't use her left arm properly, but nobody had mentioned it. No one had really said that maybe she wouldn't get fully back to normal. I wanted to help her. I couldn't stop the pain in my throat, so I lay back on the bed and closed my eyes. "Dizygotheca elegantissima," I repeated out loud until the pain passed.

Grandpa took me to school on the Wednesday, with Grandma. They spent the day in an art gallery and a free concert, then we went to see Lily after school. Kamal was supposed to come, but he was off school sick.

It was my big chance to be the best I could possibly be with Mam. I went to her and gave her a hug.

She patted my back and said, "You having a nice time?"

There was no question she'd gone mad. Lily seemed very well, but after jumping up and down and kissing me, she went off to play with a school friend who was there. I thought, *Doesn't she know I'm only here for a few hours?* I went to find her.

"Shall we check on the rose bush, Lily?"

She took my hand and led me all the way to it as if I were blind or didn't have a clue where it was. "Please don't poon it." She told me that she and her friend, Ava-Jane, were only allowed to do colouring but that she had wanted to water the plants because I was not there to look after them. Ava-Jane stayed inside while we tended to the polyanthus, which amounted to Lily smelling the blooms and saying, "Mmmm! Aaaah!" even though there was not really any fragrance at all.

"I wish you didn't go to Grandma's, but Mammy told me you got to help fix their garden for them because they get hurt if they have to bend down because they got all quite old. You are very kind, Oliber, but it's not fair."

I knew she was probably just thinking about herself, but it seemed such a caring thing to say that the wretched wells started again. I was starting to feel pretty pathetic, to be honest.

I forced a smile and said, "You're a sweet one, do you know that?"

"Sweet like a polyanthus?"

"Hey, you're good at words, I'll tell you that!"

"Will you tell me all the funny, long words for the flowers? You can write them for me, but they might be hard for me because I can read quite actually a lot but I'm not on the red books yet so I don't know. What is the funny word for forget-me?"

"Forget-me-*nots*, they're called, not forget-mes!"

"Forget-me-not—that's funny already. Let me not forget me not. Let me not forget me not, let me not forget me not."

"You're crazy. Myosotis is the Latin name."

"Mytososis. Mytosausage."

"Nearly. You know how I remembered it?"

"Tell me."

"You have to think of a boy called Myo with a tray of forget-me-nots which he is selling. He manages to sell them all, so you think, 'Myo sold his.'"

"Myo sold his, Myo sold his, Myo sold his, why so cold is!"

"You're too clever, Lily Ethel. So then to say the words 'Myo sold his' shortens to—"

"Myosotis," she said clearly!

"Genius, Lily balilee!"

"I might forget, forget, forget. You can learn me it again tomorrow."

"I will, but I have to—"

"Oliver!" Mam shouted from the top patio. "Time to go."

Lily scrunched her forehead and frowned. It was so over the top, I couldn't tell if she was putting it on or not, but she started running up into the house.

"Wait Lily," I said, at the same time as Mam shouted, "Don't run!"

Once outside the front, ready to leave, I hugged Mam and said, "Can I come home, Mam?" I was really no help at all being in an entirely different place. "I'll be really good... I can help you as much as I can."

"It's a good set-up for now, Oliver. It's all arranged, so just go with it if you want to help. Lily really does need calm. Wait till she's properly better."

She barely even looked at me when she spoke. I missed Lily like hell, but I started feeling that maybe I *was* best off not at home.

Just as I was getting into the van, disappointed that I hadn't said goodbye to Lily or even seen Sam and Nathan, I heard a squeaky voice from an upstairs window. It was Lily hanging out of Nathan's bedroom, so I got back out.

"Myosotis, Oliber!"

"I won't. And hey, how come you can say these amazing words, but not 'Oliver'?"

"Close that window this instant!" Mam said.

"I like saying it."

"Get in now!"

"It's my favourite word!" she said.

"Mine is 'beautiful,' beautiful."

"Bootiful, bootiful, bootiful! Bye bye, bootiful!"

"Abyssinia," I said, smiling and I climbed back into the van as she answered, "I be seein you too!"

Although the longing to be with Lily at home never left me, I got into a routine with Grandma and Grandpa; I had to, really, to avoid going insane. I amassed, in my room, useful and interesting items from around the house including a teeny TV, a really good dictionary, a family photo of Lily's fifth birthday party, and an exercise book in which I started a diary. I thought to write the diary for Poppy. Nathan had got me her email address, and it was such a relief when I heard from her.

I had every evening free because I did my homework on the long journeys to and from school. Most days Grandpa dropped me at the train station (and yes, I used Nathan's train pass), but two days a week he took me all the way to school. On those days I did hardly any homework during the journey because we talked the whole time. He put on jazz music like Miles Davis and Dave Brubeck and kept saying, "Listen to this bit, Ollie!" and "Let's hear that solo again!" and, my favourite, "You've got good taste, Ollie, just like your old grandpa. Grandma doesn't let me put this on. She can't stand it."

One day he even gave me a CD. He said, "You'll play like this guy one day. You must keep this CD. Have you heard of Courtney Pine?"

"No, I haven't. Who is he? Sounds American."

"Brilliant British saxophonist; parents were Jamaican immigrants." He said 'Jamaican' in a funny accent and I laughed. He's pretty cool, Grandpa, because next he said, "You'll like his recent work: tries to fuse drum and bass and garage with contemporary jazz."

"Wow! How have you even heard of stuff like that? What's contemporary?"

"'Of the moment,' 'the current time,' 'modern'... like you and me!" And we both looked at each other and smiled.

I did love the music, and I've never met anyone else who actually encouraged me to play the drums on the dashboard.

I had to accept that I was to stay at Grandma's during the Easter holidays with occasional visits home. I honestly couldn't fathom it, and I was plagued with yearnings—to see Lily more often, to see Poppy at all and to check on the greenhouse and garden—but at least it was a calm and caring environment. Nathan came to stay one night, but most evenings, I would see Punky Pete—that's what Sam called him—next door or he would come to mine. He was really good on the guitar and keyboards, and he managed to get hold of a saxophone for me to try out because his dad was a music teacher. I kept trying to play Courtney Pine music from the CD, but I could hardly even get decent notes out of it, never mind a tune. Pete was older than me, but we liked the same music. They had the Internet, too, so it was cool to hang at his.

One night, Pete smoked a 'magic cigarette,' as he called joints, out of my bedroom window and Grandma smelled it. She came up and pretty calmly asked him to smoke outside in future. But I thought the chances were I would now be sent away from the place I'd been sent away *to*, which, in my mind, was pretty rock bottom in the dismal stakes. I was glad Pete hadn't been banned from the house anyway, because Kamal hadn't come to stay. Turned out his aunt and uncle said he wasn't well enough. But I saw him at school a lot at that time because of the play. I ended up being part of it, you see.

Shopping With Lily

On the last Thursday of the Easter holidays, Grandma, Grandpa, and I drove to my house for the day. Lily had run up to me and flung her arm round my neck, and I scooped her up. We'd spent about fifteen minutes tending to our new plants when Mam called Lily. She'd promised to take her to the supermarket with her.

"I'll come, Mam," I said.

"Okay but no messing around. It's just a quiet, short trip. Lily's very tired—she hasn't been sleeping at all well and having nightmares. I'm worried she... I shouldn't though."

Once in the supermarket, I held Lily's hand and we read the shopping list together.

"I'm off to get the veg, Oliver. Will you take the trolley and Lily to the tins? And don't let her reach up for things. We need lots of beans, tuna, and tomatoes, and your dad wants borlotti beans—it's all on the list anyway."

We found aisle thirteen.

"They don't sound very nice, botty beans," said Lily.

"You're funny, you are."

"Botty, botty, botty beanies! Botty, botty, botty beans!"

"You'll get us thrown out, you loon."

The cans of tuna fish were on the top shelf, and Lily wanted to reach for them.

"Mam said—"

"Just lift me up, Oliver, pleeeease."

She'd called me Oliver. Must have been because of what I said. She was growing up. Moving on. As I held her up, she shouted, "Ow!" and I dropped her straight back down. She told me her eyes were hurting, and she clenched them closed. I got down and grabbed her face in front of me and got her to open them. She frowned and told me she had a headache. She looked weak, so I sat her on my right knee and stroked her back. I kept her like that for a few minutes before Mam appeared and walked towards us.

"Are you okay?"

"She's complained of a headache."

"It'll be the lights in here. Could you take her out? I'll just pay for what we've got so far."

In slow motion, I helped Lily up from my lap, but her face looked like a ghost and her eyes were wide open.

"She doesn't look right, Mam. She's not right!"

Her face then went into spasms, her teeth clenched, her head jerked back, and her right arm flung out, crashing into cans of soup on the nearby shelf. As the tins cascaded from the shelf and clattered and rolled on the floor, Lily's eyes went back in her head, and I dived to stop her falling onto the floor. I held her jerking body in my arms.

Mam said, "She's supposed to lie flat on the floor! Lie her flat!"

"No! I'm not putting her on that filthy, cold floor."

A crowd gathered as Lily continued to fit.

"Ring an ambulance, somebody!" I shouted.

Mam started shaking. Everybody around stood with their mouths open, like extras in a horror film. A box of soup had burst open and splashed on a man's trousers. He tutted as he wiped them with his handkerchief. The sickly sweet odour cut through the air and made me retch.

Lily's spasms lessened, and Mam hung onto the nearby trolley with her left hand, as the right clamped to the side of her face. A shop worker approached her and put her arm round her, which made her sob out loud.

"It'll be okay, Mam. It'll be okay."

On the Monday, back at school, Kamal was waiting for me as Grandpa dropped me off.

"Hiya, Oliver. How's Lily? I heard she's back in hospital!" Even Kamal was calling me Oliver now.

"She was only there two nights before they moved her to a different one."

"Oh. Is that good then? Is she getting better?"

"It's supposed to be a much better place, so I think they know what they're doing there. Yeah it'll be better, I think."

"So, they know what's wrong?"

"I don't think so, no."

"I thought...?"

"No, Kamal. They don't know—well, they're not sure."

"So they might know, then? They should have worked it out by now. Surely—"

"They haven't..."

"It so doesn't make sense. She's been ill for so long. Doctors don't really know much at all. You'd think—"

"No, Kamal! Drop it! They don't know, okay."

I was due to go home for tea and to see Sam, but when I got there at four thirty, Mam, Dad and Nathan were at the front of the house with their coats on.

"Where've you been, Oliver? We're all ready to go." Mam was unlocking the car as she spoke.

"Where're we going?"

Nathan seemed irritated and matched Mam's tone saying, "Do you never listen to anything? We're going to the new hospital."

No one had told me. It wasn't something I'd have forgotten. I needed the loo and was hungry, but I got in the car without saying anything.

The hospital seemed quite far away. "It's smaller and she'll get better care," I remember Dad saying, which was good, because it meant she was going to get properly better at last, I hoped.

"Make sure your phones are switched off. It's a very peaceful place here. And none of your inappropriate behaviour, Oliver, touching equipment and climbing on the bed," Mam told us.

"Why are you talking to me like I'm three years old?" I said to my mother. "I don't spend my entire time in hospital like you, but I do know how to act in one."

She didn't even answer. Perhaps she was angry with me. She must blame me for the relapse, I thought. It was my fault.

The rooms were colourful: bright sofas and cushions, paintings on the walls. The people there were so kind, too. Lily had more tubes than ever, including one into her stomach to feed, but it was a calmer place and there was stuff to do—TV, table tennis, computer games, and loads of arts and crafts equipment. I just couldn't believe my funny, bright, beautiful sister was flat on her back ill again.

A lady called Pauline came to play the saxophone at Lily's bedside. She was really cool. She went into all the kids' rooms just playing music.

"While Lily's enjoying the music, I'll show you a really special room that she might move into in a bit."

As he suggested this, the man was beckoning my mam and dad out of the room. Nathan went too, but I stood at the doorway, watching them all wander off up the corridor and I wondered when or if Lily might move into this 'special room.' She'd always been such a good patient that I felt she had a good chance. She must be quite far up the list, I thought. Then, looking back at her lying in bed, the mellow music washing over me, I noticed that she was doing the twitch-smiles again, but they seemed different. Were they somehow longer? She looked quite puffy, and one doctor had told Dad the illness had taken her sight now, and some doctors thought she couldn't hear either, but her eyes were slightly open and had a sparkle in them; they seemed to me like listening eyes. As the man had said, I think Lily really was enjoying the music. I walked through the soothing saxophone sounds. They filled the room and almost made your skin tingle. It was like a sort of sweet electricity. I moved towards the bed and knelt down next to Lily, so I could reach her hand.

"Do you like that, Lily? Is it making you go all tingly?"

Pauline nodded, as if in Lily's place, somehow knowing how much I wished my sister would answer. I squeezed Lily's hand, and she twitched hers back. She twitched a smile, too, and with it, the sigh I had heard so many times before at the last hospital, but this time it was stronger—more like a cat than a bird. So I climbed up onto the bed and lay next to her. I put one arm around her and stroked her matted hair with the other, and we just lay there, kind of wrapped up in the music together. Even though her mouth was busy playing the peaceful tune, I saw Pauline's eyes smiling; it was like all three of us were smiling. It sounds mad, but I thought of us as being three winged pigweed plants (frizzy-haired, green, bushy things, though obviously we didn't have green hair... and weren't that bushy). I told Lily this, knowing how funny she'd find the name, but I'm not sure if she picked it up.

I didn't feel the slightest bit embarrassed to talk to Lily in front of the musician.

"I love this melody. Do you, Lily? I'm glad I came here. Do you remember Poppy Teasdale? She's nice, isn't she? She loves looking after you, you know? She went away for a while, so I don't think she'll be able to see you very soon. I like her a lot. I don't want to make a fool of myself, though. I mean, Kamal—you love him, don't you —told me to recite poetry to her! He's a funny one, isn't he? Mind you, I used to recite poems to you, didn't I? Shall I... which one would you like?"

The saxophonist nodded again with her smiley eyes. Lily seemed like a rare and delicate bird that needed a lot of care. It was as if her feathers were so matted that they needed a lot of smoothing. But she wasn't free to fly off. I wished she were free. I wished I could make her better and whoosh her into the air. I remembered a poem Kamal had taught me which used to make her smile.

"Shall we do 'The Swallow'?"

I recited it to her, tucking my face in next to hers:

> Swallow, swallow swooping free,
> Do you not remember me?
> I think, last spring, that it was you
> Who tumbled down the sooty flue

> With wobbling wings and gaping face,
> A fledgling in the fireplace
>
> Remember how I nursed and fed you
> And then into the air I sped you?
> How I wish that you would try
> To take me with you as you fly.

The name Ogden Nash, the guy who wrote the poem, had made her laugh before, and she'd made up rhyming words like 'dogs 'n' mash'. The music seemed to echo the words even though Pauline pretended not to notice. I held Lily gently, and when I heard my parents' voices getting louder and louder in the corridor as they approached Lily's room, I gave her a big squeeze and she made a slight sound.

"I'll be back soon," I whispered to her before sliding off the bed, back to a kneeling position on the floor.

"Have you been having a nice time with Lily and the music, Oliver?" Dad asked.

"Yes. But her hair's so sticky. We shouldn't leave her with such sticky hair."

The kind man who'd taken Mam and Dad to the special room said, "Don't worry. She'll get a lovely bath after you've gone."

I must have sounded stupid, but I heard myself saying, "The water won't be too hot, will it? And will you put nice-smelling bubbles in like Mam does? She seems really delicate."

"Why you being so hyper? She'll be fine, Ollie," Nathan said. "They know how to look after her here."

He sounded like a teacher or a priest or something. I wouldn't be surprised if Nathan did end up being a teacher... or even a priest, at a push, I suppose. He'd have to start going to church every Sunday, but they say it's never too late. He'd have to give up skateboarding... No, he could be the first ever skateboarding priest; he'd be known round the world for it. He'd skate around to parishioners: a wee drop of whiskey at one house; jump on his skateboard to visit an old lady with a bad hip; whizz off to hospital to visit a sick boy, still drinking his cup of tea with too much sugar; back to the church to flatter the two flower arrangers on duty that week, thrilled by his compliments because they're both secretly in love with him; roll up the aisle at breakneck speed, kick-flipping up onto the altar, and starting eleven o'clock mass with seconds to spare.

That's a point: he couldn't have a girlfriend if he were a Catholic priest... He'd have to be Church of England or Muslim or Jewish... probably Buddhist, come to think of it.

Dad said, "Why don't you and Mam bathe her? That way you can be sure she gets the best treatment. Nathan and I'll play pool in the games room."

Mam loved to bathe Lily at hospital, but it had been ages since I'd helped.

"What about your work, Ben?" Mam looked at Dad.

He gave his response just by shaking his head. The thing was, the nurses probably gave sick children baths every day, and it wasn't like they needed to be supervised, but I suppose I was thinking a lot that day. And I suppose I didn't want to leave her that day. I wonder if there exists a spiky plant that turns to mush when you touch it.

Before Pauline left, she told me that the tune I loved was a lullaby called 'Sweet Baby, Sleep'. I'm telling you, you wouldn't want to sleep through a tune like that. I decided then that I'd find it on the Internet, download it, and Lily and I could listen to it over and over.

Mam and I went about the careful business of getting Lily and the bath ready. The shame and awkwardness I felt with Mam quickly subsided. She carried Lily into the bathroom, and I wheeled the drip behind her. It didn't seem right that Lily's hair was so matted, and I remembered how different bath time at home was: singing plus squeaks and giggles echoing in the bathroom; Dad kissing Lily's nose as it poked out of the too-big fluffy towel; Lily sitting on Mam's knee in front of the fire, all cozed up, by now wearing her favourite pyjamas and a pink dressing gown; her smile as Dad played 'Baby Beluga' on the guitar; the soothing sight of Mam brushing Lily's wet hair; the transformation of wet wool into luminous locks as the heat from the fire and Mam's hypnotic strokes worked their magic. It seemed to me that now Lily's hair had forgotten how to shine.

Once Lily was safely in the bathtub, Mam talked and sang to her constantly. I think it was because silence, bereft as it was of Lily's squeaks and giggles, was unbearable. I realised this when Mam left me alone with her for a minute. She felt all heavy with limpness and drugs. I held her body in the white water, gliding her back and forth just slowly. I hoped that the warmth and the frothing foam would be some small comfort to her. I prayed that she wasn't hurting. She lay there, long eyelashes clamping her swollen red eyes closed now, hair floating around her puffed-out cheeks. I kissed one of them and her mouth opened. "I miss you, Oliver," I thought she might say, or perhaps she would sing 'Baby Beluga', but there was nothing, just cruel silence exploding in the damp air. Maybe she *was* saying something but it was in whale language and I couldn't hear it. I found myself starting to sing myself:

> Baby beluga in the deep blue sea,
> Swim so wild and you swim so free.
> Heaven above and the sea below,
> And a little white whale on the go.

I'm not sure, but I think I saw a twitch smile. I bet she could definitely hear me. I carried on: "Remember, Lily, the guy who sang this? Called Raffi? Remember laughing at his nice, funny name?"

Baby beluga, baby beluga,
Is the water warm? Is your mama home,
With you so happy—?

Then, suddenly, my throat hurt so badly, I had to stop; the last thing I wanted was for Lily to see me upset. When Mam came through the door that second, I asked her to hold Lily and I ran to the toilet.

In the car on the way home, everyone was quiet, and I mean really quiet, like it seemed loud—a 'deafening silence.' Kamal once used that phrase when he was describing the moment he asked Becky Bailey on a date for the second time and said using an opposite adjective and noun was called an oxymoron. A deafening silence—that's exactly what was filling the car. Our heads were filled with opposites too. Dad's head was filled with worry, Mam's with sadness, Nathan's with those things plus skateboarding, and mine, those things plus the tune 'Sweet Baby, Sleep'… and wondering where Poppy was.

When we got home, I rushed upstairs and typed in 'Sweet Baby', but all the wrong stuff came up. Maybe Pauline had written the tune herself. By the way, I realise now I'd missed out the word 'sleep' when I typed it in. I ran downstairs and asked Mam to help me, but she didn't respond. She sat at the kitchen table with a glass of wine, staring into a candle. I swear she didn't even look up.

"Will you find out tomorr—?"

Then she turned to look at me with eyes that said, "I don't want to talk to anyone."

I shocked myself with how I reacted. "I just want to know the name of the bloody tune for Christ's sake, Mam! I'm asking you a question. I can't find the sodding name... I need to know what it is. I want to—"

"What are you talking about?" my mam finally said. "Why are you shouting and swearing at me?"

"What am I—" I stopped myself. "Do you ever even hear me anymore? Are you glad that I'm hardly ever here now? I may as well be invisible. Over here, Mam." I started waving like a crazy person but she just looked more puzzled, so I went back upstairs. Mam shouted me to come back and I took delight in ignoring *her* for a change.

Once in my room, I closed the door, leant against it, sighed and contemplated going back down to apologise or try to talk to Mam, but I couldn't face it. I typed in 'Pauline saxophone Rachel House' (that was the name of the little hospital Lily was in), but it came up with a man called Paul Rachello or something who played the saxophone. I'd remind Mam the next day, and then Lily and I could hear it again very soon. It might be hard, but I wondered if I could learn how to play it on an instrument. If we listened to it loads, could it possibly help her recovery? Mam would surely be pleased with that idea.

I thought of the nurse at the new hospital, but it wasn't Celia. Why hadn't Mam told me we weren't going back to Newcastle hospital? I should have said goodbye to Celia. I'd have quite liked that, well not that I never wanted to see her again, but you know what I mean. I hoped I hadn't disappointed her.

Celia-mail 5

Dear Mam,

I've been a bit disappointed, as I didn't say proper goodbyes to Lily's family and the boy, Oliver, I've talked about. More than disappointing is that she had a major relapse and has been admitted to Rachel House. You know what that means, don't you?

It's been playing on my mind that I want to contact the boy. His eldest brother left his jacket last time he was here, and Mam says he'll come in and get it, but I had the idea of dropping it round at their house. What do you think? No, I think I will do that. I'm keen to see how they are. Hang on a minute, Oliver is still staying with the grandparents as far as I know. Perhaps I'll have to let it go. I get too involved, I know.

I hope Emily wasn't too upset with our little chat about changing the party idea. She did seem to understand that the cabaret act was a step too far and that you wanted that Frank Sinatra tribute band. It's now booked, so you can relax! Yes, she looked up to heaven when I told her you wanted vol-au-vents, quiches, and sandwiches instead of her fancy canapés, but it was best to sort it out before it got out of hand. She seemed pleased that there was still going to be a dress theme anyway. Can't believe she seemed so miffed when you told her you wanted to be the only Snow White.

Must dash. Have to nip into Newcastle to buy some trainers. Got my aerobics tonight, and I thought I'd put them in my bike basket, but I don't know where my mind was because when I got to work and took them out, I'd only gone and put my slippers in by accident.

Much love,
Celia x

Drama Club

I worked out that if I could only get involved in the school play, I could move back home, because even though I liked it at Grandma's and no one would probably even notice if I was back home, I wanted to be nearer Lily.

A miracle did happen. At the beginning of my first drama club, when I thought the tough decision I would have to make would be whether to plump for helping with props or costumes, Miss Pratt announced that Bill Owusu had become heavily involved in jiu-jitsu and had dropped out of the play, leaving the role of Laertes open. Enter yours truly! Kamal kind of secured the part for me, convincing Miss that I was perfect for the role. This part was way more challenging than a crow would have been, and I feared I'd bitten off more than I could chew, but I was so flattered, I accepted. I think Kamal's motive for recommending me was more his excitement at the thought of our fight practices at my house rather than any faith in my acting skills.

Before I forget, I will say that even though the cast was years seven, eight, nine, *and* ten, most teachers thought Miss was deluded and over-ambitious to try to stage *Hamlet* (especially since last year's play had been a devised piece about pupil gripes, called *What! No Loo Roll?*).

There were only two scenes where Kamal and I got to act together, but they were both what you might call 'meaty.' We got to jump in a grave in Act V Scene (i), and in Act V Scene (ii), we got to have a sword fight. To say Kamal was enthusiastic about the sword fight would be an understatement. I was slightly in the mood for a fight too.

I was excited the first time we looked at my scenes with the character of Hamlet. Apart from anything else, it was to be the first time I'd see Kamal acting, so I could get some first-class ideas and tips from him.

My character, Laertes, can't bear that Ophelia's funeral is so basic, and at the actual funeral, I say, "Must there no more be done?"

Miss told us it's kind of backwards talk in Shakespeare plays a lot of the time, a bit like Yoda from Star Wars. But she taught us that if you look at the words carefully or more or less spend ages on it, it makes perfect sense.

She wasn't too happy with my acting.

"Say it like you mean it, Oliver! What does it mean? What do those words *mean*? 'Must there no more be done?'"

"Uh. Does it mean, 'Is this all we're allowed to do? Can't we do any more?'"

"Yes, yes! Good! He can't believe it, can he? Is that it? 'Is that *it*?!' he's thinking. What does he feel at this point?"

"Angry..."

I know she wants more, but I feel a bit nervous.

"And?"

"Upset?"

"And?!"

"He's angry and upset." I realised that this wasn't the heart-wrenching stuff she was after, and I noticed Kamal looking to heaven. That irritated me more than it should have.

"What the hell's going on here, Oliver? Anybody?"

She asked this a lot: "What the hell's going on?" It meant you had to think hard about the action and any confusion with feelings and stuff. Kamal was double-keen to give his slant on the whole thing:

"Can't you see what's going on, Oliver? It's obvious. Can't you feel it? His sister's being buried, and he can't believe that there isn't a huge ceremony with people giving speeches and crying out. The priest won't conduct a stately funeral because it has been mooted that Ophelia may have taken her own life and that it wasn't an accident, which is a mortal sin. He feels resentment and directs it towards the priest and—"

"Right, Kamal!" said Miss. "Now we're getting somewhere. How do you think—" but I interrupted.

"I *do* know what's going on! It's my sister and I know more than any of you!"

This was *my* question and I only had a few scenes. Kamal was in loads and never shut up about Hamlet's character, and now he was trying to tell me what *my* character was about! I suddenly felt *real* anger. I'm still not sure what happened because I think I must have hit my peak here (disappointingly since it was the very first run-through), but I somehow got into the flow that day.

"Tell us then! What's going on, Laertes?" Miss Pratt said, palms out and facing upwards, her body crooked forward at the waist. Her words and stance spurred me on:

"Is this it? Pathetic, pitiful excuse for a priest! Ophelia's worth a million of you! Her soul will fly and her angelic arms will float in heaven as yours will face nought but the flames of hell! Flowers shall grow from my sister's pure flesh as worms devour yours! She deserves a grander funeral than any of you here! Any of you! Her death is not clear, so you lead this sorry ceremony? Who amongst you understands death, never mind of one so sweet and young and perfect...? She's more worthy of love and honour in death, sad priest, than your miserable self will ever be on this earth! Than all of you!"

I carried on because I couldn't quite believe I might have said something good and I'd learnt my lines.

> Lay her i' th' earth;
> And from her fair and unpolluted flesh
> May violets spring! I tell thee, churlish priest,
> A minist'ring angel shall my sister be
> When thou liest howling.

My eyes were stinging and my throat was tensed. I knew I'd definitely over-acted in my desperate attempts to outdo Kamal, and Miss told me I was somewhat out of control and to go and work on the scene with Kamal, but he continued with the script: "What, the fair Ophelia!"

Then Lizzy Smith, Kamal's mother, Queen Gertrude, said, "Sweets to the sweet; farewell!" Then she threw some plastic flowers in the air. She continued:

> I hop'd thou shouldst have been my Hamlet's wife;
> I thought thy bride bed to have deck'd, sweet maid,
> And not have strew'd thy grave.

Then everybody, including Miss, clapped. It turned out okay in the end, and everything seemed right and all matched up—'synchronicity,' Kamal had said it was, a meaningful coincidence. Miss Pratt said we were starting to get it now and we must try to remember our physical response to anger and pain and stuff.

Kamal gave me a compliment about how I'd acted. My self-esteem boost was short-lived, though, because he quickly followed it with some director-type tips:

"Now use that anger and fire when we're grappling in the grave in the next bit! You need to have consistency in this game."

I was interested to see what Kamal was going to do with *his* lines. I'd never seen him really angry. I didn't want him to try to control how I acted my part and I felt resentment mounting and felt like saying to him, "And how are you going to act anger and pain?" I felt aggravated with Kamal that day.

Miss took us aside as others worked on individual lines. We had a first run-through of a section of Act V Scene (i). One of my lines was:

… Hold off the earth awhile,
Till I have once more caught her in my arms.
[Leaps into grave]

I had to jump into Ophelia's grave—well, a rectangular space marked out with skipping ropes—then Hamlet (Kamal) jumps in the grave, too. They're fiercely arguing about who loved Ophelia more because now Hamlet finally spells out that he *was* in love with her. When he jumps in the grave, Laertes says, or rather I say, "The devil take thy soul!"

I loved this line and thought to make a devilish face here, though it wasn't too much of a stretch, as I did sort of feel like killing Kamal in real life at that moment.

And he responds:
Thou pray'st not well.
I prithee take thy fingers from my throat.

I know I'm being mean here, but when Kamal acted these lines, he sounded and looked like he was saying something massively trivial like, "Fart not, crude fellow! Your stench disgusts me!" rather than being afraid for his life.

We carried on fighting; I practically strangled Kamal for real, and he screwed up his mouth and nose, as if to quell the fart smell. When we got split up and dragged out of the grave, Hamlet's mam, Queen Gertrude (Lizzy Smith), tried to calm him down:

    HAMLET : Why, I will fight with him upon this theme
        Until my eyelids will no longer wag.
    QUEEN : O my son, what theme?

(Lizzy was impressive here, hands outstretched, "conveying a sense of longing yet apprehension," Miss had said afterwards.)

    HAMLET : I lov'd Ophelia: forty thousand brothers
        Could not, with all their quantity of love,
        Make up my sum...

Talk about a come down from Lizzy's line! I tell you, it was such a let-down that Kamal wasn't that good. He may as well have said, "Why didst thou devour the last fried egg? Knowst thou not, of Haribo sweets, it holds the most elevated place as my most favoured?"

I'd need the emotion library to communicate this disappointment I felt in Kamal. He'd always been into acting, as long as I'd known him, and I so much wanted to be blown away by his talent, but I felt nothing except deflation. I mean, he loved acting and he was intelligent, so I just thought, well no, what did I know anyway? If Miss had praised his efforts, I would have known I was wrong, but as it turned out, she said much worse than I was thinking:

"Good first try, everyone. Excellent work, Lizzy. You *feel*, don't you?"

She smiled. And Kamal and I smiled for a different reason: Lizzy had been teased after Alex Beaumont caught her feeling Danny Rodd's knee during a lesson. I wouldn't care, but it was in Religious Studies. Kamal looked across at me, and we had to immediately separate our gaze to stop laughing.

"She did really feel it, really got to grips with it, Miss. I wish everyone could have seen it," Kamal said, which was too much for me and I had to laugh. His smugness crumbled as quickly as it had built when Miss Pratt commented:

"That works okay, Oliver. I was starting to believe you really loved her, and well, that's what it's all about here. I'm not sure that you and Kamal might not be better swapping roles." Kamal actually sat down at this point, and I felt embarrassed, too.

"Kamal, you think too much. I need to see you letting go a bit."

The disgust from Kamal! And then, the situation became cringe-worthy as Miss asked him, "Is there anyone you miss? Anyone you wish was here? In real life, is there someone who's moved away or even passed away? Can you think of someone?"

His blinking eyes looked like a micro-train, speeding back into his mini memory stations, but the platforms were all empty. It must have been too hard for him to say, "My parents."

"Well, tell me someone you love: probably someone in your family."

"Ghandi."

Everyone laughed, but he was deadly serious.

"Is that a pet?"

Her relief turned to bewilderment when Kamal said, "Pet? No, the first question. I just needed time. Mahatma Ghandi, Miss. I miss *him*."

Lizzy thought this stupid in a cute way: "But you didn't *know* him, did you, you daft thing? She's talking about someone real, you know, like your granddad or something."

Kamal did not at all take kindly to this. There's nothing he detests more than being made a fool of (who *doesn't*, I suppose?). He said, "Don't you see the link between Hamlet and Ghandi—the struggle for freedom?! To free the people from treachery and free his mind from torment and free his heart?"

"Ah!" the teacher held her right index finger up, facing towards him. "Torment of the heart. Yes. We're talking feelings here, not intellect, do you see? I want to see the love."

This was something she said a lot, too—"Where's the love? I want to see the love."

She continued what now seemed like her interrogation of Kamal:

"Tell me someone you love right now. Give me a name."

She was really pushing it, and I was seriously hoping she knew that both his parents were dead. Not that he could remember them as, like I said, they died when he was a baby. She obviously didn't know. His face now looked determined and a little wild.

"Like your uncle, Kamal?" I said.

Even though he had been brought up by his dad's brother and wife as if they were his parents, he had always called them Aunt and Uncle. He was their only child, and they gave him everything he wanted, but they had not wanted him to call them Mam and Dad, which was probably what Kamal wanted more than anything in his whole life. I never understood why he was forced to call them 'Aunt' and 'Uncle.' Wouldn't it be a constant reminder that he had no parents? He need never have known, I don't think. He told me once that his uncle had explained the decision: he needed to honour his brother's name. Do they think 'Honour' is more important than people being happy? I just thought it was selfish, daft, and cruel.

"My uncle, Miss," he said.

"Good. Okay, so imagine how you'd feel if you lost him."

I wasn't comfortable with where this was going. If this was what acting was about, it was all too gruelling for my liking. I was worried about what would happen if Kamal *succeeded* in imagining his uncle, his dad really, dead.

"Okay. Let's try that again. And *feel* it! Really *feel* it. This is an intense scene, guys."

This time when it came to "I loved Ophelia: forty thousand brothers / Could not with all their quantity of love, / Make up my sum...," Kamal spoke the words like the stuffing had been knocked out of him, even though I hadn't strangled him anything like as hard as the first time. He seemed sorrowful and confused. And it worked. I don't know if he'd taken on board anything Miss had said; I think his mood had just changed dramatically, but it came out okay. Miss was pleased and looked chuffed that her directing had seemingly had some sort of impact.

As Kamal walked me to the station to get the train to my grandparents', he was quiet. He said, "So Lily's not at home and... and nor are you. Seems—"

"I know," was all I said. Nothing made sense, so I just let myself be dragged along with it all.

"Shall we practise the sword fight at the weekend if you're back?"

At that moment, I could only visualise him fighting with something very flimsy, like a feather.

"Yeah. Sure. It'll be a good laugh. And very soon, we've got the trip to London. That should be brilliant."

"Should be," Kamal said.

In bed in my yellowy-green room that night, I wondered if acting might be the thing I was going to be halfway decent at, though it seemed to have brought out some major negativity in me and towards my best friend. Kamal didn't deserve to be treated badly... not after everything else. He could be annoying at times but can't we all? And there wasn't a 'bad bone in his body,' my dad had once said of him. And his acting wasn't that bad. The teacher didn't seem impressed with either of us, but I wanted to improve. I could go to drama school maybe—live in London. Lily could visit me at weekends. I could get a part in *Eastenders* or something; that was Mam's favourite. Imagine how proud she would be if I were on TV?!

I'd ask Mam soon. I wondered if she'd be pleased. I seemed to have few chances to please her at all about anything whatsoever, to be honest. Perhaps this would be the thing to cheer her up. She'd say, "I knew there must be something you were good at, Oliver. Finally, there *is* something!" Or perhaps not.

The trip to London! I could see if I liked the place. Check it out. I'd probably have to live there to be an actor, you see. I see now that my head was all over the place, but I thought that perhaps I would find a way of staying in London for a bit... not come back on the coach with the others? I might not see Lily for a while, but how cool would that be if I didn't go back! There would be a chance my mam might actually notice if the coach turned up at school minus her son.

So, there was the crazy paradox: the play and thoughts of acting in London distracted me from Lily, even though being near her was my main motivation for getting involved in it! Mental times.

London

By the time April was coming to an end, I wasn't being so pathetic about Poppy even though it looked like she wouldn't be coming on the trip to the Tate Britain Art Gallery in London. The first thing I wanted to do when I got home every day was to send her an email, but I decided twice a week would be the least stalkerly option. Well, the first week that is; from the second week it was more like three times, I think. She only wrote to me once a week, but she wrote a lot. It was a new feeling—my heart racing each time I saw she'd sent me a message. Her last message before the trip to London was the most dramatic:

Thanks for your fourth long message this week! So glad the play is working out for you, and you ARE good at it—you know you are, you Mugwort. I don't know about drama school though. I don't think you'd fit in.

I miss England a lot, but it's lovely and warm still here in Port Macqaurie. Got my hair cut short, like my new friend, Muriel, coz I'm on the beach a lot and doing heaps of sports. I'm learning to surf and it's five-star fun. You would look good with your long hair and baggy clothes. A lot of boys have long blond hair. They're always messing with it, and that reminds me of you, only they've all got tanned bodies. One boy I'm getting on really well with is Sean Tobias, who plays rugby and is in a band. He's got massive muscles. He's brill on the guitar and likes The Editors and The Fauves (not that manic dance stuff you like)! [It isn't just dance music I like at all, by the way.]

Going to a party tonight.

So glad that Lily seems to be much happier and getting better, though I can't believe she's had to go back into hospital! She seemed back to normal. No, it doesn't sound daft you telling her poems and singing, and you should ask that music teacher who comes to school about that special tune you and Lily like. I so, so, so wish I could visit her. I forgot how funny and cheeky she is, but she has that cute delicate side to her. I know you think it's too soppy, but I still like to think of her as a fairy rose, just like her special 'tree.' The new hospital sounds really good anyway. I will go with you as soon as I get back. I miss reading her stories, Sam swinging her in the air, seeing her laughing on your back and that massive chuckle she does when Nathan pretends to fall down. It won't be long before she's doing all that again, it sounds like!

Here is a list called 'Things I Miss about Oliver Timothy Campbell':

- *funny way of talking like about plants*
- *lovely face*
- *floppy hair that he can't stop flopping*
- *shiny blue eyes that he hides*

- *the way he sometimes looks at the floor when he's talking to me*
- *five-star sense of humour*

You say you miss me, so why don't you write a list like this for me?

My gran has not got any better, and Mum says we're not getting the flights back on Sunday. It's going to be another two weeks.

Write back and tell me all about the trip to London.

Poppee xxx

The coach picked us up from school at five in the morning; several pupils who'd missed the trip the year before were there, too, but not Poppy. It took us six hours to get to London. With every hour that passed, I felt more and more free. I was moving on. I wished I were going to London for a long time. I could still find a way of staying, maybe.

Being at home, before the move to my grandparents', had irritated me, but now *not* being at home felt wrong too. It was because of Lily that I was not at home, and now she wasn't even at home. Yet she still dictated everything that went on and completely took over my mam's mind which is probably why Mam didn't realise I should be back. I wanted to stop worrying so much about all of it and being away from my family seemed like a relief.

Throughout the journey, Kamal talked and I drifted. When someone shouted that we were in London, it took another whole hour to get to the art gallery. Just how big *was* this place? How would I know whereabouts to live?

Half an hour into London, I asked Kamal, "Where would you live in London? Which part?"

"Hmmm? It would have to be Notting Hill… or maybe Brixton or Hampstead… or Primrose Hill—you get all the intellectuals there. Imagine sipping amazing coffee outside one of those delightful cafés, discussing French films or the plight of the Aborigine."

"How do you know all that stuff, you loon?"

"I've taken many trips with Uncle. His friend has a shop in Notting Hill."

"Is it cheap in those places, you know, to rent a flat?"

"God, no! No, no, no, not at all. The opposite."

"I thought intellectual people were poor," I said.

"Not all," said Kamal. "But even the poor ones still sit in cafés or on other people's roof gardens. The ones who mix, that is. Then, of course, there are plenty of spots in *south* London, too, south of the river Thames."

"Where's cheap?"

"We'll study a map on the way back. Why are you so interested?"

"I might live here."

"When? You're not moving are you?"

"No."

"Oh."

"Just making plans. Thinking about the future."

"Don't think too much. You're not even fifteen yet. There's only so much you can plan. Mostly life happens to you."

"You think?"

"Well, no. The decisions you make *are* vitally important—major decisions like where to live—but sometimes life thrusts its plan onto you. Look at me. Look at Lily," he said.

"What do you mean?"

"Why is she ill? Who did what to make her ill?"

"No one did anything. You know that. Don't talk… Don't say stupid things."

"You were the one talking about big decisions!" Kamal said.

"No, I wasn't. Anyway. I'm just thinking out loud, that's all."

We'd eaten our packed lunches ages before we got to the Tate Britain, so we had about four hours to go round the gallery before we were due back on the coach. Our teachers took us round a lot of rooms, and we had to fill out worksheets. We'd been doing 'portraiture' and 'stylised landscapes,' and our teacher loved David Hockney (maybe because the artist came from Bradford, which is also in the north of England, even though he lives in Los Angeles now), so we spent a good while looking at his work. I liked a funky-looking painting called *Four Flowers in Still Life*. It was done in a much more modern way than those boring old paintings of just a bunch of flowers in a vase on a table with a dead partridge or something in front; Kamal had one like that in his house. We then spent some time in the portraiture room before eventually being allowed to do our own thing at about three o'clock.

"Have a wander round, then meet at the entrance at half past three. And, like we said, stick in pairs or groups. Don't let me hear someone's gone off on their own!"

I couldn't believe our time was nearly up. I wanted to stay much longer; I was nowhere near being ready to go home. People always telling me what to do. My life being mapped out.

Kamal and I studied the plan. The words 'Pre-Raphaelites and Painters of the Ideal' caught my eye. Just the word Pre-Raphaelites looked interesting to me, but I'd remembered too that my Auntie Margaret used to love this kind of art; she used to have a poster with that word on it. So, I pointed to Room 14.

"Let's go here. I really feel like going there."

Kamal did not agree and said, "Waste of time! Pre-Raphaelites? Mamby-pamby nonsense. Girls' stuff—all pretty faces and floaty hair."

This didn't put me off. He carried on, "Look, you said you liked John's work, didn't you, so I don't mind seeing some abstract paintings, but then let's see some solid art—there's a Henry Moore collection here, you know."

I vaguely recognised the name, but I didn't want to sound ignorant so, as usual, Kamal had hooked me in.

"If we have time, I'd love to squeeze in some Constable, too," Kamal squeezed in. I could guess that Constable must be the name of an artist, but I couldn't hold back the visuals of Kamal hugging a policeman.

We made our way to a room called 'Abstract and Concrete.' The paintings were pretty cool—reminded me of paintings my mam did. Well, she used to. I thought her work was amazing, but she stopped when Lily got ill. She still drew lots of patterns—I don't mean doodles, I mean really fantastic designs, but she didn't paint on big canvases any more. I kept telling her she should at least design cards or something, because it's hard to believe that you can go into a shop which sells cards and nothing else and the entire selection is crap. Every single one. The arty ones aren't arty, the sad ones aren't sad and the funny ones aren't funny. I tried to find one with a guitar on for my dad last year, but it seems dads are only allowed to like beer, football or tits. And don't get me started on the rhymes inside—they should have sick bags at the end of each shelf. Imagine at the interview—"You think all art is bollocks... good. You sum up the gender difference here with, 'Women like shoes, men like poos'... excellent. And I see here you think old women's breasts are hilarious... perfect. Try and stop me hiring *you*!" Anyway, Mam never listened to me. And I don't think she believed in herself... or anyone... or any*thing* those days.

I'll tell you, arty people are blinking complicated! I can't find anything I'm good at, but can you imagine being really good at something and not doing it? Actually, I bet there are more people who are really *bad* at something and *are* doing it. I mean, you only have to watch those TV talent shows. Even half the pompous twits *deciding* if the contestants are good are no good! My Uncle Francis is the same. He's a brilliant songwriter, but he hasn't got famous. I mean, no, he's different because he *does* do it, write music, I mean, but he hasn't got that cockiness a lot of music people seem to have. Mind you, I think he's too clever to want to be famous.

The pictures that reminded me of Mam's were by an artist called Piet Mondrian. They were made up of blocks of colour and lines. I suppose the room was full of work that you hear people mocking, "My five-year-old could have done that!" or "I could have done that!" But they couldn't and they won't.

"I like this one, Kamal, do you?"

He shrugged and nodded his head, but with a turned down mouth as if to say, "I suppose so, but not especially." I felt like shouting, "Are you mad? Can't you see it?!" I realised how great but lonely it was, to love something that someone else, even your best friend, couldn't care less about.

The oval picture on deep blue background was by someone called Arthur Jackson—real name Jack Hepworth, it said—and was a bit like the Mondrian paintings with blocks of colour, but not geometric shapes like squares and that. It had irregular, swirly, overlapping shapes, and it felt peaceful, a bit like a sort of multi-coloured floating egg. That sounds weird, but that's what it made me think of... and feel like somehow.

"Poppy would like it, I bet," I said.

"I wouldn't exactly class Poppy as a connoisseur of art!"

"What would you know? Anyway, I'm just saying I feel something when I look at it."

"Haha! Oh very nice. No thoughts in your head, then, just feeeeelings?"

"Why are you being so annoying? Just shut up for once, will you?"

"What's got into *you*, Olby?"

"And shut up with the dumb, lame nicknames as well!"

"Whoa! You love that!"

"Do I? Says who?"

"I know you have to take your anger out on something, but don't start treating me like a punch-bag because I won't stand for it."

"Leave me alone. Just go and do your own thing," I said.

I would have a really good look round, I thought. Kamal would have to go off and do his own thing then. But I kept seeing him out of the corner of my eye, checking his watch furiously in between crossing his arms and tapping his foot, no doubt desperate for his squeeze with Constable.

My other favourite was *Construction, Intersection* by John Piper. It had some skinny rods stuck on canvas and consisted of overlapping and interweaving planes of colour. I thought John, Sam and Nathan's dad, would have liked it. Maybe he already did.

Kamal had stayed with me, and our second port of call was Room 20, Kamal's suggestion of Henry Moore. I could have kicked myself, but I gave my ignorance away by blurting out, "Is he dead famous, then?"

I had a niggling thought that he was going to reply, "Do the bears… " (you probably know the rest!), but he said, "Doesn't your mother teach you anything? Hasn't she supposed to have done an art degree?"

"What d'you mean, 'supposed to'? You're such a…!"

While he was throwing his eyes to heaven, I screwed up *my* eyes to read the name of an artist on a sculpture next to us and quickly added, "Anyway, I prefer Bernard Meadows." I was relieved that my eyes hadn't tricked me into saying "Bernard Matthews," which is a make of turkey food products. "And Barbara Hepworth." I'd just read something about her and she was definitely a famous sculptor.

It was becoming some sort of daft game of intellectual tennis.

"You should have said that in the first place!" Kamal said.

"I don't 'should have' done anything."

"You can't say that."

"I've just said it!"

"Ooooh! What's wrong with you, Olby, honestly?"

He was really getting on my nerves now, and his pointless nicknames were getting on my nerves, too, but I decided to let it drop for fear of losing it and flinging him into a sculpture. That would've been something—if he'd disappeared into a piece of art, turned into a lump of marble maybe.

"I'm going to take a look at some of these Bernard Ma... Meadows sculptures. It's quarter past three now, so we've only got fifteen minutes."

"What?" Even though he must have looked at his watch twenty times in the last five minutes, the significance of the time or even the actual time had not registered. "Right, let's dash round here, then skip quickly round the Constable! Five minutes, okay?"

I found my own eyes going to heaven now, at the same time as the image of Kamal, wearing a pink tutu, skipping round a policeman, flashed into my head. When I turned to look at *Startled Bird* by Bernard Meadows, I laughed. I don't know why. I felt guilty, even though I knew it wasn't a mocking laugh. It just provoked that reaction. I checked around me to make sure nobody was looking disgusted, and a woman of about seventy smiled and nodded knowingly at me, so maybe it had been okay to laugh. It was a metal sculpture of a really cute and quirky bird with bits all poking out, yet it seemed quite vulnerable. Then I came upon *Large Flat Bird*, which made me smile at first; then I felt sorry for it. I glanced over at the Henry Moore sculptures. They looked powerful and solid, but I think the lie I told Kamal about preferring Bernard Meadows was in fact the truth. Their spikiness and lack of smoothness appealed to me.

When my gaze fell upon *Fallen Bird*, I felt odd. Emotion library needed. Its mouth was open, like it wanted help, but it couldn't say anything, well, sing anything. I wanted to stand it upright and breathe into its mouth and say, "You're fine now. Off you go. You're free." I was in a kind of trance, and my visual path to the poor bird was only broken by Kamal's hand, waving vigorously up and down in front of my eyes.

"Wake up! Constable beckons!"

As we left Bernard and the birds, I stopped briefly to read the description of Meadows's life, but all I had the chance to take in before Kamal grabbed me by the arm and pulled me away was that he was born on February 19th, same day as Sam.

I checked my watch—twenty past three. The thought of going back 'home,' of facing everything again, of being on the coach with Kamal for five hours depressed me, and I wondered if I could be strong enough to run off somewhere.

Kamal said, "Come on! I know exactly where he is! Follow me!" And he broke into a semi-skip. I found myself striding behind him, like I was a robot under his control. Art sped past us, like a colourful history film.

Just as Kamal shouted, "Next room on the right!" something made me stop. I watched him run ahead. I looked above the door of the room we were about to leave—'Pre-Raphaelites and Painters of the Ideal.' I would forego Constable. *This* would be my last room.

I stood still for a moment, then swivelled quickly round as if someone had tapped me on the shoulder. Directly in front of me was a group of pupils blocking my view of a painting they were looking at. I could have approached any of the other paintings, but I had an urge to see *that* one. I ambled up to the school group (all girls—perhaps Kamal had been right) and tuned into the teacher's voice:

"She was hanging a garland of flowers when she slipped and fell into the stream. Her brain was in a very disturbed place, and she couldn't think how to get out. See how peaceful Ophelia looks, as if she is singing? Do you think she is still alive here, girls? She is certainly in a strange and fascinating state of stillness, floating here, her hair like seaweed around her face. Millais painted the figure of Ophelia in his studio, but went to the countryside to paint the stream, then put the two together. The model, who posed for it in a bath, became ill from being in the cold water for so long."

I thought to myself, *Kamal should take a job like this*—rambling on to only half-listening people. But *I* actually *was* listening. The female teacher's voice was deep like a man, and engaging. I found myself sidling up to the back of the group.

"You see that bird, there, Miss Mirkovitch? Is it a symbol?" asked one of the pupils.

Cor! I thought. *What a cool question!*

"It's a robin, Violet, and you're quite right to be thinking along those lines. Legend has it the robin redbreast is associated with divine sacrifice and rebirth of the spirit. Perhaps the bird is Ophelia's spirit about to fly up. In mediaeval Europe, the robin was sometimes depicted with baby Jesus, a hint of its future mission: to pluck the thorns from Jesus's crown, ending only in the tragic bird's own demise, ripped about the breast as it was by the very thorns it sought to pluck with its beak from Jesus's head. The red feathers, then, are believed to represent the honour of this divine connection. Remember the little robin's position in the painting, girls, for a sheet I'm going to give you tomorrow in school. Several of the flowers depicted here are symbolic, too; we'll look at that in more detail tomorrow."

"Could you tell us one now, Miss Mirkovitch?" I couldn't believe I'd said it. What a prize dork. The whole group turned in slow motion to look at me. Just as I was saying, "Sorry," the teacher laughed and said, "I'm glad someone's listening! The girls are going off now. Why don't you come to the front? Go and gather round *The Blind Girl* please, girls!"

With that, they dispersed quietly and smoothly, gradually revealing the painting bit by bit. First, ornate foliage to the left, then decorative flowers and rippling stream water to the right. There she was—Ophelia. She was lying in a stream. Her dress was all billowy in the water, her face was pale and calm, and she was surrounded by long floating wet tresses of hair. I glided nearer to the painting and the teacher.

"Look here. The nettles represent pain."

"Do they? Oh, I see. Thank you, Miss."

"Do you see these daisies? Innocence. And pink roses here floating by her cheek—"

"Love and beauty," I said.

"... Well done! Yes, I'd say so, young man. In the actual Shakespeare play, *Hamlet*... Do you know it?"

"Yes, Miss."

"Good. In the actual play, Laertes calls his sister here 'rose of May.' There's sure to be a link there, don't you think?"

"Yes."

"One more flower I think... which one...? Here, the vivid red poppy—"

"Papaver."

"Sorry?"

"Latin for poppy."

"Well I never! And did you know it symbolises sleep and death?"

"Oh? No."

"I personally prefer the association with magic and eternal life, don't you?"

"Absolutely, Miss. Yes, definitely."

"Must be getting on now, young man. Enjoy the painting. You must get a postcard in the shop! You seem terribly fond of it!"

"Thanks very much, Miss Mirkovitch."

"You remembered my name," she said, with a smile. "Most people can't even say it!'

There was something magical about the painting. It seemed real—the colours so vibrant. I moved closer and closer to it so that I could have reached out and touched her face. I don't know what came over me but I said, "You'll be fine." Yes, I said it out loud to the actual painting, well the person in it—Ophelia.

"What? You crackpot! You talking to paintings now?"

Kamal.

"Come and see the Constables. Amazing clouds."

"This is Ophelia. From *Hamlet*. It's your fault she's dying."

Kamal burst out laughing, saying, "You really are going bananas! It's fanciful nonsense, anyway. She was as crazy as you are. Shakespeare would have had her thrashing about like the barmpot she was, not all pretty and still!"

I felt like hitting him. I looked at my watch. Half past three. I said, "You go and put your head back in the clouds. I'm going outside. It's half past three."

"What? Half three!"

He never failed to amaze me.

But I didn't go outside. I ran and ran till I got to the gallery shop. I found myself easily at the postcard section. I bought a Piet Mondrian card for Mam called *The Tree*. Even though I knew Mam loved bright colours, I had an urge to buy this grey one for her. I got Arthur Jackson's egg-shaped work just called *Painting, 1937* for

Poppy, David Hockney's *Four Flowers in Still Life* for Lily, Bernard Meadows's *Fallen Bird* for... well, I didn't know who for, and John Everett Millais's *Ophelia* for me. And, at the last minute, a peaceful-looking seascape caught my eye, so I got that, too. It was by someone called John Brett. I slipped the paper bag into my backpack.

15:45.

I was late.

Deep breathing.

I'd get into trouble.

I thought of the long coach journey. Five hours of shame for making everyone wait. Five hours of Kamal. Five hours of going back... *I don't want to go back. I won't go back.*

I scanned around the shop. No one looking for me yet. I needed to get out quickly. *If I don't go back... if I stay here. I'm staying here. I'm staying in London.* Pneumatic drill battering my chest.

I had my phone, money, a map.

"Run!"

Who was saying that?

"Run you useless git."

It was me. I was saying it.

"Come on, think!"

"Meet at the front steps at three thirty." The front steps. Okay. There's got to be another exit.

"Ask someone. Ask someone, you useless... Excuse me!"

"Are you all right, young man?" an elderly lady asked.

I forced a smile and said I needed to meet my mother "... at the side entrance. Not the front. The *side*. I'm late."

"I see, dearie."

Hurry up.

"Do you see over there? Go out there and follow signs to the café. You'll want the Manton Entrance on Atterbury Street, I imagine. I always use that one because my daughter's in a wheelchair. We come at least—"

"Manton Entrance. Thank you."

"Yes. Manton."

Café. There's the sign. There's the sign. Look around. Look around. Keep checking. Café. Café. There it is.

"Manton Entrance!"

I ran and ran. Glass door. Archway. I was outside. Bright sun blinded me. The traffic noise was like a truck bulldozing my brain. My eardrums were about to burst. Everything was about to burst. Left: a ramp leading towards the front of the building.

"Stay away from the front!"

Right: steps leading towards the back. Yes.

I leapt up the steps then turned back. No one. *No one must find me.* I put on my sunglasses to hide myself. I wanted to carry on running. My body pulsated with energy.

"Take a moment. Act normal," I said out loud.

I needed superhuman strength to stop myself running. I was on Atterbury Street. I might need to remember the name. *Remember it. Commit it to memory. Okay.*

"Come on!"

If they found me they'd want to batter me... batter me then bury me. Batterbury. Atterbury. Okay. As I walked north, I noticed a huge yard across the road to the left, flanked on three sides with fancy red brick buildings. Looked like the buildings were wearing matching grey skirts. A solitary young tree in the left-hand corner and another one in the right-hand corner. Like the Mondrian—the postcard for Mam. Standing alone, but strong. The yard was laid to grey cobblestones, but a square carpet of lawn lay bang in the centre. Looked weird and out of place. Young people on it (the lawny bit), lounging and stooping in the sun. Colourful people. Students? Catching the next flight on the magic carpet to Utopia—the ideal world. *Any tickets left? What time's the flight?*

15:55.

I had to get off the street. I was exposed on the streets. I needed to hide away. I carried on to the end of Atterbury Street, my heart still thumping in my ears. *So many trees for such a huge city.* I reached the corner of the Tate Britain. I looked right. Who was that? I stopped dead. Looking straight at me. Bicycles in a very long toast-rack and some guy staring at me. It was a statue. The white plinth matched the Tate stone, but who was it? Who was on it?

"You haven't got time, stupid!"

Maybe now, that was exactly what I had got. I turned to look ahead and there, in front of me, a park! A small park, but a park. One of those havens of tranquillity someone really clever and kind thought of. But first, I ran right up to the statue.

… *It's him!*

Ophelia's painter!

John Everett Millais.

"What you doing back here? You following me?"

Or maybe he was doing the same as me.

I crossed the tree-lined street and looked back. I was on John Islip Street now. And there was the main John—artist John—hiding behind the gallery. I walked right. Where was the park gate? Maybe it was private.

"No. Please!"

A gate! An open gate. I took a sharp breath in and blew out as slowly as I could and entered the garden. A few dogs. A few dodgy-looking characters. I spotted a bench and went to sit down. When I crossed my legs, I felt my foot shaking, so I flung it onto firm ground. Was I going to sleep here? Seemed safe enough.

Thomas

16:00

Checked my phone. Missed call from Kamal. Turned my phone off. Closed my eyes and tried to calm my breathing down. In, out, in, out, in… out… in… out…

"You okay? Someone runnin' after you?"

I jumped out of my skin as my eyes sprung open. A man of about sixty stood in front of me. I'd never seen such a grimy coat and face. His eyes looked like they'd lived about ten lives.

"No… No, not at all. It's me," I said.

"You? You wha'?"

"It's me who's running."

"Ohwww!"

"I've run away."

"Ain' we all, little feller. What you run away from then, eh?"

My eyes started stinging and I clenched my teeth and throat.

"Nothing... everything."

He sat down and I didn't mind. He put his arm on my back, and I didn't care about that either even though it crossed my mind that he could be a murderer or something.

"Must be somefin, little feller, eh? We've all got our crosses to bear, ain' we?"

"I'm not going back."

"You ain' got the look of a messed-up kid, mind. Look at that shiny face o' yours and them teef!"

"What's yours?" I asked.

He opened his mouth, and it looked yuk, like a dead person's: black, ulcerous, with two or three dark brown twisted teeth.

"Four or five I fink I'm down to nah."

"I mean your cross. You know—your 'cross to bear.' What you said before."

"Ohwww! You don't wanna 'ear that. How come you's askin' me all these questions? You a spy or summin?"

I smiled and said, "Don't be daft."

"Thomas," he said. "Thomas Diamond. Pleased to make your acquaintance!" He looked somehow radiant with his dead eyes trying to smile and his pokey brown tooth jabbing his elephant-skin bottom lip. "Can't 'elp bein' daft. It's in me nature!"

We both laughed.

"Not 'Tom' for short then?"

"Don't you start! Always Thomas; it's what me muvver called me. Ain' seen 'er in donkeys, mind. Not since I run away."

"Did you save up to run away?"

"Don't make me laugh, little feller! Save up! You make me laugh, you do. I was headin' for the sea. Always wanted to go to the seaside."

He dropped his head backwards and clenched his eyes and his whole face. Then he started moving backwards and forwards in a sort of jerky way. I thought he might be having a fit, but I didn't do anything or say anything. I just sat there watching him, taking in the waves of smoke and toilet wafting towards me with every sway. His hair didn't move when he did. It was like he'd found some old wig rotting in a forgotten costume box in a disused theatre. It had experience, but no life, if you know what I mean. In some way it calmed me, watching Thomas and his rhythmic rocking. I could have watched him for hours, so it was a bit jolting when he stopped sharply, whipped his head towards me and said:

"You 'ad a fight wiv your mum, I bet."

I was brought back to earth and could feel anxiety creeping around me. "I'm on a trip. I've come from Newcastle-on-Tyne with the school. We went in there." I pointed.

"Where?"

"That huge building there—the Tate Gallery."

"Come 'ere all the time but we ain' allowed in the likes o' them places."

"Course you are!" I said. "So how old were you then, when you first saw the sea?"

"I dint make it, I told you. You never listen. None of you ever listen. What's your name anyway?"

"Oliver."

"No, little 'andsome feller, I never saw it in the end, the sea. Must be summin else! All that water spreadin' out in front o' you instead o' walls! Never wish you lived by the sea? Wha' was that line again from that film? 'He's not wavin', he's drownin'!' Funny line that, eh?"

"Yeah."

"They should take you to the sea, them poncy teachers, not a blinkin', poncy, farty art building! Shunt they? What's your name again?"

"Oliver. I love it there," I said.

"I dunno. All that money for a few pictures! Least they're proper—takes time to paint."

"I mean the seaside. I mean, I love it at the seaside."

"Blinkin 'ell! You been, then? You been the seaside?"

"Yes I... once or twice. I love it. I even just bought a postcard actually in—"

"What's it look like? Does it really make that sound like in the films?"

"It really does. And you can smell it, too."

"Smell it! You're 'avin me on!"

"It's the truth."

"When I get me dog, I reckon I'll get meself down to Brighton."

"You should do. You will, I hope."

I looked at my watch. 16:20

"Gotta get somewhere?"

"They've gone now. I'm not going back with them. I'll be in such trouble. But I'm not going back."

I explained about the coach and half past three and I told him about Lily and Mam. I told him loads, actually, even though he was a stranger. Thomas told me he'd had a younger sister. He said she'd have been about thirty this year; then he changed it to forty, so he could have been just making it up.

"You ain' the baby no more. Sounds like this littlun needs 'elp. You gotta sit this one out, little feller. Don't wanna give your mum any more grief, do you?"

When I looked at my watch again, Thomas said, "They're still 'ere, you do know that, don't you? Teachers won't leave. Not wivout a boy like you. Police'll find you soon. Not too late, is it? What is it? What's the time?"

I shuddered at the thought of the police, and my whole body tingled as I imagined my teachers being called to pick me up from the cop shop! Maybe Thomas was right and I should cut my losses and run back to the coach... if it was still there. I showed Thomas my watch, but he just shrugged.

"I'm an hour late now. It's half past four," I said.

"That's a good amount 'o time to be late by. You wanna leave it another hour and 'av 'em all jeer at you or go now to claps and cheers?"

"Claps and cheers? I don't think so."

"You come in a big bus, then?"

"Yeah. I was supposed to meet the coach out the front of the gallery."

"Come on, I'll take you to the front. Say I stole your bag or summin and you done one 'o vem citizens' arrests."

"You are a nutter, Thomas Diamond!"

"You ready, little feller? I'll go and tell 'em meself if you won' come."

"I'm not even any good at that, then," I said.

"Wha'?"

"Running away. I can't even get *that* right."

"Stop feelin' sorry for yourself. You're stronger than tha', little... What they call you, again? Good home like that! Don't know you're born, some o' you kids!"

"Maybe I shouldn't have been born."

"Ay! Now that's enough. Pull yourself togever. You're a good lad, now come on! Time to face the music!"

I was in a dream as we made our way back down Atterbury Street, but not before I got a passer-by to take a photo of Thomas and me next to John Millais's statue. I was in some weird movie. There was a new batch of students sitting ready for the next flight.

"Looks like a magic carpet, don't you think, Thomas?"

"Blinkin' 'eck yeah, it don't 'alf! Never fought of that. You got some head on you, little feller! Art college that is. Par' of Chelsea School of Art."

We reached the end of Atterbury Street. We had to turn left onto Millbank to walk the final plank yards to the coach, but I stopped for a moment.

"I'm gonna be in such trouble. I'm so stupid."

"You're bloody clever if you ask me! Now, trust me… Wha' they call you? Blinkin 'ell, Oliver! It is, ain' it. I suppose you fink I'm too scruffy to trust?"

"No. No of course not. Okay, then, I suppose."

"River Thames that is on the righ'; runs all the way along 'ere."

"I didn't realise how huge London was, but I still might live here soon."

"Huge all righ'! Wunt live nowhere else, mind. Maybe Brighton. Come on, Oliver."

I took a huge breath in and blew it out very slowly. No one was outside the coach, but it was definitely our coach. Thomas was right. They had stayed. I hoiked myself up onto the first step of the coach. I turned my head to the right, and they were all there. Claps and cheers. Thomas was right.

"Where the hell—?" Mr. Wetherill said, but Thomas scrambled up onto the coach, too. There was a whole range of vocal responses from sharp intakes of breath to "Urrgh!" and "Eh?!"

"I nicked 'is bag, but he's such a fast runner. He caught me in the end and done one 'o vem citizens arrests. Police was all over me, but Oliver 'ere said he'd forgive me if I come 'n' explain it to the teachers."

At this point the two other teachers arrived back at the coach and heard the end of Thomas' confession.

"So they dint arrest me coz I come 'ere and he says his teachers are nice and kind and they'll understand."

Wetherill was first to say his piece. "We should call the police immediately. There's been some sort of abduction. This doesn't make any sense."

Miss McGinty said, "For pity's sake, let's just leave and just thank God Oliver's all right. You're all right, are you? Thank God."

Everyone cheered again.

I followed Thomas off the bus.

"Where are you going now?" Miss McGinty said.

"Can I just have a quick word with T... with the thief?"

Miss Shah answered, "No. Get on the bus now. Why would you want to talk to a dangerous man, Oliver? Come on. I'm sorry, sir, but our pupil has to leave immediately. You've made us very late."

Miss McGinty had a different response: "If you stand just here, we'll wait a minute, but we'll have to watch you. Go on. Be quick now."

"Dint I tell you?" Thomas said.

When I said, "Thanks so much, Thomas," and gave him a kind of half-hug, he went all stiff, as if I was going to hurt him. Then he relaxed. His cardboard coat hung loosely over his fragile frame. Like a delicate bird, trapped in a sack. I fumbled in my bag.

"Here, Thomas. I'd like you to have this."

"Wha' is it?"

"You don't have to have it. It's just a picture. You could look at it and imagine you're there, you know?"

I handed him the postcard of the seascape by John Brett. It wasn't much, but I wanted to give him something.

"Blimey! It's the sea! And look at them—like angels' swimming pools!"

His bottom lip started to quiver.

"You all right, Thomas? I haven't upset you, have I? Thomas? I don't want to upset you."

"I'm happy, you block'ead!"

A trickle cleansed its way through the dirt on his left cheek.

"No one's give me a present since my fortief six year ago. Coat from Oxfam: this," he said, patting his chest.

"It's lasted well. Got a lot of character. Has it seen any soap suds?"
"What *you* fink?"
And we both laughed.
He looked closely at the card, then turned it over. "What's it say 'ere?"
"It says 'The British Channel seen from the Dorsetshire Cliffs, by John Brett: glitters with light and happiness.'"
"Nice, that. I know! When I ge' me dog I'm gonna call 'im that, Oliver.'"
"Good idea. Cool name for a dog, Brett."
"Not Brett, you block'ead, Glitter."
"That's even cooler!"
"See, I'm not totally useless, little feller!"
"Come on, Oliver!" shouted Miss Shah's head from the coach door.
"Go on, little feller. Be good. And whatever 'appens, be kind to your mum, all right? Sit it out. She'll come back."
"I can't see that at the moment."
"She'll come back. Trust me."
We both smiled, and he shook my hand. His was like frail leather. I grabbed a pen from my pocket and wrote a message on the postcard with my name and address before getting back on the coach.
"Bye then, Thomas. You're not on your own, are you, by the way?"
"We're all on our own, Oliver."
As we pulled away from the front of the Tate, I sat next to Kamal and leant over him to smear a patch of condensation on the window, big enough to look back at Thomas. He was waving with the postcard; then he held it to his chest. Waving, not drowning.

On the way back, I pretended to fall asleep so I didn't have to talk to Kamal. All he managed to say was, "I've never been more worried in my life, you numbskull!"

I told him I was exhausted and closed my eyes. But I really did fall asleep. I had a nightmare and woke up panting and coughing.

"You okay, Oliver?" That was one of the few times Kamal had ever called me by my actual name. "We were supposed to study the London map. You've slept nearly all the way. Missed Alex Beaumont pooing into a Tesco bag. Miss McGinty and Bill Owusu held blankets round him for privacy. You must be the only one who hasn't taken a photo. Jade's put it on Facebook already! Can't really see anything though, apparently. I had no one to play 'Pub Legs' with, not that there were many pubs on the M1! You okay? "

Somehow Kamal's prattle was comforting.

"I'm always missing stuff. Let me see the photo."

It just looked like Alex in a sari.

"'Pub Legs' it is, I suppose," I said. "I'll take the right side of the road."

"Aha! Bad choice, my man. Look what's coming up on the left! The Three Bulls! Starter for twelve! Bring it on!"

But this was followed by a poor run for Kamal with The Rising Sun, The Crown, and The Ostrich Feathers. He pulled two back with The Dirty Duck, but I soon beat his fourteen with my winning streak: The Red Lion, Man on the Moon, George and Dragon, Lion and Lamb. I thought it was in the bag, but the coach driver had to take a detour and we passed Cricketers on the left. To my thinking, that was four points, as the sign depicted two men in cricket whites, so four legs. But, get this—Kamal reckoned Cricketers meant the whole two teams, twenty-two players, forty-four legs, giving him a grand total of fifty-eight!

He wouldn't accept that there had been only two cricketers on the picture and that it should have been eighteen a piece. He said, "We're going on the name, not the picture, so the least I should get is the fifteen cricketers who'd be on the field while a match is in play. That's thirty, so gives me forty-four."

"I give up. You win." I was losing the will to live at this point, never mind win the game.

Kamal gave me a sidelong stare. With his eyes still on me he asked, "Am I a bit annoying sometimes?"

I wanted to laugh because he'd never said anything like that before, but I said, "Is the Pope Catholic?"

And, just then, as we were pulling up outside the school gates, we both said, at exactly the same time:

"Good use of rhetorical question!"

Then we both did laugh.

All the parents knew about us being late, and about me and the thieving 'tramp,' so I wasn't in trouble. What's more, some parents even stroked my head when other pupils pointed me out.

I was very surprised when Mam was there to pick us up, even though the plan was for me to actually stay at home that night. She was usually at the hospital in the evening. She had heard the story, so I hoped she would be pleased to see me.

"So it was you who got yourself into trouble again, was it?" she said.

"No."

"Oh? I heard you got involved in a chase."

"No."

"It *was* him, Mrs. Campbell," said Kamal, "but he was more of a hero than a silly boy."

"I don't quite get how you work that out. Everyone's safely back. That's what counts. Good, was it?"

"Yeah. It was okay," I said.

"Good," she said.

But once in the car, Kamal wasn't about to leave it at that: "Yes, we took in so much in the four hours we were there. Your son was taken with Bernard Meadows, and I even caught him speaking to one of the paintings! He's a well-known—"

Mam surprised me again when she interrupted—more because she had been listening than because she actually said something interesting.

"I *know* who he is."

"Do you?" I said.

"He was born in Rotherham."

"Really?" I said.

"Didn't exhibit much. Didn't believe in himself. He actually stopped painting. He studied at Hull School of Architecture."

"You studied art at Hull, Mrs. C?"

I couldn't resist showing Kamal up by saying, "She's *supposed* to have."

I turned to look at Kamal in the back to catch him shaking his head.

"What do you mean, 'supposed to have,' you cheeky sod?" Mam said.

"Only joking, Mam."

"It was something we were talking about before," Kamal said.

"Well, I'm not in the mood for jokes, as it happens."

So that went well. I wanted to get back on the coach and drive it to London myself.

But I was stuck back home now.

"She'll come back," Thomas had said. "She'll come back. Trust me."

I couldn't see it.

I needed to throw myself into my acting. If Mam could see me in the play… I'd have to work hard to get my performance up to scratch. Mam and Poppy and Lily in the front row! Standing up, clapping, cheering. "Bravo! Bravo!" Poppy would shout, and they'd all look at each other, smiling and happy, wiping tears of joy from their reddened cheeks. Maybe that was pushing it a bit, but I had to think big.

Before getting out of the car, Kamal said, "See you for our sword practice tomorrow, Oliver. You're staying till tomorrow night, aren't you?"

"Yeah."

"Don't sound too keen!"

Kamal got out of the car, and Mam and I made our way back home. She hadn't been listening properly which somehow totally annoyed me; it was obvious as she said,

"More gardening? I wish you'd do something active from time to time, like your brothers."

"Gardening *is* active. But we're not doing... it's not gardening, it's—"

"In the garden or stuck in your room at home and stuck in your room at Grandma's. What do you get up to for so long?"

"We'll be outside tomorrow, Mam. I'm not going to be in my room. We'll be rehearsing."

"What?"

"We'll be outside."

"Okay. I'm tired."

"I don't even know how you would know where I am, anyway— you're never around. And when you are, you're always tired," I heard myself saying.

"I've got enough on my mind! Stop whining, will you?"

"No. No I won't," I said. "By the way, that story about the homeless man's not true. I made it up because Thomas wasn't trying to steal my stuff."

Mam didn't say anything. She turned to look at me with fast-blinking eyes which waited for an explanation.

"I ran away," I said. "I didn't want to get back on the bus because I didn't want to come home because I'm sick of everything and I'm sick of you and don't expect I won't try it again if I get half a chance!"

I didn't look at Mam, but the air changed. She pulled over by the side of the road and switched the engine off. Still without looking at her, I asked if she wanted me to get out and walk home.

"Why are you saying that?" she said. "No. Of course not." She took my right arm, but I pulled away. She looked at me and said, "That's the truth, is it? Did you try to run away?"

She must have seen the answer in my face because she said, "Christ, Oliver, things aren't that bad. Not for you, anyway. Are they?"

She read my face again and said,

"Why didn't you talk to me? To Dad?"

"Don't tell Dad! He'll go ape!"

"He won't. But don't keep things to yourself. I'm sorry," she said. I couldn't believe my ears. "I hadn't realised… just sorry we hadn't noticed things had… Things seem to have got quite bad, have they? We'll have to have a proper talk when I get the time. I thought everything would be easier for you at your grandparents'."

She held my arm again, and this time I didn't pull away, but I still didn't look at her. As we drove home, there was a weight lifted: Mam had listened, at least a bit, I think.

"How's Lily?" I asked.

"I can't tell any more. Why don't we go to see her, the two of us, tomorrow?"

"Yes. Definitely, Mam. I've been so worried." And then I hung my head and said it. "You don't think that it was me, do you? I mean my fault, in the supermarket? You do."

She squeezed my arm again and said, "No, Oliver, no."

And a pain of relief pushed from the back of my eyes.

Celia-mail 6

Dear Mam,

Only three weeks to go now till the big party! I've had replies from nearly everyone, and there's going to be a great turnout. I've arranged the sign interpreter for your deaf friends as well. The 27th day of July will be a special day, I'm sure, even though it's a Sunday party!

You know I've been going on about the young Oliver with the sister who's very ill in Rachel House? Well, his big brother, Sam, came by to get his coat that he'd left, and I had a nice chat with him. The young lad is still at his grandparents, apparently, so I decided to ask for the address. Sounds like it's all too much for poor Sam now, and he can no longer bring himself to see his little sister so ill. He said he'd tried to go in several times but keeps making excuses to Anna, the mam. He's staying in Durham with some friends, I think. He tells me the middle boy, Nathan, is putting everything into his skateboarding, but that Oliver has become very distant and depressed. Sam tells him off because he's started to complain that Lily gets too much attention, but I suppose he's right.

Anyway, Sam told me Oliver was in the play, *Hamlet*, at school, so I bought a card of that famous Ophelia in the water, by John Everett Millais. I hoped it wasn't too gloomy, only it's got quite a few flowers in and I know he enjoys horticulture. I spent ages thinking what to write last night and had pages of words in my head, but in the end I just wrote, 'Good luck with your play at school.' Then I woke up in the night and added, 'Sorry I didn't get to say goodbye properly. Hope you're okay. Hang on in there and you'll be fine. If you ever feel like letting me know how things are going, or a haircut, do get in touch!' and I wrote my email address and mobile number. Then, in the morning, I said to myself, "What am I thinking? I can't send that," so it's propped up on the mantlepiece wondering what to do with itself! I suppose I'll have to let the whole thing drop. We're told not to get involved anyway. And the poor lad probably wouldn't even remember who I was!

Got to pop out for a stroll and fresh air. Been sick at work—think it's these herbal fertility drugs I've been taking.

Much love,
Celia x

Lily Love-Stone

Nearly two months had passed and Mam never got the time for a proper talk though she said a few times that she hadn't forgotten. I once overheard her saying to Dad,

"I lie awake in bed and amongst the myriad of other plans, I see a quiet lunch for us, just me and Oliver, in a peaceful corner somewhere. I see him laughing." I found fleeting solace in her words. "But I wake up and the next thing happens, you know? The next cannon ball is rolled at great speed at my feet and it's all I can do to stop crashing, face first, to the ground…" I suppose she was hardly with me because of Lily, so it wasn't that surprising that we hadn't talked. She did try to give me more attention and actually smiled in my direction occasionally, but it seemed false… sort of forced in a way. It was like she'd been reminded I was there, but she still couldn't really see me. Her mind was just too taken over by her sick child.

Everything was about Lily. We were all in purgatory as she didn't seem to be getting better, and it's all Mam cared about.

I was at Grandma's and Grandpa's a lot of the time. There didn't seem to be a plan for me; sometimes I was at home, sometimes I was at Grandma's, and that was it. When Grandma tried to talk about anything like me properly going back home, Mam snapped at her, so things just plodded along. She practically lived at the hospital, so I didn't even get the chance for a not-proper talk. But I sensed that I'd be home before too long.

Miss Pratt had taken ill, so even the play rehearsals had been put on hold since May. We were supposed to perform at the end of July, but there were rumours that it would be cancelled or postponed till the next academic year. I'd learnt all my lines and was desperate to get back into some acting, but I found my plants were all that held any sort of promise at that time.

A week into July, I did something a bit weird. I was in Newcastle with Kamal to go to Waterstones; he wanted to buy *I Have a Dream: The Story of Martin Luther King* and I wanted to buy the ridiculously long-titled *Planting & Caring for Your Rose Garden: Who Else Wants to Discover the Amazing Secrets to Growing Beautiful Roses Anytime, Anywhere—No Matter What Your Experience Level?* While Kamal was paying, I overheard someone talking about the dreaded Newcastle Infirmary and it made me think of Nurse Celia. I then had the urge to go and say hello… well, goodbye, I suppose. I wished I'd picked some snapdragons from the garden, which had flourished in the last week, but I borrowed some dosh from Kamal to get her some delphiniums instead and we made our way to the ward.

"It strikes me as a tad odd, taking flowers to a nurse you hardly know," said Kamal.

"I know, but I sort of got on with her; she was nice to me, that's all. She's probably not even there."

And she wasn't there. I left the flowers for her, my address at Grandma's (though I didn't really know why), and a note. I discovered I still had the Tate Gallery cards at the bottom of my bag, so I wrote on the back of *Fallen Birds* by Bernard Meadows.

"Bit of a depressing card to leave for her, isn't it? I thought you said she was a jovial sort."

"Yeah, well, it's all I've got. It's a sweet little bird anyway."

"More like a frightened little bird. Or is it actually dead—an ex-bird? They've got a shop here, you know."

"I've done it now. Let's just go. Don't like this place."

By the third Saturday in July, I was back home properly and school was over for the summer. Kamal texted me to say that Poppy Teasdale was finally back, too. I had thought she was never coming back. She hadn't told me herself because she'd stopped communicating. She must have fallen in love with someone or I must have said something, I thought. But surely it couldn't work with him living so far away! I mean Sam had split up with Sarah for the same reason. ("Long-distance relationships, Ollie. Impossible.") And she only lived in York.

Her gran must have died, but she hadn't told me. She hadn't contacted me. She obviously hadn't really wanted to keep in touch or even find out how Lily was doing. That's what surprised me most. Now she was back, she'd probably need a shoulder to cry on, I thought.

Kamal's text telling me she was back played on my mind. A balloon was gradually inflating inside my head. The pressure to text Poppy or ring or run round to her house mounted. Surely it would be *her* who'd contact *me*. I walked to my bedroom window in search of distraction, but thought I saw a plane trailing a banner emblazoned with, 'Poppy Teasdale Is Back!' I turned back to my room and saw POPPY'S BACK in neon lights on the wall above my bed. I sat on the bed and closed my eyes. Then, I heard one of those vans with megaphones blaring out, 'Breaking news! Poppy Teasdale is back in town!' I kept my eyes shut and blocked my ears. I heard knocking and a voice shouting, "Oliver!"

"Poppy?" I shouted back as I opened my eyes.

"What? Why are you saying that?" said Mam as she opened my door. "We're all going to the hospital—Lily's taken a bad turn."

Lily was in a constant bad turn, it seemed to me, so I knew this turn within a turn must be pretty serious. I had got bored with the drudgery of going to the hospital and seeing Lily ill, and for some reason I was even getting angry with her, but this time, I wanted a distraction and did want to be with her. I longed, for a moment, that there stretched before me a long, hot summer filled with Poppy and Lily properly better and Mam laughing.

Rachel House had bedrooms for families to stay in, so, as we had done twice before, we all stayed the night that Saturday; I say "all," but it was just Mam, Dad, my aunties and me. Nathan had gone to stay at a friend's house, and Sam was in Durham at his dad's. I didn't want to be the only kid there, but my brothers wouldn't come and Mam didn't force them. My aunties Colette and Margaret had been up from London since the Thursday, and they stayed the night as well.

It was a sunny day, so we all spent some time in the grounds. It felt like a secret garden; there was no one there but our family. Rachel House was a pretty peaceful place, you see—there was only room for about ten sick children, so it was more like an actual home, and it was quite likely that you might have the whole of the outside space to yourself.

We wheeled Lily out in her special pushchair and stopped at various spots within the six-acre landscaped gardens. The weather couldn't make up its mind: windy with dark clouds scuttling across the sky, then a stretch of blue, then white puffy clouds, then dark again and even a few spots of rain. But the air was fresh and clean. Dad put Lily in the wheelchair swing first and pushed her, my auntie Margaret swaying the drip she was holding back and forth, mirroring the rocking motion. It looked like some whacky and perverse new sport. I followed Lily's movement, as in a tennis trance, hypnotised by the arc her body drew over and over. I imagined her taking off with one of the upward swings and waving down to us as she flew up into the sky.

I loved the cave corner. It was like playing house: so warm and sheltered with a musty smell that was strangely pleasant. The ferny floor was all crinkly and welcoming, like a crackly fire. There were bamboo beams, making a kind of ceiling that slow danced above us. As we rested on the furniture—rope seat, logs, stumps —I felt as though we were protected there; nothing could harm us. It was a cool sort of humble haven with blood-red colours everywhere: berries, freshly cut roses in a vase, and a small glass lantern with a calming red candle flickering inside (even though it was daytime). I slumped over Lily's chair as best I could, my arm wrapped around her bloated body, and we both listened to Mam and our aunties singing. They could sing in harmony—sounded really soothing.

"Come on Oliver, you're a good singer," my mam said at one point. I was happy where I was and being silent, but my heart sang, delighted as it was with Mam's warm words. My breathing moved with Lily's. Everything was slow: every sound, every move, every glance, every blink. This day had a real stillness about it, like it would last a week, but I didn't mind; I wanted to stay in it forever. I wouldn't have been surprised if everything had just frozen: that time had ceased to flow.

When the time came, it was with a wild unwillingness that I moved on with the group to a new section of the grounds, to sit round the fountain. There was a weird feeling of opposites in the air—of things being perfectly ordered yet nothing making sense, if you know what I mean. So when Auntie Colette washed some crystals in the fountain and lay them carefully out on the low wall around it, to dry in the sun, it seemed nothing out of the ordinary. It seemed equally normal that, once dried, she laid the largest crystal on Lily's lap.

"Are you trying to heal her or something weird like that?" I asked her.

"No, love. Well, not in the way you're thinking," Auntie Colette said.

"She's a bit mad, Oliver. That's all," Auntie Margaret chipped in.

"Some people think crystals have powers, you know," Auntie Colette said, "healing properties, but for me, it's just interesting. It's just a vague interest. I think there's definitely something positive about naturally grown crystals, though. They're not all crystals, just called gemstones really. Let me ask you this: do you like *flowers*? Or maybe that's a funny question."

"He's a funny boy, Colette!" Mam said. "And you know he does. Anyway why shouldn't boys like flowers?"

"You saying *I'm* weird?" I said, half-smiling at Mam. Our eyes met with a sweet lightness that I hardly recognized.

Auntie Colette pressed me, "Just tell me, though, why you think people like getting flowers and plants?"

"Because they have lovely names and they're appealing to look at and you can smell them and touch them... and they make people feel good. And they teach you about colour and texture and stuff.

They're innocent. Innocent. Even the ones that kill. And nature takes you away from the boredom and the anger and the loneliness."

"Okaaay. Don't know how the word 'kill' got in there, but yes... " Auntie Colette approved of my answer. "You see? It could be all that?"

"Because gemstones are just cool things, you mean?" I said.

"Yeah. They're supposed to have different vibrations, like colours probably do. So maybe they can affect you like colours can. Come and look at these, Oliver."

My auntie beckoned me down to where she was kneeling, next to the low fountain wall and the line of stones she'd laid out along it. There were about ten of them, all different shapes, colours, and sizes, the sun gleaming through them. I thought of the gleaming glass I'd seen at John's exhibition and Sophie Sunstone.

"Which ones do you like, then? Which one's your favourite, do you think?"

Auntie Margaret jumped in with, "I like the green one. What's that called, Colette?"

"I think I like this one best," I said, as I picked up a shiny mottled stone of dark green, beige, and salmon-pink.

"That's called unakite. And yours is called aventurine, Mags. You see? Everyone likes a different one! I bet Anna likes the pink one, for instance."

"Yeah, I do actually."

Mam was very close to Auntie Colette, and they always knew exactly what the other would like: clothes, music, art, books, ornaments, candles.

"Do you know what it is, Anna?" Auntie Colette asked.

"Quartz or something, isn't it?'

"Yeah, rose quartz. Love crystal's another name for it.'"

"Let's give that one to Lily then," Mam said. "I want to make a necklace. How can we make a necklace, Mags?"

Auntie Margaret had done an art degree like Mam, and she was a primary school teacher, too, so she was good at craft stuff.

"We'll need some glue and a ribbon."

I was in outdoor mode, so a natural alternative sprung to my mind.

"I could make a teeny basket for it with grass and make the chain from flower-stems tied together," I said.

While I rummaged about in the growth looking for necklace-making material, my auntie started talking about the gemstones we'd picked out.

"You see, Mags, your aventurine is supposed to be good for balancing the heart and reducing anxiety and fears."

"I could do with some of that!" Auntie Margaret said.

"And the rose quartz or love stone, well, what it says on the tin—it represents unconditional love. It's said to help you let go of anger and jealousy. It's supposed to encourage forgiveness, too, and even help you sleep if you put one by the bed."

"I've got a big one of those somewhere," Mam said. "I must find it."

"And wash it. It needs to be cleansed, they say," Auntie Colette said.

They seemed to be taking it all pretty seriously considering it was just a vague interest, I thought, but Auntie Colette hadn't picked one herself yet, so I asked her, "What about you then, Auntie Colette? Which stone do you like best?"

"Out of these, I kind of like the look of the carnelian today, the yellow one, though normally I'd say amethyst, and the tiger's eye's rather gorgeous."

"Hey come on! You said pick *one*!" I said.

"I'll go for tiger's eye then. And that's not just because it brings good luck, wealth, and success! It's supposed to protect you and help build confidence."

"I think you've got enough of that!" Auntie Margaret said.

"What's that one you laid on Lily's lap, Auntie Colette?"

"It's a clear quartz crystal, known as the master healing crystal. I put it there because they say it promotes harmony and helps you to see your way clearly."

"She can't see now, though," I said.

Mam said, "She doesn't mean 'see' literally, Oliver. It's like when you say, 'See what I mean?'"

"I don't *see* how a little stone can help Lily when none of the doctors in the world can help her," I said, starting to feel irritated with it all.

Mam said, "We're not trying to cure her, Oliver. It's just something nice to do."

"Well, it's a bit stupid. It's not nice putting weird stuff on her."

I felt bad saying that because Auntie Colette looked offended. She said, "I know it's stupid, but there's nothing wrong with it. I just think the stones are beautiful. I suppose that chain for Lily's necklace is out of the question now you've decided we're all insane!"

"Just you, Colette, actually," Auntie Margaret said.

I'd been making it while they were talking, so I surprised them all with the finished article—three bits of tall grasses tied together for the chain and a tiny mesh pocket thing I'd made out of some leaves.

I put the love crystal in the little pocket then hung the necklace round Lily's neck and kissed her puffy cheek saying, "There you are, Lily, and don't worry; it's nothing weird apparently. Can we go in now, Mam? It's getting cold now the sun's going down."

It *wasn't* getting that cold, but the sun *was* beginning to disappear, despite my wishes for it to never stop shining that day.

"Of course. It's been a lovely day, hasn't it?" Mam said.

I looked at her poor smiling face glowing like an angel in the golden sunlight and longed for it to stay like that. And as we looked at each other, we found the sweet lightness again, so much so that my throat clenched up and I simply nodded and looked up into the sky.

That evening, I watched TV and drew some cartoons and talked a bit to a boy called Max whose brother was in Rachel House. Even though Rachel House was such a positive place, he made it sound like a prison, asking me, "What's yours in for?"

I didn't properly know, so I just said it was her brain, and I didn't understand what he said his brother had. It was two very long words with about ten syllables. I didn't really want to talk to him at all, so I was glad when he suggested going on the Xbox because that meant we didn't have to say anything or look at each other.

Dad went upstairs on his own, while Mam and my aunties sat in the conservatory section, drinking wine and talking.

After finishing the game with Max, I wandered down the corridor to Lily's room. The door was open, and a nurse was with her. I leant against the doorframe and watched. Lily's eyes were still closed, and the nurse was fiddling with a machine. There were splashy paint pictures mounted on black on the wall behind the bed and some cards stuck on the wall, including the two new ones she had just got from my aunties. Her polar bear lay next to her head, and behind her, on the upsloping bed, was a box of tissues, an oxygen mask and a little plugged-in fan, trained on her face.

The nurse said, "Oh! I didn't see you there. You gave me a fright. I was just leaving, so why don't you come in for a while?" So soft and gentle, the people who worked there.

I didn't say anything. I walked towards the orange sofa with the blue embroidered cushions as the nurse left the room, leaving the door open. I sat down, my gaze fixed on my little sister. She was so still and she seemed incredibly weak.

"I'm sorry I never found the 'Sweet Baby, Sleep' music, Lil. I'll try to find it for next time... I said I'll try to find it for next time."

A dribble was growing out of her mouth like a pupa from larva, so I stood up and wiped it away with my sleeve. I took it as a sign she was communicating with me, but something inside me needed to speak to her in a new way.

"I don't think you're going to get better, Lily. I'm so sorry to be the one to tell you. I'd do anything to... I know you can hear me, so I'm just saying it's okay, you know. You've been ill too long now. I'm just saying it's okay, I mean, if you have to go. Okay? I've put you some flowers in a little vase here. It's a pink polyanthus and a few forget-me-nots. Myosotis... Remember? Yours haven't come out yet; I picked these by the river Tyne. Not many coz you shouldn't really pick wild flowers. We have to conserve the countryside don't we? Save what we can, eh Lily? They're not weeds anyway, are they? They're beautiful and bright and delicate, like you."

The left side of her mouth went up into a smile, and she sighed. And I lay down next to her. "Stupid doctors can't work it out, can they? They're not clever like you. I don't want you to go, but you're so ill and I can't bear it anymore... to see you like this. Or maybe you'll be sitting up tomorrow when I come to see you, will you? Sitting up looking at your new necklace that I made for you. And maybe we can learn all about The Millenium Seedbank Project when we go to Kew Gardens? Shall we change the lawn into a meadow full of bright wild flowers, eh? And watch all the insects and the bees come to play there? We'd love that, wouldn't we? I'd love that. I hope... I wish... I love you, by the way, Lily Ethel Campbell. An incredible amount that there are no words to explain. You know that, don't you? Forever and ever and ever. And I'm just saying it's okay if you feel it's time... you know...?"

So many opposites scrambled together. It had been like magic to see Mam almost happy that day. She even talked to me quite a few times. It made me not miss her so much. And the selfish anger towards Lily had lifted.

I fell asleep next to her that night, but apparently Dad lifted me up to bed. I wish he hadn't.

Lily Still There

The next morning, my aunties had left very early in the morning, and when I got up at eight o'clock, Mam and Dad weren't in their room or at breakfast. When I found them in Lily's room, sitting on the orange sofa, Lily was out of her bed and in Dad's arms. Tubes out. Machines off. He was rocking her. I stood in the doorway. Mam stared through me.

"She's going into the special room today," Dad said with shell-shocked eyes. But it wasn't what I had thought. This is the hardest thing I've ever had to say in my entire life, but the thing that Lily had to do to be allowed into the special room was to die.

On Sunday, July 27th, my little sister, Lily, not yet six years old, died.

I couldn't believe it. That's what was special about the room. After a person dies, you could go to this special place, called the Cold

Room I found out, and just sit and say goodbye. I didn't. Lily had died in my dad's arms. He had rocked her to sleep for the last time.

"Shall I stay in the room or not?" came out of my mouth.

Nothing back.

I stayed at the door. Mam took Lily in her arms, and Dad got up and walked past me, crying. I went upstairs, stood at the window, looked down at the fountain, and saw a little bird hopping a few inches before flying off. *A chaffinch or a robin? Which one? Male chaffinch or female? Which is the brighter one?* I sat on the bed. I looked at my watch. I went back to the window. I saw Max with his parents and his brother with the complicated illness. He was laughing—the brother. Laughing.

I went to the toilet. Nothing happened. I brushed my teeth for too long. I sat back on the bed. I looked down and saw my hands. I checked my pulse.

I crept back down the stairs and sort of floated to Lily's room in a daze. Mam was still holding Lily.

"Oliver, do you want to—?"

I didn't want to hold her. Mam looked back at Lily, so I went back upstairs and sat on the bed again. I went back to the window. Max was helping his little brother walk to the fountain. *So he can even walk as well, this brother.* Max spotted me and waved and shouted something. I was watching a play at the theatre, so I didn't respond. Max cupped his hands around his mouth and shouted my name several times. I opened the window.

"Hey, it's dead warm out here. We're gonna paddle our feet in the fountain. D'you fancy it?"

I tried to say no, but nothing came out of my mouth.

"What? Bring your sister, eh?"

I closed the window and waved a 'goodbye' wave (not an 'I'll-see-you-in-a-minute' wave). "Bring your sister." "Bring your sister." The words stabbed every part of my body then strangled my stomach, and a foul feeling rose to my throat. I ran to the toilet. After cleaning my mouth and brushing my teeth, I packed my bag and sat back on the bed. I did that thing when you pull all your fingers one by one, even though mine don't make that clicking noise. I found myself rocking back and forwards, chewing my right thumbnail, chewing my right thumb knuckle. I fell into a sort of trance. I stayed like that for ages.

I went back downstairs. My mam must have been holding my little sister for hours by now even though Lily had... you know. I stood at the doorway, and a nurse came up behind me. She put her hand on my head, then said to Mam, "Do you want to put fresh clothes on her or pyjamas, love? We'll help you all we can. We'll need to take her to the Cold Room, Anna. You can carry her."

Mam said, "No. I mean will you dress her, please? I mean no. I have to speak with Ben. I'll ask Ben... about clothes. I'll have to check with him. I don't know."

"*I'll* get him, Mam," I said.

Mam looked puzzled like she didn't know who had spoken.

"Mam. I'll get him."

She looked at Lily, lying still in her arms. "Shall we put your clothes on, darling, or shall we make you snug in your pyjamas?"

"I'll just go and..." I said, but she couldn't hear me.

As I walked away from Lily's room, I wondered if they'd given Mam some drugs. I didn't have to go far before I saw Dad. As I turned left, off the corridor, I saw him leaning head first onto a wall, his shoulders shaking. I quickly stepped backwards round the corner, out of sight, my back up against the wall, like a spy on the tail of an assassin. Then I went back round.

"Dad!" I shouted as I stepped round the corner again. He gestured for me to go to him. I walked up to him, and he wrapped his arms around me, telling me we'd all have to help each other. I felt like we were acting in a play.

"Do Nathan and Sam know?" I asked.

"Mam wants to be the one who rings them. Soon, Oliver."

"She needs to see you," I told him.

We walked back, my arm around Dad's waist, who was trailing his feet like an old man. I imagined I was visiting him in an old people's home and was taking him back to his room to help him on with his slippers and make him a cup of tea.

A random, selfish thought came into my head—that we were all supposed to be going to Kew Gardens the next week and what bad timing this was. I wanted to blame someone.

Once back to the room, the few minutes' distraction with Dad made the sight of Mam and Lily shocking, so I ran back up to my room. I dropped to my knees next to the bed and threw my face into the bedclothes. Then it hit me.

Lily will never come home again.

I will never hold Lily again.

Lily will never smile again.

Lily will never laugh again.

Lily will never hear Sweet Baby, Sleep again.

Lily will never eat curry or dance or sing or tend to her roses or say my name or even twitch again.

Lily will never, will never... see me *again.*

I wished I or someone else could have given a new brain to Lily, because that was where her disease was. I would have felt so angry, but my head was numb.

When I went back to Lily's room and stood in the doorway, no one was there, not even her cuddly toys. It wasn't Lily's room. It had never been Lily's room. It was waiting for its next victim. A death factory. An infirmary.

"Hi, Ollie... You okay?" Nathan had turned up, even before Mam had phoned him, so I don't know how he knew. He rubbed my head and asked if I would go to the Cold Room with him. Mam and Dad were there. Turned out we all had to stay another night, as Mam and Dad had to register the death and meet the funeral director the next day.

"You coming?"

"No!" And I meant no to everything. As he walked with a plodding gait, robbed of his sister, to the fridge room, I set off in the opposite direction, to the Games Room, and texted Kamal to tell him the news. Then I texted Grandma and Sam, even though they already knew. Then I texted Poppy. Then I texted Celia, who'd amazingly sent an Ophelia card to me a few weeks earlier with her number in. I went outside to rock on a swing. A bloke came out and asked me if I wanted anything. I knew what I wanted, but I couldn't say it. The text replies I got were:

Kamal: "Oh no, Oliver. Your poor mam and dad and family. So sorry, mate."

Grandma: "We knew this day would come, but it must be so awful. It has hit me and your grandpa hard, too. Be strong for your mam and dad. We'll be with you soon, pet."

Sam: "What a shit day. How will Mam cope with this? Good that you were there. I couldn't face seeing her like that any more."

Poppy: "I can't believe it. I'm in shock. Can I come and see you? Your mam must be a mess. I loved Lily so much."

Celia: "Oh, Oliver, sweetheart, what sad news. You will feel so numb for a while and maybe anger will come before the grief, but remember you were the best brother a little girl could ever have had. You gave her so much happiness. There's nothing you could have done. You have been kind to life, but it seems to have been cruel to you. That will change, I'm sure. You deserve a great life. Thinking about you, love."

Odd that I remembered 27th July would always be in Celia's diary, too, because it was her mam's birthday and she was having an eightieth party that day with a Snow White and the Seven Dwarves theme. She'd mentioned it in her text back to me after I said thanks for the card. I texted her back late that night, "Thank you for your kind words. You don't know how much it means to me what you said. How did your mam's party go? Who did you dress as?"

She wrote, "Amazing that you remembered that with the day you're having. You really are an extraordinary chap. It went very well, apart from a man in a Sleepy costume falling into the cake, very drunk. Emily had one too many champagne cocktails and licked cake from his arm! All a bit shocking at an eightieth! I went as Dopey. Try to stay peaceful, and perhaps your gardening will help you in the coming weeks, love."

That night, even though I was glad, at least, that Nathan shared the room with me, I couldn't sleep and felt alone. I wouldn't unpack my bag, so I lay awake with my clothes on. I crept to Mam and Dad's bedroom and crouched outside, my ear against the door. I wanted to sleep on their floor, but I didn't want to disturb them. It must have been about two in the morning, but they were still awake.

I remember hearing Mam say, "Our baby's dead below us and we're going to sleep."

And I heard Dad say, "Oliver hasn't even cried, I don't think. It hasn't hit him. He doesn't believe it."

And Mam answered, "None of us believe it, Ben. I don't anyway; I don't know about you. We're all different, I suppose."

I had fallen asleep against my parents' bedroom door, and a nurse had helped me back to my bed at about four in the morning. I knew this because Nathan told me he was woken up and he couldn't get back to sleep. We were already out of synch, it seemed.

We were all sitting at breakfast in this strange place, in this strange mood. We usually only ever had breakfast away from home when we were on some sort of holiday. It was like a nightmare holiday, the discussion not about what time the coach tour was setting off but about what time the funeral director was arriving. I say 'discussion,' but mostly we didn't say much at all. Mam was the only one who said anything, now I think about it. She said she couldn't believe she was eating breakfast like nothing was wrong and that she'd stayed up late the night before smoking and felt sick today. She had run out of cigarettes, but stayed up drinking coffee and telling anyone who would listen that her only daughter had died that day. A dad who was staying at Rachel House, too, gave her a whole pack of cigarettes which were far too strong for her, but which she puffed her way through anyway.

For some reason, I decided I wanted to meet the funeral director with Mam and Dad, but I wasn't allowed. I made a bit of a scene about it, and Nathan had to calm me down and insisted we play football outside, which we hardly ever did, even at home. Max joined in, but he didn't say anything apart from, "What team shall we be? Liverpool?"

Nathan and I were several years older than him, so it seemed a pointless yet somehow refreshing idea to pick a 'team'. Without consultation, we both said, "No! Newcastle United!" and half smiled at each other. I immediately felt like I'd committed a mortal sin, smiling while my parents were discussing my sister's coffin.

Another journey home. The last journey home. The worst journey home. Every revolution of the car wheels felt like a violent jolt away from my sister. And the tarmac behind us melted and buckled and plunged into hell, because there was no going back now. It was as if we'd all been drugged and in our trance had been told, "Go now! Do not turn round! Do not come back! There is nothing here for you now!"

My mam was the only one who spoke. But it was as if she were someone else, talking about someone else:

"I think that was a good choice; a basket's much nicer than a casket. He had such a selection of materials in that swatch! I'm glad we went for the pink silk lining. She'll like that. Would make a beautiful dress. That's a point, what should she wear? Mam and Dad are coming over later, boys. That'll be nice. And Sam's back this afternoon. I'll meet him at the station. I'll drive up there for him. Shall we all go? No, that's pointless. What would he think?! I'll go on my own. Or perhaps the boys might come? No. We'll see anyway. I'll have to get planning tonight. I'll have to have people staying. I'll make food. How many shall I cook for? I don't know. How many people will come, Ben? I suppose we have to invite them, don't we. Do you invite people? I don't know. I've never... How is everyone supposed to find out about it? Who's going to... ? Ben, will you? I'll have to make a plan. Mam'll help me. She knows what to do. I'll have to choose some music. Colette will help me. Does she know? Does everybody know? I rang them, didn't I? Did I? Who did I ring from the hospital, Ben?"

Dad and Nathan made some appropriate noises, but I desperately wanted to block my ears.

I dreaded being in the house. How would everyone be? How would Mam be? How would she be that afternoon? That night? The next day? The rest of our lives?

Always With Me

Grandma and Grandpa arrived at about three o'clock. I didn't see them at first, but I heard Mam crying with them in the kitchen. I heard Mam crying on the phone to my aunties.

I don't know why, but Sam didn't come home that day. I'm sure Mam was expecting him, but he didn't come till a few days after Lily died.

I was the only one who went with Mam to the station to collect Sam. We exchanged no words. It was more just to get out of the house than anything else, but no sooner was I at the station, sitting in the car while Mam stood at the exit gate, waiting for the train to come in, than I realised I didn't want to be there at all. I almost got out of the car to run home. I would have to witness my mam seeing Sam for the first time since the terrible day.

When Sam eventually arrived, he ran to Mam, dropped his bag, and they stood hugging while everybody else walked past them. I didn't want to see, but I looked nevertheless, at this time-lapse photograph—blurred passers-by and a still couple in the middle. The clock froze for them I think, because by the time they'd come out of each other's arms, ours was the only car and we were the only people left at the station.

I was glad the family were all back together, but our connectedness seemed flimsy. That first night, when Sam got back, Mam, Dad and him spent all evening in the kitchen, drinking and listening to music. I went in occasionally to get something to eat, but wasn't interested in their drunken tears and hugs. I couldn't get drunk. What was I supposed to do? I think the drinking in between the days was supposed to help, but it seemed to me that things couldn't be worse.

The oddest thing was that when Poppy texted me a third or fourth time, the same day Sam came back, I felt very flat. I'd been dying for her to get in touch, but she asked if she could come round, as if everything was all right, you know, and I just thought it was all a bit sudden and she hadn't explained anything. I mean, she hadn't contacted me for months. When I didn't text her back, she texted again saying, "So sorry about your sister. Mam said I couldn't go and see her because she was too ill." I didn't believe her. She could have seen her if she'd really wanted. I decided to leave it and not answer till I felt clearer about stuff. I realise now I was being stupid, but Poppy even sent another text begging to come round to see me and saying it would be 'five-star', which I ignored as well. Nathan said I was off my tree and that I was only putting Poppy off because I was enjoying the attention.

Apart from the funeral that we were all dreading without saying it, the future seemed dead. So when Mam wasn't in bed, which she seemed to be a lot of the time, she busied herself with preparations for people coming to stay and plans for the day. She alternated between being hyperactive and hardly being able to function at all, so she had to lie down a lot. Sam said that she kept going to bed because she felt lonely, empty and "dead inside." When she could put her mind to practical stuff, she certainly seemed alive. Once, when we were in the supermarket together buying food and candles and fizzy wine, she said, "I can't believe I'm shopping for my child's funeral party."

I didn't know what to say, so I didn't say anything.

That first week, Dad spent the days gardening. He seemed very confused about everything. He said he found the earth a comfort. I worked with him and on my special garden patch. We allowed the soil and plants—their textures, colours and smells—to hypnotize us.

Sam played the guitar and travelled between home and Durham, trying to be the sensible, 'together' one. He was the luckiest, being able to get away so easily, though I doubt very much he'd use that word.

Nathan was desperate to make things better, but he had to accept that he couldn't, and he immersed himself in his skateboarding.

I had my mind and my nightmares and was now at home for good. I loved my plants and flowers and trees, but I wasn't good at anything, not like my brothers, and I couldn't distract myself enough to stop anxious thoughts like *Is everyone thinking it should have been me?*

Maybe that's why nobody asked me my ideas about the service for Lily. I would have liked to choose some music. I could have perhaps read out a poem or a letter. I could have written a letter to her. Mam talked to her sisters, my aunties, about it all, and they decided on everything.

Auntie Colette and Auntie Margaret had visited Lily in hospital quite a bit more than the other siblings and Dad's siblings, so I suppose it made sense that they were involved at this point. All the grandparents had visited sometimes, by the way, but you could see just how much they couldn't bear being there. They looked like they had some terrible itching disease, so uncomfortable did they seem in their own skins. No one knew what to say, and when they tried, it was so easy to say the wrong thing. I don't think any of our cousins came to visit Lily. They were mostly very young, you see, so I suppose the parents wanted to protect them from the upset... or protect themselves from the upset. I know that the two aunties who came the most were the only ones who didn't have their own children. Maybe that's how they could visit so often, even though they lived the furthest away. I don't know. It's very complicated. Who actually wants to stand in a hospital, next to a bed of a young child who is dying? I certainly hated going. I had to prepare myself. It was like entering a stage. You had to brace yourself and remember your role and not be afraid or angry or upset but just try to stick to a sketchy script and improvise a bit.

Kamal kept texting to ask if he could come round. I didn't answer. He came round anyway. We watched TV.

Just before he left, he asked the beginnings of four questions, all of which I answered. It felt like a game—"I'll name that question in two words!" "*I'll* name it in one!"

"When—?"

"August eighth. Next Friday."

"Can I—?"

"No. I... I want to be on my own."

"We'll send fl—"

"They don't want flowers. Donations to Rachel House."

"Rachel—?"

"Rachel House, the hospice. Not a hospital. It's where you die."

Kamal stood up now and made towards the living room door. He started on another question. "Do you—?"

"No, I don't want to practise *Hamlet* till after... till a few weeks time, you know, when everything's over. I thought it was cancelled anyway."

"No. She's starting again when we go back in September. Do you want this card, I was going to say?"

"Oh. What is it?"

Kamal looked at me like I'd said, "Which planet is this we're on?" I realised, then, what the card was for, but it was such a weird, alien time, nothing much made sense. It didn't really even feel like it was me talking. It was as if I were hearing somebody else.

Kamal put the card on the arm of the sofa, and I saw him to the front door. He squeezed in another half question.

"When will I—?"

""Tomorrow," I heard myself saying. I wanted to be alone, but I had said "tomorrow."

"Oh right, good. We could go on the moor... or stay in. It's supposed to be hot, though... out, you know, so we, well, we could still just stay in and go on the Xbox or something if you want. Or in the garden... we could take some—"

"Just text when you get up, all right?"

"K, see you."

I could sort of be on my own and still have a distraction from myself when I was with Kamal, if that makes any sense. I was grateful for that. I should have let him come to the funeral, but I wanted to block it out. I didn't want to go myself.

It didn't *look* like a funeral: pink pillar candles flickering on the floor and no one wearing black or holding lacy handkerchiefs or anything like that. And I organised bunches of dried statice flowers dotted round the room, and wrote, 'I miss you' on little cards; seemed sick that fresh flowers were flirting about the place somehow. A cruel joke. But there was no getting away from why we were all there. Not that I felt like I *was* there. I felt like I was acting in a horrible play as some bizarre punishment for I don't know what. I tried to distance myself mentally, but there was no getting away from the room full of heavy hearts either; the ground might have crumbled and tumbled into the centre of the earth with the weight of them. I imagined a sort of vapour of pain pervading the space and choking every inch of it.

Hanging in the hot and humid air was this vile poison of fresh flowers, aftershave, incense, smoke, and sweat. Stifling.

It did *sound* like a funeral: melancholy music, crinkling of Orders of Service Sam had handed out, nervous shoe shuffling, and then readings breaking the sniffing silence. Stifling.

A man came to the front. He opened his mouth and words came out. He'd never even seen Lily in his life. How dare he speak of her that way? It was *not* her time. As if he knew all along because he was 'like that' with God, but us poor sinners had been duped by the devil into thinking she'd be around forever. "Let's celebrate her life," he said. I thought. *No, let's watch a speeded-up video of Mam and Dad trailing themselves back and forwards to the hospital, lashed about by 'God's plan'. There, back. There, back. There, back. Ad nauseum. Let's watch a speeded-up video of Lily being taken out of and put back into her bed, to endure endless, pointless, painful tests. Stabbed with needles. Tubes inserted into her fragile flesh. Up and out, back down. Up and out, back down. Up and out, back down.*

My aunties went to the front. They opened their mouths and words came out.

Then my dad's turn... I wanted to block my ears, but instead I gritted my teeth. *Dizygotheca elegantissima. Dizygotheca elegantissima. Brugmansia sanguinea...*

Four other things I remember about the funeral are:

- Mam's face was red and blotchy, and people kept helping her to walk and stand like she was a cripple. And I heard her say, "She was my baby."

- My uncle Francis had written a song called *Always with Me* that was played during the ceremony. I normally thought his music was great, but I tried not to listen to this song because the lyrics were horrible lies, saying Lily was still there in stars and trees and daft things like that. Anyone who had not cried up to that point did when they heard Uncle Francis's song. I didn't.

- My two biggest hugs were from Nurse Celia and Grandma. I had to fight with every ounce of strength I had not to lose it. "The anger will pass," Celia said.

- Poppy Teasdale.

She was there.

I didn't see her till afterwards. She came up to me with her mam. As they approached, my mind flashed back: her arms flinging around my neck at the hospital; her spoken words, "I thought you said she was better"; her written words, 'Things I miss about Oliver Timothy Campbell.'

She moved, slow motion, towards me, and my eyes, aching with the effort not to cry, saw her afresh for the first time in ages: silky pale pink dress to her knees, usual dark make-up round her eyes, new short bleached hair (with a bright pink flower in) sitting on bronzed cheeks. But she wore an awkward expression: smiling mouth, sorrowful eyes.

"Ollie. I'm so sorry."

Hearing her speak reminded me of how much I'd missed her, how much I'd wanted her there through everything. It wasn't enough to me, just saying "sorry." I thought, *Sorry for what? For pretending to like me? For leaving me? For leaving Lily?*

"We just got back."

I didn't say anything. I had a load of things I wanted to ask her and tell her, but I said nothing at that point.

"It was Gran. We stayed to look after her, like I wrote to you. Up in the mountains."

Thing is, she hadn't written to me. Well, not for two months. I'd check to see if she'd emailed several times a day, but nothing. So I stopped sending my daily messages. I wasn't *that* stupid.

"She's fine now. She had an operation."

Did she really think I cared about her gran? I didn't want to feel it, but for the first time, I thought of her with a kind of distaste. I felt like I was an idiot. I'd even got that wrong: the girl I was so keen on seemed to be stupid and thoughtless.

"I'm going to find Anna," Poppy's mam said.

"Your hair's five-star—got longer," Poppy said with an awkward grin as her mother left us.

"Lily's didn't."

"Oh."

"It started falling out in the end. You wouldn't have known." I couldn't stop myself.

Her gaze dropped to the ground and she bit her bottom lip. It was wretched to see Poppy so uncomfortable, but something gripped me and made me carry on with my unkind words.

"I cut a bit of it the last night I saw her, you know, at the new hospital you were supposed

to visit. Well, not hospital actually, a hospice, where people go to die. She couldn't even see in the end."

She pursed her lips as her head hung, and tears began splattering themselves in dark spots on her pale dress.

I felt like a swine making her cry, and I wished I could have hugged her and said sorry; but something perverse was taking hold of me, and I convinced myself she was putting on an act. In my anger I told myself she didn't care about me. She didn't care about Lily. So, I decided, I didn't care about her.

As I walked off, though, I couldn't help looking back. Her mouth was open, as if in shock, and her eyes, by now pinker than her hair flower, focused on me. Her right hand went to clutch the gold heart necklace she was wearing. She probably got it from that Australian boy she went on about, I thought. I turned away to walk off to the car to wait for the others. It was like I'd cut my own wrists, hurting Poppy and leaving her so upset, but somehow, in a messed-up way, it lessened the pain of Lily.

It seemed like the end of everything.

The rest of August is a bit of a blur. The main thing I remember was that Mam went away. Dad said that she couldn't bear to be in the house. *I* couldn't bear to be *anywhere*. It would have been easier for her if it had been me who had died because at least then she would have still had two boys, I found myself believing. Of course, she hadn't *said* that, but why else would she have left me?

She went to Cornwall the day after the funeral with Auntie Margaret and Auntie Colette. A great friend of theirs, Rose, lived there. Rose's sister had died many summers before, Dad explained, so Rose and her mother, who lived there, too, could help Mam a bit or at least would understand.

"Anyway, she's been tied to the hospital for God knows how long now. She needs a holiday."

No matter what Dad said, I couldn't understand it.

Sam told me that the loss of Lily had caused Mam and Dad to fall out of love. He said that Mam could not begin to cope with Lily dying, never mind take on Dad's grief. Mam and Dad had been so close that she had felt like she couldn't breathe in the house with the stifling silences and the "perpetual gloom," as Sam described it, so she had to get away.

Kamal came round the evening after Mam left.

"You look like a shell," were his words as I opened the door. He followed me into the living room where I was watching a programme on the impact of climate change on plants.

"You seriously watching this?"

It was dad who had put it on for us, but he'd got up after a few minutes to fix his bike.

"How did... Was the...?" He could see I wasn't going to answer. "Are you okay?"

Stupid question.

"I've got you that book you wanted to borrow about drama schools."

I wasn't interested.

"Hey! Got hold of two cool swords for our fight! Uncle got me them at a car boot sale! Not bad, eh? For our fight scene... Ollie?"

I didn't care about our fight scene.

"I know you don't feel like rehearsing just yet, but maybe it... How are your mam and dad, anyway?"

I turned to look at him.

"What? What, Ollie?"

"Gone, of course," I said.

"What do you mean, 'gone'?"

"She's left."

"Oh God! Really? I mean, *really*? Where on earth has she gone?"

"Does it matter?"

"Yes, of course it does. What the hell's happened? Where's she gone?"

"I don't care. She doesn't care. She's been waiting for the chance to get away from us for ages. It doesn't matter, does it? It doesn't *matter*, okay."

"No. I just thought she'd be here. She should be helping you."

"She shouldn't 'should be' doing anything. She does what she wants. She's lost… she's lost her child, remember?"

"And maybe you're feeling like you've lost them *both*."

I couldn't dwell, for even a second on his terrible words. I said, "It doesn't matter now. Nothing matters now, does it?"

"No, I suppose it doesn't matter… if you say. I saw Poppy last week! What a tan she's got from Australia. Have you seen her yet?"

"Poppy?"

"Yes. I'm asking if you've seen her. You okay?"

I forced words out of my mouth: "It's all over. Don't talk about her. I hate her."

"Jesus! Why are you saying that?"

"I'm just saying it."

"She didn't have the Internet when they took her gran to the mountains. What do you mean it's over? She was dying to see you."

"I can't believe that. Why are you saying that? She didn't even bother to see Lily. She stopped contacting me."

"She wasn't ignoring you, mate. She *couldn't* contact you."

"She could have written. A letter, I mean. I've a bag of letters to *her*, just no address to send them to. She doesn't give a… She doesn't really care, does she, I mean, you know, I've realised that."

"She *does* care and you're being… You're experiencing great loss and grief and that's to be expected, but don't shut her out… *us* out. I think you're punishing yourself, and you don't deserve it. We simply want to ameliorate the situation."

"What? Amelia what?"

"We want to try to make things better... easier, or just sit with you and talk... or not talk. Whatever you want. What *do* you want?"

"I don't know. Just be on my own right now."

Poor Kamal started coming round less often. He didn't usually stay for long either. I said very little. He talked, of course, but it was like background music.

When she came back, I hardly spoke to her—Mam that is. Part of me hated her. No one noticed, though, because I think everyone had a lot of anger and they didn't know what to do with it. Some of the time Mam and Dad got rid of it onto each other. I used to think, *Why are they fighting each other instead of hugging each other?* I remember one day asking Sam, "Do you think they're going to split up?" and he told me, "No, Ollie, but their hearts are broken. There's no one to blame. Imagine the agony of that frustration." I didn't have to imagine it.

Even though I didn't want to, Nathan and I had to go back to school after the summer. Mam and Dad didn't feel ready to go back to work. They didn't go back till about five months later, in January. I partly liked having them both around for a change, and though I loved watching my mother draw her intricate designs and Dad kneeling in front of his flower beds, it wasn't always calm at home. In fact, there were days when I was very glad to be in school. I had the play to focus on.

Grave Rehearsal

When I started year ten in September, our form tutor said that she hoped we were looking brightly to the future. She used the phrase 'raring to go.' It wasn't exactly a phrase I could connect with.

In the first half term, in PSHE, we had to write about what career path we might explore: Kamal wrote about being a politician; Jade Hilton wrote about 'being famous'; Bill Owusu wanted to be a professional jiu-jitsu fighter (though I'm not sure if that's even possible); Lizzy Smith filled pages about why she wanted to be a nursery school teacher; Becky Bailey wanted to run her own company and travel a lot. Lisa Comrie made it clear that she was already on her chosen path as a model—there'd been a photo of her in the local paper, at a fashion show in the Town Hall, organised by her dance club, Dance Attack.

I wrote brain surgeon and drew a cartoon. We weren't supposed to draw, so I got a low mark, and the teacher wrote, 'This is not what I asked you to do.' Maybe he hadn't known much about what happened in the summer. I think it was too painful for my mam to keep telling everyone. In the cartoon, I discovered the cure for Alper's brain disease, which is what killed my little sister. Once I'd written the cruel words, I got this urge to scream and howl, but my brain and my heart still felt sort of numb.

Nathan was in his last year in the sixth form. Though we never talked about it, I noticed that he'd changed quite a lot. After Lily died, he became afraid of random activities, like reading in class. Mam said he'd developed a phobia. He would start to worry on Sunday about whether he would have to face the fear of being asked to read during the next week. Sam said Nathan was having something called panic attacks too. I didn't really know what it meant—well, I could guess, but I didn't really understand, so I never asked him about it.

"Can you read okay in class now?" I asked Nathan after about two weeks of it going on.

"Yeah, it's fine. It was just a daft thing, you know."

"Well, what's that pass you've got to leave the class?"

"What pass?"

"Matthew Murray's brother told him you keep going to the front of the class. Says you show a card thing, then leave the room."

"Just doing errands for the teacher."

"So why do you show the card to the teacher?"

"What's it to you, anyway?"

"Just that someone said it was to go to the toilet. A couple of lads were making jokes about it, so I just wanted to check, you know, that everything's all right."

"It's just a stupid thing. And who's been laughing at me? Have they been giving you a hard time? I'll put a stop to that!"

"No! I just wanted to check you're not ill or something. You wouldn't keep it a secret, would you? I mean, if you got ill, you would, you know—?"

"Don't worry, man. Everything's kosher. I just get a sudden feeling like I have to go to the loo, but then as soon as I leave the classroom, the feeling goes away. It's off its head, you know, but I still want to keep the pass, just in case." He must have felt so embarrassed about it all.

"Do you get it when you're outside? Like when you're skating and that?"

"God no. Honestly it's nothing, and it's just when I'm in class. Hey, I know I keep asking, but what's your problem with Poppy? I'm fed up with her asking about you."

I knew I was harming myself, not contacting Poppy, but I'd become sort of addicted to it. It channelled some of my feelings away from Lily, but there's no way I could explain it. I lied to him saying,

"I'll go and see her soon. Cool that your toilet thing doesn't affect you out of school."

At least he still had his skateboarding. In fact, he was becoming highly skilled at it, and he kept winning competitions.

Sam started to take a keen interest in his education and switched from the course he was on to a music course. He threw himself into that and was at home less and less frequently.

The *Hamlet* rehearsals started up again with a view to performing at the end of September, and I decided I'd throw myself into that.

It was only the second week back at school, but Kamal was dead keen to carry on rehearsing our fight scenes. On the Saturday, he came round. When Nathan opened the front door to him, he shouted up to me, "Ollie! There's half an arm and a plastic sword at the door for you!"

By the time I'd come downstairs and got to the door, Kamal was stepping inside saying, "Sorry, Nathan. I thought Ollie would have answered." Then, spotting me, "You *were* expecting me, weren't you, Laertes?!" And he held up two plastic swords saying, "Choose your weapon!"

"Come on, let's go to the bottom garden," I said. It was a warm day, so I thought we could rehearse outside. "Mam's made lemonade if you fancy some."

"Bottom garden! Home-made lemonade! Sounds like something from Jane Austen!"

"Who?"

"The famous writer? Sounds posh like something you'd do in a great manor house with acres of landscaped grounds. You'll be telling me next that we're to shoot grouse before tea!"

He put on an upper-class accent and I nearly laughed. I didn't want to spoil his fantasy, so I didn't let on that it was the first time Mam had *ever* made lemonade and that her idea to do so had only been triggered by the bogof on bags of lemons at Asda.

As for the 'bottom garden'—perfect for ball games, picnics, or sword fights.

I filled some cups with lemonade before leading Kamal to the bottom garden.

"We should start with Act V Scene (i)," Kamal decided. "Ophelia, Laertes's sister, is being buried. That's when he—you—leaps into the grave followed by Hamlet, who professes that he loved her just as much. Then we have to grapple, which I think we should choreograph properly, don't you? If we get that right, we'll go on to the sword fight in Act V Scene (ii). Agreed?"

"We don't have to make it that complicated, do we? Don't I just basically try to strangle you?"

"'Just try to strangle?' It's a delicate operation, acting that effectively!"

"If you say so, but as far as I see it, I've got one pair of hands and you've got one neck! I mean, there's nothing delicate about me going for your jugular!"

"Ollie, you puttock, we have to think of our audience! They have to see the action, see the expressions on our faces, the intense battle of minds and hearts! It's got to be staged properly or there's no point in doing it. We'll have to work out where we're standing and how we move—that's what I meant by choreography."

"Well, let's just get on with it then. Where's the grave?"

"I was thinking that for the actual performances, we could fashion a headstone out of cardboard; then the space in front of that would represent the freshly dug grave. But for the moment, let's just mark it out with twigs."

Dad had some wood leaning against the shed, so I went up to get some planks. We laid out a rectangle to represent a grave (Kamal insisted on lying down and me laying down the sticks so they left a foot of space at either end of him). He then made a crucifix out of twigs and grass and stuck it in the ground where a headstone would be.

We were making good headway and by the third run-through, I had been happy with my "Lay her i' th'earth, / And from her fair and unpolluted flesh / May violets spring!"

I felt a frisson of excitement when I imagined the play working really well, so well that Mam was actually proud of me. We were in full grapple. I had a strong but loose grip on Kamal's neck with my face and body turned slightly out to the audience, as instructed by Kamal, when Mam appeared with a jug of lemonade.

"What the hell's going on?" she shouted.

"We're rehearsing, Mam!" I shouted back.

"What are you talking about? Rehearsing? Rehearsing what, for Christ's sake?"

I had told her about it. I had sat at the kitchen table while she was putting away groceries and I had told her about it. She had made the right noises and even sounded vaguely interested which I had noted with contentment. Misplaced contentment, it seemed.

"Drama club, Mam! You know? I told you!"

"What drama club?"

"Do you never listen to anything? Just leave us to get on with it, will you—you're being embarrassing."

"You've told me nothing! And stop shouting at me and being so rude! I can see exactly what you're doing, Oliver—you're fighting! And what the hell is *that*?!"

As Kamal took some steps back, for once correctly gauging how little he should involve himself, Mam had spotted the 'grave'.

"Are you both insane? You stupid boys! What have you done? What the hell have you buried? Is this some sort of sick joke?!"

I shouted, "Nothing! We haven't buried anything! And you're the stupid one because you've got it utterly and completely wrong, as usual! Because you don't listen to me! You never listen to anything I say! I hate you! You never—"

"Right! That's enough! Calm down! Calm down right now and explain this properly, please."

The jug of lemonade should have smashed, so severely did she plonk it onto the wall. Her arms reached out to me. For a nano second I thought *Right, I've got her now, I can explain it, explain EVERYTHING honestly and calmly*, but my mouth had other ideas.

"No!" I said. "What's the point? You don't care one inch what I'm doing or what I did yesterday or what I'm doing tomorrow! You don't give a—!"

"Oliver, that's *enough*, I've told you. You are the one being embarrassing."

"No! No, I'm not, because he knows what's going on, don't you, Kamal? He knows you wish it were me who were dead instead of Lily and that's why you ignore me and can hardly stand to look at me and probably, I wouldn't be surprised one tiny bit, HATE ME!"

For the first time since Lily had got ill, I saw my mam: confused, scared, shocked, desperate. From wearing all these emotions, I saw her face transition into robot mode, so that moments after being on the brink of screaming tears, she said,

"Kamal, you'd better be on your way! This is out of hand now and I need to deal with it. Off you go home, please, if you don't mind."

I said, "*Deal* with it? Oh really? You can't deal with anything because I know you can't. Because I *have* noticed. See, Mam? I actually notice stuff, notice *you*—notice you *not* noticing me, for instance, as in EVER!"

"Oliver! This is too much now. Stop it! Kamal, please?"

"You stay right here Kamal! He can hear all of this because he sees how you are!"

"Kamal, please, I'm waiting for you to leave us now. And I don't think you should come back here if you're getting Oliver into these outrageous games."

But Kamal seemed frozen to the spot. Mam then slipped back into desperate mode and lost it: "Go away, Kamal! Leave! Now! And don't you ever play these terrible games again!"

Kamal's eyes welled up for the first time, well, the first time I'd seen. But he still didn't move.

"Anna! What the...? What are you saying? Don't talk to him like that!" Dad had entered the scene. He'd heard the commotion and had come down to the lawn. My heart was thumping in my chest, and my teeth were grinding together. I really felt like I wanted to hit my mother.

"I bloody well will! Have you seen this sick game they're playing?"

"They're in a play at school. This is a scene from *Hamlet*. Christ, Anna."

Mam picked up the jug as if for protection, pressing it to her chest with shaking white-knuckled hand and stood there, her left hand on her hip.

My dad continued, "Oliver's got a part in a play, Anna. They're rehearsing a scene from a play. Shakespeare! For God's sake, woman, get a grip!"

Mam finally grasped the situation properly: "Well, well, I don't want this nonsense in my garden, then. It's unbelievable that he thinks this is okay. I mean, is he on a different planet? Is he not part of this family?"

"No!" I said. "Obviously I'm not because you said it!"

"Get inside, Oliver! Now!" Dad said.

"No!"

"He's not doing it anymore," Mam said. "That's it. Finished! And I won't be spoken to like that either! In fact, if your friend won't leave, I'm bringing you inside. I'll bring you in myself."

She let the jug tumble onto the grass, the lemonade gushing out in slow motion. She ran to me, grabbed my right arm and tried to yank me forward, but I jerked my arm back, and Mam tripped over the grave sticks and fell to the ground, catching her right cheek on the cross made of twigs. Dad ran to help Mam up, and when I saw a trickle of blood crying its way down Mam's face, I looked at Kamal and he knew what I was thinking.

I ran up the steps, along the passage at the side of the house, Kamal close behind, and continued to run along the road. Once round the corner, Kamal shouted me back:

"Stop!"

I stopped running and turned around.

"You've got to think here!" Kamal said. "Look at you! Your eyes are like a crazed mad thing. I'm going home and I think you need to go home, too."

"What?! You're joking! I don't want to ever go back there! You've seen how much she hates me! She'll kill me now anyhow. I've hurt her."

"Exactly. She's very upset. You *have* hurt her, and you have to go home whether you want to or not."

"Well, she hurt me as well. You saw! What about the way she talked to *you*? Just because you're my friend, you get all that?!"

"She didn't mean to get so angry. It was just an unfortunate incident. It may even be for the best in the grand scheme of things. Please, please, just take a breath and think."

"The way I'm feeling at the moment—"

"Maybe it's okay to shout sometimes."

"Ah! You're a psychologist now? Classic!"

"I'm just telling you, if you go back now, you'll see that this whole thing isn't as monumental as it may appear now. Please, for me, Ollie, will you just try it? Go home, will you? Please?"

"No."

"Well, I'll stand here until you make up your mind. Look, mate, you have a mam and a dad. They love you and something terrible's happened. That's it. That's everything. Right there."

"Do they? They hardly know I even exist."

"That's not fair. Stop feeling sorry for yourself. You have a mam and a dad, Ollie. You have your parents there in the house, desperately worried about you. And your mam bleeding from her face because of our stupidity! You have a mam, there in the house, bleeding from her face, waiting for you!"

And he put his fingers to his eyes to try to stop tears.

"Hey. Don't get—"

"You have a mam, Ollie!"

And he turned and leant his head on his arms against the wall.

There was a sort of shift in the air then. I didn't expect Kamal to get upset as well. He was supposed to be the calm, in-control one.

"Hey, come on, Kamal. I didn't mean for this to... I never thought you'd... I'll go back then. Maybe I'll go back and sneak up to my room."

"Good," said Kamal, with his head still leaning onto his bent arms and by now his shoulders shaking.

"I said I'll go back, then. I *will* go back home."

"Good," said Kamal, this time turning away from the wall to look at me, wiping the skin behind his glasses with the backs of his thumbs. Drips hung from the end of his nose and his orphan eyes.

"Go back," he said, not caring about how he looked.

"Yes."

"You've lost Lily, but don't lose sight of the precious family you *have* got. Okay? Talk properly to your mam. Off you go. And text me, will you?"

I watched his scrawny frame zigzagging up the hill. He turned around and said, "And, um, I'm sorry."

"*You* sorry?"

"Sorry, it might have been a crackpot idea, rehearsing at your house, in retrospect."

"Oh. Yeah. Mental, I suppose."

"Good luck."

We stood facing each other until he turned away again and made up the hill. I dragged my feet back to my house and felt very small indeed. I made my way down the side alley, but when I got to the end, I could hear Mam and Dad talking on the bench in front of the kitchen window.

"Have I really been such a bad mam? For God's sake, he thinks I hate him." And she started crying, and I mean a really loud sort of blubbing. I leant backwards against the damp alley wall and dropped my head down so that my chin nearly touched my chest. I tugged at my hair. The blackened stone seeped through me. This was all my fault. I'd made everything worse.

"What possessed the teacher to have Oliver play that part? I mean, are they trying to send us all round the twist?"

Dad said, "She didn't know anything about our situation, and this has been going on for a long time—before—"

"Well, he can't continue with it. It's too awful for him… and me, us."

"But it's something he has his heart set on, Anna. It'll be over soon. They're performing in a few weeks."

"Well, how will he feel when I don't go to see it? I don't want to disappoint him any more than he already is."

"Hey, come on; it'll be okay. Go along and wear your iPod under your long hair if it's going to upset you listening."

They both laughed sort of gentle, slightly repairing laughs. I sighed with relief that Mam had stopped crying and whipped my head back, hitting it too hard (on purpose) against the wall.

"It could well be a solution, though a crazy one. But he thinks I ignore him, doesn't he, so I couldn't do that. Do I? Do I ignore him? I give him attention, don't I?"

"Perhaps he hasn't had much *positive* attention."

"You think? Oh dear, I don't know. I promised we'd sit down and have a good talk. I mean Jesus, Ben, he tried to run away. Run away and leave us with everything. It's awful but I thought it was selfish at the time. Didn't he know it would have brought us more pain?"

Dad said, "We're all struggling, Anna. *I* want to run away sometimes. You did go away yourself, darling, and… well we did send him away. Perhaps it was a mistake. And I haven't really talked to him properly either. Yes we talk about the garden but—"

"Will he be all right?"

"He's with Kamal. What do you think? He's with Mr. Sensible."

"I hope so. I'm exhausted, Ben. I'm going for a lie down."

"Well, lie on your left side to let the air to that scrape; it's not too bad, darling."

Mam walked inside. When I heard the door closing, I sheepishly stepped round the corner, and my eyes met Dad's. I had to drop my gaze immediately, out of shame. I was waiting to hear words of chastisement and punishment, but Dad just said, "Mam's gone to lie down."

"Is she—?"

"She's fine now. I think you'd better go and have a rest, too. I'm going to carry on weeding the steps."

"Sorry, Dad."

"This is all new for us, all of us, but you have to think about other people."

He shook his head and pulled on his gardening gloves.

It had all been too draining for Mam, so that even though she came up behind me and stroked my hair while I was having breakfast the next day, which she hadn't done for yonks, we didn't 'properly talk' about it. I didn't even respond to her touching me; I became mute and just hoped that she picked up the sorry I tried to send out of my back. I felt terrible about what had happened, so I potted one of my special plants I was growing in my mini greenhouse to give to her. I gave her the Physalis, or Chinese lantern, which was just flowering for the first time. The flowers are kind of heart-shaped—really cool, bright orange papery things. I had been growing it for Poppy, but I knew Mam would like it. In the end I wasn't entirely sure if she did actually like it because Sam told me she put her hand to her face when she saw it. Kamal had tried to help me with a poem to go with it, which was getting all gushy and long. It wasn't working, so I just wrote, 'Hope you like this Chinese lantern.'

Mam had scribbled under my note, 'It's perfect, Oliver. Thank you.' The word sent pain to my eyes. 'Perfect'. I felt sorry for it—trying desperately to be upbeat when really everything was quite definitely imperfect to an extreme.

There was what I would call 'an atmosphere' between me and Mam after Gravegate (Kamal had called it Twiggate at first, by the way, but had admitted that it was trivializing the event and that he wasn't too happy anyway with the double 'g' as the word could have been mistaken for Twitgate). I sensed that Mam and I both wanted to hug and make up, but neither of us could bring ourselves to mention it. Kamal said that Gravegate was 'an elephant in the room'. I loved the expression and when I asked him what it meant exactly, he said, "Seek insight from our dear trusty friend, Wikipedia."

I looked it up that night and it said it was an 'English metaphorical idiom for an obvious truth that is either being ignored or going unaddressed. The idiomatic expression also applies to an obvious problem or risk no one wants to discuss.' Aha. It was certainly that. But Mam did make an effort to speak to me more about other things.

A couple of days after the terrible incident, Mam said, "I've been meaning to say, you must ask Kamal round for tea."

"Okay."

"And you must carry on with *Hamlet*. I'm looking forward to seeing you in it. Do you get to sing?"

"Sing? It's Shakespeare, Mam, not Richard Rodgers!"

It sent shards of light into my heart when her smile almost broke into a laugh.

"I'm not that uneducated, cheeky; I just thought school productions usually put a different slant on things."

I don't know what came over me but I so wanted to prolong the lightness that I picked up an umbrella which was leaning against the kitchen wall and used it as a cane to do a mock song and dance routine. I stuffed a cushion up my sweater too.

"To be, to be or not to be. I said tubby, tubby or not tubby? That, I say, is the question question, that, my friend is the ques-ti-on."

Then I suddenly felt like an idiot before the silence broke with the dancing notes of my mother's laughter filling the air like a million twinkling stars. As she set to her drawing again at the kitchen table, she said, "I'll never understand you." And I said, "I'll never understand *you*." And like a hypnotist had clicked his fingers, the elephant lumped his way back into the room. But we had communicated, connected, even joked and it sounded like she was definitely coming to see the play. Then, with her eyes still firmly on her art work, Mam said, "You reminded me of Lily just then."

"Did I?"

"She would have been good at singing and dancing... she *was* good at singing and dancing."

"And making stuff up with funny words," I said. Then she raised her head from her drawing, looked at me, and smiled again, saying,

"And making stuff up with funny words."

Everything was still too raw, so within moments, Mam's eyes were back down and a second elephant had been summoned to the room.

So Mam was going to see me in the play. Not only had she stopped ignoring me as much, she might now even be proud of me. We'd been given dates of the performances too: it was to be on the weekend just before my birthday at the end of September, well a bit longer than a weekend—Thursday, Friday, and Saturday.

Lily Talking

I think I can say that the play was a triumph (to be honest, I would never have used that word, but Mr. Hickey kept calling it that and it's stuck in my head). My part went okay, though I was so nervous I sort of changed my mind about acting being my thing. I thought people must be quite mad to put themselves through all that pressure over and over again, to be honest. Miss Pratt said she wasn't too sure if I was right for drama school, but that if it's what I really wanted, I should practise more and go for it. I think she was just being nice.

There were only two things that went slightly wrong with the play, and it's hard to believe, but they were both Kamal's fault. The first screw-up was when he mucked up his lines. He's the last person you'd think would mess a line up, but when he had to say, "O, that this too too solid flesh would melt, / Thaw and resolve itself into a dew!" he said, "O, that this too too solid flesh would melt, / Thaw and resolve itself into a stew!" I have a very slight inkling that he did it on purpose to lighten things up. The funniest thing was that nobody seemed to notice. A more obvious cock-up was when Kamal stumbled to his death after being poisoned. He made a meal of it (which he had been warned not to do in dress rehearsal) and tumbled off the stage. There were gasps from the audience, but a sense that his fall was possibly the result of a much-rehearsed stunt. Only, he clambered back onto the stage and 'died' again, which ruined the whole thing because the audience then laughed. Again, it crossed my mind that he may have done it on purpose.

My dream of my favourite people shouting "Bravo!" came partially true. My mam and dad, Sam and Nathan sat in the front row on the last night. I was going to say that of course *Lily* wasn't at the play, but I like to think that somehow she was.

I must say that I was the one who came close to providing the worst goof-up. Before the grave scene, I kind of froze. I stalled because I desperately didn't want to upset Mam again. There was a hush—a 'pregnant' hush, as Kamal/Shakespeare would say—in the audience. For a moment I thought it was going to go horribly wrong. But then, I caught Mam's eyes in the front row, and her head was madly nodding up and down to me. And what was hilarious was that Miss Pratt shouted out a prompt twice to me. She so didn't need to—I knew the lines like the back of my hands. Anyway, I got an adrenalin rush when I saw Mam urging me on, so I went for it. I was so relieved and happy that she was okay with it that I think I overacted in the end (except Kamal said it came out right because mostly I *under*acted so that when I thought I was *over*acting I was actually just 'acting').

I was dying to see Mam after the play and could hardly believe it when she gave me a hug

and a bunch of lilies. It may be a surprise, but I was pretty embarrassed getting flowers in front of my school friends. She told me I'd done well but it was Dad who said,

"We're all very proud of you."

"Yeah, ace, Ollie!" Nathan said.

Sam said, "You're not just a sissy plant boy after all. Hey, I'm kidding. Nice work, bro. Good stuff."

As we were leaving school and making our way to the carpark, I trailed behind, letting the flowers dangle from my right arm and starting to regret asking Kamal to put Poppy off coming. Just as I was thinking, *Idiot*, Poppy appeared like an angel with a single rose. My eyes lit up and I went to hug her. At the same time as I said, "I'm sorry," she said, "You were five star." I said,

"Poppy, I don't really know why I—"

"Oliver," she said as she shook her head and she carried on shaking her head, saying nothing. I was about to ask, "What?" but as our eyes stayed connected, and we stood very still, I realised that we both knew what the other was thinking. A sweet smile began to paint itself on her face and just as an urge to kiss her surged through me like a wave of warm honey, Mam's voice broke the silence:

"Come on Laurence Olivier!"

"Who?" said Poppy

And now I found my*self* the smiler and the head shaker.

"Good to see you, Poppy," Mam added.

Poppy blew a kiss to her then handed me the red rose. *Yeah,* I thought *Very very good to see you.* I wish I could have bottled the high I felt on the drive home and drunk from it every day for the rest of my life.

By the time my birthday came at the end of September, I'd never felt less high or less like a celebration. The combination of the play being over, and the feeling that the rest of everything else stretched

out like an endless, Lilyless, empty road in front of me, created a nothingy sort of head mulch, like I couldn't see the point. I was fifteen. Growing older. Yet, thing is, I felt like I was shrinking. I'd had a Poppy relapse too and couldn't face dealing with how I felt, though I was trying (probably not that successfully) to be 'friends.'

I didn't want to have my birthday, or Lily's birthday in November, or Christmas. I didn't want to be 'there' for any of them. Everyone was pushing me to have a birthday party. I didn't have one. I decided to throw myself into a solitary hobby—the playing of a musical instrument—and that way, well, I could practise as much as I wanted, and what's more, no one else could get upset. Maybe that was the thing I could be good at.

I asked if I could have a saxophone, but Mam said no; they were too expensive, so she got a recorder and a mouth organ. I thought it was some sort of a joke but Mam said, "Oliver, the recorder's good to start on. Great for breath control. It's a delightful instrument!"

I knew money was a bit tight because Mam and Dad had lost a lot of wages from not going to work, so I didn't moan or anything. I'd give it a go, I decided, but I couldn't think of an un-cooler instrument to learn. I imagined myself sliding across a huge stage, head rocking, hair flying everywhere, madly improvising on my descant recorder, but it didn't inspire me. The way things were going I'd get a triangle or some castanets for Christmas. My career in music was going downhill before it had even started.

The highlight of my birthday was when Kamal made up a mental dance. He played the recorder at the same time as doing this Irish-type pointy-toed jig. I remember that because I think it was the first time I'd laughed, like a lot, since Lily died.

I didn't even talk to Kamal, or Poppy for that matter, about Lily, though they tried regularly. Poppy'd look at me with a serious expression and say, "Are you okay?" and I'd always reply, "I'm fine," but who wants to hear how you really feel? I mean, you don't know how you really feel anyway yourself. I appreciated the way Poppy's look lingered every time I said, "I'm fine," though, like a mental hand on the shoulder. It was all I needed from her, I decided.

Poppy brought me a card and present. She'd written 'Strelitzia' instead of my name, on the envelope, which is another word for bird of paradise, which is not a bird at all but an exotic orange flower. She'd drawn a weeping willow on the back of the envelope. The card said:

Hope you can manage to keep going even though it's a sad time. Please can I come and see you more often? We could just sit if you don't want to talk. I bought a gold heart locket for you in Australia, and I wondered if you would accept it even though it sometimes seems like you're still angry with me for letting you down.

I wanted to give it to you at the funeral, but it was obviously the wrong time. I thought you could put that lock of Lily's hair in it. I'm sorry for not being there for you. I suppose I'm not as confident as you think. I hope you feel a lot better soon about everything because I love the way you were and it's still in there somewhere. I'll wait. There's no rush. I've written a new 'miss list'.

Things I miss about Oliver Timothy Campbell:

  - Oliver Timothy Campbell

Please forgive me and let's be five-star friends forever,

  Poppy xxx xxx xxx

I felt stupid for messing her around, and what she wrote was so kind, but she had said 'friends'. So that's all she ever wanted to be. Not that I loved her or anything, or maybe I really sort of did, but she would never be my girlfriend, so what was the point? I didn't know if I could bear to be friends. It wasn't worth the pain. What if she started up with another boy? How would I stand that? I couldn't just suddenly stop being friends, so it was best to stop it before I made a fool of myself.

I still put the card under my bed in my special box, though. Sounds twee and babyish, I know, but it's just a white shoebox. When I first thought of it, I was eleven. I had written 'Keep Out' on the lid at first, but then realised that those words were more likely to entice someone into opening it; so I found another lid and wrote 'SHOES' on it, but realised that was also suspicious; so I found another lid, which was red, and I wrote nothing on it. Sounds corny, but I keep a box of important stuff, well, things that seem important to me, or did at the time. Poppy's card joined another one which she'd sent for Lily after she died, but which I hadn't opened. The box was filling up nicely: the concert programmes, some dolphin earrings Poppy had left in the kitchen ages ago, the lock of my sister's hair, a miniature copy of *Hamlet* which Kamal had given me after I'd gone loopsville in the garden, the necklace I'd made for Lily which I sort of stole, and the order of service which I'd ripped into four pieces and taped back together. Plus there were three photos: the one of Mam and Dad smiling, holding me as a baby; the one of me and Thomas Diamond with John Millais outside the Tate; and the one of Kamal, Poppy, and Lily in the garden. I wanted to get this last one framed.

When Lily's birthday came on November 7th, it felt like the day would never end. She should have been there, and she should have been six. I should have jumped on her bed far too early and too excited and tickled her, and Dad should have come in, rubbing his eyes saying, "Go back to bed, you daft things!" but Lily would have climbed into Mam and Dad's bed anyway, and Dad would have snuggled her up to him and smiled as he squeezed her closer.

Everyone sent birthday cards, which was stupid because Lily wasn't there to look at them. I don't mean proper birthday cards, though, just cards with flowers or a pattern or something, you know. I woke up with a numb brain, zombied about all day, and went to bed with a numb brain. Mam and Dad cried... a lot. I didn't. I wanted to make things seem more bearable for Mam and Dad, but I had no words of comfort either. Sam wanted them to move on and said something like, "It'll get easier over time." But this just made them more upset.

At Christmas time, Mam and Dad were grief-stricken about Lily, and my brothers and I knew we couldn't do anything about it apart from get on with life and try to be upbeat. They invited Uncle Francis, Auntie Isobel, and Auntie Colette with her husband, Uncle Chris. Even though there was much pouring of tears along with the wine, having family members was a distraction from their grief.

On Christmas day, I saw a box under the tree with my name on it. Instead of grabbing it and tearing off the paper, something made me kneel down slowly and very carefully unwrap it. When I lifted the lid off the box, it was like opening a treasure chest; I was dazzled by gorgeous gleaming gold... It was a saxophone. Dad had watched me open the box, and when I looked up at him standing over me, his eyes were watering and he said:

"That's what I was most looking forward to today—your happy, smiling face when you opened your present."

Of course, I wasn't happy, as in 'in my life in general', but I was certainly really pleased. I sprang up and gave him a hug. I felt a suffocating squeeze in my throat.

"But they're so expensive, Dad."

"Grandpa," Dad said.

I started lessons after Christmas and threw myself into my playing. I loved it. More than once, when I was practising, I caught Poppy out the corner of my eye through the window of the rehearsal-room door. She never knocked, and I never acknowledged her. Sometimes I even felt her there without seeing her. I don't really know why she was there. I practised before school and at breaks and lunchtimes.

Kamal told me I should join a band or form one, but I told him he was being daft because I'd only just started to learn. Anyway, I wanted to be on my own. I reminded him that people always fall out in bands; you could connect amazingly with someone and get very close, then fall out terribly and leave the band and the magic you thought could last forever would be gone. He said the Sex Pistols was a bad example of a bitter break-up as there probably wasn't much love involved. So I offered Liam and Noel Gallagher as another example.

"It would be from elation to despair," I said. "People would start siding and blaming, and

it would sting you and kill your spark."

Kamal said I was getting carried away and being melodramatic and that a lot of musicians and so-called artists were egotistical twits up their own arses (his exact words), but I told him that you hear of people who are perfectly decent, cool people in bands who fall out deeply over stuff and break up forever, or until they're about a hundred and think their days are numbered so they may as well make up and reform. He said it was high emotions connected with artistic ventures and that it was their egos which led to wasted precious years.

No point being in a band. No point getting close to people. No point being close to Poppy. Kamal, I would have to stick with for the time being, as it was too far gone with him, but even he would probably leave in the end, so it was best to start pulling back, I thought.

"You should be good the amount of time you're spending on your saxophone!" he had said one lunchtime. "Couldn't you just practise at breaks and lunch? Then we could walk to school together again."

"I have to be focused if I want to be any good. It's the only way to be halfway reasonable."

At my seventh sax lesson, my teacher, Miss Milne, had finally brought the music for 'Sweet Baby, Sleep,' which I had asked for at my first lesson. It turned out that it was written by a famous composer called Ralph Vaughan Williams (quite a cool name, I thought—better than Bach, which I suppose is marginally better than being called Oink or something). She said it was far too hard for me to play and thought it a strange request, but I surprised her with my enthusiasm and by making not bad progress with it.

I had been pretty dedicated with my practice, but now that I had the music for 'Sweet Baby Sleep' that Thursday, there was no stopping me. I got down to practising that Thursday night, Friday night, and all day Saturday. I would have practised Sunday, too, but we had to travel to Wales to a country cottage for February half term. Mam said we couldn't really afford it, but that we needed to get away. She'd been talking about going on holiday since Christmas, and I'd been praying she didn't mean that she wanted to go off on her own again.

Although Mam talked to me a bit more and I was glad to be back home, she had whole days of being in her own world so that even when I asked her a question directly, she didn't seem to even hear me. Sometimes I felt like shaking her to get a reaction. And when she did talk, she wouldn't shut up about Poppy. She thought we were going to be girlfriend/boyfriend and she kept pushing me to ask her over for dinner. But that's exactly what I *didn't* want to talk about. When I asked her to talk about something else, she usually laughed, which made me feel like punching her. I mean, she hardly ever laughed anyway, so what was so funny about that? I was making an effort to pull away from Poppy, but Mam wouldn't respect my decision. She thought I was wrong. She couldn't understand me. I wanted to please her, but I always felt she needed more from me, like I was a big letdown. I wondered if getting away from home would help Mam to see things in a new light.

On our first night at the cottage in Wales, I couldn't sleep. I looked at my watch and saw that it was four thirty in the morning. It was a ridiculous time to play the sax, but I had a desperate urge to practise my lullaby, 'Sweet Baby Sleep'. I slipped out of bed and tiptoed to the window. The thin, fusty-smelling curtains were still open. The moon was full and bright, lighting up water that glistened at the bottom of the huge garden. I pulled on my sweatshirt and trainers and crept down the stairs with my sax. I found the back door, turned the key, and stepped out into the prickly air. Apart from a distant owl, the night was still and calm.

I reached the water at the end of the garden—it was a brook. I found the perfect tree stump to sit on and got ready to play, but I realised I didn't have the music.

I stared into the stream. I wondered how deep it was. I could hear the gentle gushing of the water over mossy rocks and twigs caught between stones. I wondered where it had come from and where it was going. Where might it take me if I just offered myself to it?

I started to play 'Sweet Baby Sleep'. Somehow, the tune flowed from me without the music, and it sounded sweet to me, echoing among the trees and melting into the stream and the moon.

Then it happened.

As I played more and more easily and gazed into the water, I clearly saw Lily's face, big and bright and smiling, her golden tresses floating in the water, her pink silk dress buoying her up in the stream. Flowers all around her. A poppy on her chest. But this time it wasn't a twitch smile—it was a proper, real, beautiful smile that looked like it would last forever. I continued to play, but became blinded by the water as it flowed into my eyes, and I felt like I would never see again. For the first time since July 27th, the numbness let go of my heart. I watched her mouth making smile words: "I'm okay, Oliver. I'm okay." A warm light seeped through my body and felt like it was glowing out of me. Even with the salty streams blurring my vision, I could see Lily. I could really see her.

My mother found me just after eight o'clock in the morning lying next to the brook, hugging my saxophone. When my eyes met hers as she sat over me, she looked different. I mean, she was looking at me differently. The sun lit up her red henna hair like a fiery halo. She pushed my hair off my face and stroked under my eyes.

"They're all puffy. What on earth are you doing out here? You must be freezing."

"I wanted to play outside, that's all."

"Couldn't sleep? Me neither. What time did you come out?"

"What does it matter? Why's everything I do wrong?"

"It's not like that. I don't mean—"

"Why do you think so little of me?"

"Where on earth has all this come from?"

"You," I said.

"Am I really so mean to you?"

"Why didn't you talk to me properly after I gave you that plant? Why didn't you really say anything after the play?"

"My mind's been so jumbled, Oliver, but really, I never meant to—I couldn't find the words... I thought you'd go to counselling with us."

"Counselling. I wanted *you* to talk to me. And why did you go away after the funeral?" I couldn't believe it, but my eyes had got used to watering from the night before, and they started again. "Was Lily the only one you wanted?"

"God, no, Oliver! Please don't think that." Her eyes started to water now. "It's so hard to explain. I'll try. I will try, but... let's get you warmed up, beautiful."

Beautiful.

That word.

Had she said that?

Had she really said that?

She put her arm around me, and we glided back to the house.

"Must have been like clutching a huge ice cube all night, that saxophone!"

I never told her that it wasn't really my saxophone I'd been hugging and that it was the warmest hug I'd ever had in my whole life.

When we got in the house, Mam made me a big breakfast, which she hadn't done for ages and which I was too shocked to eat, then brought a duvet from upstairs. I felt slightly angry with her, but it still felt okay when she sat next to me and pulled the cover over our knees. We sat there on the sofa all morning and even part of the afternoon.

Dad and my brothers went on a long hike, though Nathan was in a mood because we didn't have the Internet at the cottage. We did have iPods though, and Mam plugged hers into a little speaker and we just relaxed and listened. I hadn't even sat with my mam for months and months, but she put one arm around me. We just sat there, kind of wrapped up in the music together. It was all the stuff that *she* liked—Joni Mitchell, Carole King, Keith Jarrett, Andy McKee, Judie Tzuke, Uncle Francis—but I seemed to like it, too. She hummed along to it and sometimes rocked me to and fro, a bit like I was a baby or something. "This is the last song Lily heard," Mam said at one point.

"What is it?"

"It's called 'Blue' by Joni Mitchell. Do you like it?"

"Kind of."

"I bought it when she was in Rachel House."

Then I thought of something which I decided to say. "Maybe she can still hear it."

"That would be something, Oliver. That *would* be something. And maybe she can hear *you* too, playing your gorgeous tunes?"

Gorgeous tunes.

Had she said that?

Had she really said that?

"Me?" I said.

"You're very good, you know," she said, twiddling my hair.

"Me?" I said, pulling away slightly.

"I think you've got a real talent. I'm so proud of you. Lily would be, *is* proud of you too."

I couldn't speak then, and I couldn't stop the pain spreading up from my throat and jaw and spilling onto my face.

The last recording came on. I'll never forget that song—the last one we listened to. Some music is like an injection directly into your heart, I think—I suppose sometimes you avoid it and sometimes you wallow in it. There was like a blend of sorrow and joy that seemed to well up in our hearts as we let the song wash over us. I say 'our' hearts, because even though I wasn't looking at Mam and couldn't even see very well, I knew we were synchronised, my mam and me, you know, sort of thinking and feeling the same thing.

When Mam told me it was called 'Dido's Lament' or 'Remember Me' from an opera by Henry Purcell called *Dido and Aeneas*, I automatically said:

"Myosotis."

"I'll never understand you," Mam said.

"It doesn't matter; you don't have to."

I *will* try to describe this song for Lily's sake. If this melody were a scent, it would be the heavenly odour of the delicate yet bold white stargazer lily. Its bright blooms point up towards the sky and are thought to represent something innocent and pure.

Though it was the last song we listened to that day, we stayed rocking and crying for a long time after it finished. It was like I imagine a powerful drug would be, that song; not even something I'd ever think of listening to normally, but the effects of it sort of pulsed and lingered.

Just before Mam got up to make some lunch, she said, "I love you, you know. And I'm sorry that... Well, I'm just sorry... No, I'm sorry if you think I haven't been paying you enough attention. I'm sorry I *haven't* paid you enough attention, you know, haven't been there for you. And I went away because, well, I just felt so terrible, I couldn't bear to stay still. I know it was selfish, but I couldn't bear to stay still. And... I shouldn't have sent you away. I see now I deprived you of the very last weeks of—"

"It's okay," I said as she burst into sobs.

"She loved you... you two should have—"

"It's okay, Mam."

And we sat there for more swaying and rocking. And when she'd calmed down a bit, she said,

"And I was thinking, you should join a proper acting club, too, if you want. I did hear you that day, you know. It reminded me of me, watching you. I always wanted to be an actor when I was young."

"Did you?"

"We're all connected, Oliver, you see."

"Yeah I think we *are*, but someone told me we're all on our own in the end, aren't we?"

"You think?"

"Yes."

"So you see that, Oliver, do you?"

"It's just what I've learnt, you know, what seems to be true."

"Maybe that's the hardest part of all this. But we've got each other, too, haven't we? We should be there for each other, as best we can. I'll try. I love you, you know."

I had been worrying about if Mam really did love me, and I was sorry for the negative things I had thought about her, so when she uttered those words, a warm light started to glow inside me again.

"I'm sorry, too," I said.

"No. You don't be sorry."

"Is that even grammatically correct?"

"Cheeky monkey," she said, tickling me till we both laughed.

A weird mix of laughing and crying.

Before I fell asleep that night, I wished I'd had my box to take a photo out. I wanted to tell Thomas Diamond he had been right. But I think, strangely, he probably knew anyway.

Celia-mail 7

Dear Mam,

Everything going brilliant with the baby. Joe and I are on cloud nine! Looking forward to picking you up on Sunday to come to stay. This is quick, as baby is due to wake any minute.

I've decided I'm not going back to nursing after my maternity leave. You were probably right all along that I get too involved. I'm going to look into working with deaf children. Presumably, I'll be allowed to get involved then. I've learnt a lot of signs from you, so I'm going to try the stage-one British Sign Language course.

And I think you're right what you said about Oliver. With his mam sending us the nice baby card but telling me they were very worried about Oliver, who hadn't cried since the funeral, it could be a good idea to tell him we've called the baby Lily. I didn't want to upset Anna by telling her just yet, but, well, I think I'll tell the boy.

Much love,
Celia x

How It Is Now

Now, coming up to Easter, the pain isn't quite so raw, but it feels like it's just a teeny bit down my throat, and the slightest reminder of Lily can bring it all back. You're kind of sitting on it, like it's a wild animal, and sometimes it escapes and you have to run just as wildly after it until you can grab it back and sit on it again.

I think Mam and Dad would say it isn't a question of being reminded and that it is always with them. And I don't even think they sit on it; I think you can almost see it with them. It's like a huge sack sitting on their shoulders full of swollen love.

Mam's kept a lot of Lily's things even though someone actually advised her she should get rid of them and that she should be 'getting over it' by now. But she doesn't, *we* don't want to get over it. I mean, if there were a pill we could all take to wipe the memory of Lily away, none of us would take it. That sounds insane: to choose to suffer for the rest of your life 'the slings and arrows of outrageous fortune' (that's from *Hamlet*, by the way). I can't explain it. Maybe it's the love. You can't erase that sort of thing, can you? Not for a little person like Lily anyway.

Mam likes, or I should say, needs to talk about Lily quite a bit, like talking about her somehow keeps her there. And she likes other people to talk about Lily as well. One person was so scared of mentioning it or saying the wrong thing that she crossed the road when she saw Mam coming. Mam prefers people to face it. I always imagine that the acknowledgement of her grief lets her move the huge sack a tiny bit—to settle it back down with a slight shift, a fresh place, allowing air to the sore it left before.

Someone who found out only recently about my sister dying sent a card depicting a cherub playing a trumpet.

"Brugmansia," I heard myself saying, as we all looked at it over a family dinner.

"What, love?" Mam asked.

"Angel's trumpet!" Dad said, with a puzzled smile. "How d'you know that?"

"I notice stuff, I suppose, Dad."

"You do that. You certainly do, son!"

"Don't get big-headed, Ollie! Just coz you know well-odd pointless stuff!" Nathan said.

"No chance of that in this house!" I said.

Sam had the final word on it. "It's not all pointless, is it, Ollie?" And he smiled.

Did I mention I found *Kamal's* card the other day? It was down the side of the sofa. It had a drawing on the front called *Brother and Sister* by someone called Gladiola Sotomayor. In typical, flamboyant style, he had written a poem in it! This is what he wrote:

> Set not the sickly sun, yet bright shall Lily be,
> Squawk not the muted gulls, still angels sing "Lily,"

Bloom not the barren branch, and yet this flower so rare,
Shall scent till time grows tired of sweetness in the air.

But time will ne'er turn weary of unpolluted grace,
And Lily, with such form, shall never shield her face.
Her brother's heart, though scarred, should know: through all its days,
This little sister-sun, shall blaze through it her rays.

I wasn't sure what it all meant exactly, but I asked Mam if I could put it on the special table. She made this sort of shrine to Lily, you see. It has photos and cards and candles and toys and stuff plus I placed a bunch of statice on it with one of the cards from the funeral. I think it helps her. I wanted to help her, even though somehow things between us had changed ever since Lily got ill. It was much better, but not the same. How could it be?

"Of course. That's a great idea. Put it at the front."

"Thanks, Mam. He'll be right chuffed when he sees it there."

"It's not just for me, you know, Oliver, this corner. It's for you as well, all of us."

"Yeah, I know. Thanks, Mam. That's why I put those postcards on it."

"Oh of course. Yes, I like them," she said picking them up. "*Four Flowers in Still Life*, David Hockney. Lovely idea, beautiful."

I placed it right at the front after moving a pink stone. "What's that stone again, Mam? It's huge."

"Rose quartz."

"Love crystal!" we said at the same time and smiled.

"Gosh! That reminds me. I never did give you that stone that Auntie Colette left for you! Did I? I did give it to you, Oliver. Did I?"

"What stone?"

I knew immediately what she was talking about, but I didn't want to sound soft. And of course, I had committed the name of the stone to memory—the one I'd chosen at the fountain at Rachel House that afternoon.

"I know where it is! It's in my ring drawer—I'm sure it is. I'll go and get it."

She walked enthusiastically (she rarely runs) up the stairs and returned with the gemstone.

"Look! Here it is! I knew it! After all this time. God, I feel terrible. I'm so sorry, Oliver."

"It's not like it was causing me sleepless nights, Mam!"

"What's it called again? Oh, I'll never remember. Someone must know," Mam said.

"I know. A picture of you, Lily, on a kite with a mottled pink and green background—you have to visualise the stone. You on a kite. Unakite."

"You're so funny!" Mam said and messed my hair.

"Don't know what it means, though. Auntie Colette forgot me when she was doing her readings!" I said.

"We should look it up."

"No point really. It's all a bit daft that stuff, don't you think? I'll keep it as a memento though. Colours are cool." *Another one for my box*, I thought.

Mam went back down to the kitchen, and I walked over to the bookshelves and got down a book Auntie Colette had given Mam years ago called *Crystal Healing*.

'Unakite: helps the release of feelings long held in and conditions which have been inhibiting personal growth.' I thought of Lily, squeezed the stone, and smiled.

Another thing to remind me of her.

I was just rearranging the postcards on the table when Mam shouted up, "Oliver! I just thought, you should put that photo you love on Lily's table! The one of her with Poppy and Kamal, you know?"

She started walking up the stairs to the ground floor, wiping her hands on a tea towel. As she came back into the room she said, "There's one of all of *us* there, but you particularly liked that photo of those three, didn't you, I remember, so it just occurred to me when I was looking back at *Four Flowers in Still Life* just now, you could add the photo to the table and call it '*Three* Flowers in Still Life'!"

She was beaming with her idea, but I didn't get it.

"What d'you mean?"

"Has Kamal never told you what his name means?"

"No."

"Ah! Then you'd better look it up."

She made her way back down to the kitchen. "I'm making your favourite, by the way—cottage pie."

"Tell me what it means!" I shouted after her.

"Look it up! You love looking things up!"

I walked over to the computer set up in the same room as Lily's corner and typed in 'Kamal meaning'. It said 'perfection', so I still didn't get it. I actually thought, *How annoying. He's big-headed enough as it is!* Then I saw that this meaning was linked with the Arabic, Muslim name. The *Indian* meaning was different—it meant 'lotus'.

"Lotus!"

Mam heard me shouting it and started laughing in the kitchen.

"Lily, Poppy, and Lotus! 'Three Flowers in Still Life'!" she said.

I was tickled with her idea and got the photo from my box. But I changed it a bit and just wrote 'Three Flowers' in the end, on a little piece of card. While I was 'in' my box, I spotted Mam's poem

I'd found in the drawer at Grandma and Grandpa's. I had been saving 'My Little Girl' for when Lily got better, so I wasn't sure whether to show it to Mam, but it seemed as good a time as any, so I decided to tell her I had it. Once down in the kitchen, I placed the piece of paper on the table, a strange mix of fear and smugness coming over me.

"Maybe you could put this on Lily's table."

Picking it up, Mam's eyes screwed up, and she tilted her head as she read it out loud.

> When I have my little girl,
> We'll watch the world, its fronds unfurl.
> We'll hang on branches high, and sway
> And drink the drama of the day
>
> When I whirl her through the years,
> And save my girl from fears and slurs,
> I'll heave the hurdles from her trail,
> Then safe in love she will prevail.
>
> When I feel my colours fade,
> And cannot life's cruel fall evade
> She'll watch and wait and with me curl,
> When I shall have my little girl.

"You wrote that, Mam, when you were seventeen."

The pause hung in the air like a blanket that could either snuggle or smother.

"Where did you get this? I don't remember," she said, her smile at odds with her eyes. She dropped hard onto a kitchen chair. "Didn't work out, did it?"

"No, Mam. I'm sorry. I'm stupid. I shouldn't—"

"Nothing works out if you think too much. Shouldn't wish too much. It can devour you, longing can... like a predator clawing at your stability."

She stood up again as quickly as she had sat down. "It's okay." Through her nose she sniffed in a sharp and better-acted smile, which eased away as her nose steadily streamed out the air.

"It's fine, Oliver. We're going to be fine. We have to be fine. Yes, it can go on the table. Where did you...? Never mind. Well done, Oliver. Go on, then, go up and see if it fits on the table. Good lad."

It was the last thing I'd suggest for the shrine to Lily, I thought. It was too late to say, "You know what? Let's forget it," and after all, she did seem to want it on the table. And I decided I would never tell her about Nurse Celia calling her baby Lily. Some stuff is just too... too achingly ironic. I found it kind of sweet and touching, but there's a thin line between touching and taunting in this case.

But not long after, I found myself making another suggestion for the shrine. Mam easily let me put the John Brett postcard of the seascape on the table, even though it wasn't strictly connected to Lily. Oh, I didn't explain how it ended up back with me, did I? In March, a little parcel arrived for me from Thomas Diamond. There was my postcard, a photo, and this note:

Mr. Diamond asked that this be sent to you. We asked him if we should contact anyone, and he said he only had one address. Before he died, he dictated a letter to you, so I've written it as he spoke it. He said:

"I've just got my dog and now I'm not going to bleedin' get to look after it! Reason being, I've gone and got ill. I'm off to a better place.

Talking of places, I never got to the sea yet, my little feller, but don't worry, I looked at my picture every day, so I reckon I have been. I'll tell you I can't wait to see my sister, Janet! And I'll keep an eye on your little one. [I don't know how he knew about Lily.]

Oh and look after your mam, there's a good lad.

Oh, and I did call my dog Glitter. I've given him to my mate, Andrew Higgs, so maybe you'll see him one day.

This is the big news—you was right! I was allowed in the Tate Gallery! A sweet little nurse wheeled me in last week. I'll tell you for nothing, when I seen that huge picture of my postcard, I come over all weepy. What a twerp, eh?!

Oh, and I went to see that chap who the statue is behind the gallery. Did you ever see the lovely lady with loads of hair, lying in the water with all o' them flowers? I felt all calm when I seen that, and it stayed with me so that now I'm all calm inside still.

So long, Oliver and I hope you like the photo. I wanted to send you something.

By the way, I didn't save you. You can only save yourself because we're all on our own.

Oh and none of this running away. You'll do good and make something of yourself. Not like your loyal friend, Thomas. Trust me.

Love from Thomas Diamond (Remember me? Oh, you can't answer that! And you won't know it but Remember Me is also the name of a song but it's not a question in the song. My memories aint many, but that's what comes to mind when I think of my ma. She was a singer and she loved that song. She sang it to me, to my face! Can you imagine? Did I tell you that little feller? That she was a singer. How bout that?)"

And I think he couldn't write, so he just put a cross. Or maybe it was a kiss. It struck me that the photo of him and his sister ('Thomas (11) and Janet (5)' written on the back) showed a smartly dressed pair. Made me wonder how he'd ended up on the streets in the state he was in and if he'd really never been to the seaside. The John Brett card was in the parcel, too, with my address and my message: 'Dear Thomas, Thank you for saving me. I will think of you for the rest of my life.' I still wonder how he knew about Lily.

I passed grade three on the saxophone last week, by the way. It'll be something I'll keep up, I reckon, playing the sax. My parents took me all the way to Kew Gardens *and* Barnes Wetlands Centre (an excellent nature reserve) in London for getting a good mark. I'd been going on about it for years. It was an amazing day. The Royal Botanic Gardens is the full name for Kew Gardens. It's got a hundred and twenty one hectares of gardens and botanical glasshouses, would you believe. What I wouldn't do to get a job there! Maybe that's where I'll live... in Kew or Richmond, in south-west London. I wonder if saxophone-playing could trigger plant growth? I could do some experiments. I could log my results and send a report to Kew gardens.

Dad and I listened to a talk on seed conservation. The bloke said (and this is hard to believe) that more than one in five of the world's plants was threatened with extinction. My jaw dropped when I heard that, but when I turned to Dad, he was just nodding. Lily's words danced across my brain—"Don't let it die, Oliber." *I won't, I won't,* I thought. I won't let anything die if I can possibly help it. I want to make things live. Turns out the incredible scientists from Kew Gardens are leading massively important conservation work around the whole world. He was basically saying that everything comes back down to plants. I found my*self* nodding then. I mean you just don't think of that, do you—that we rely on plants for food, clean air and even water? It was the first time I really got the idea that if we mess about with the environment, it messes all the plants up too. I said to Dad how brilliant it would be to be able to save something. I mean it's impossible to save people sometimes, but I could maybe save something, you know some plants or something. Imagine that—to save life? That's what it would be. That's what they're doing at The Royal Botanic Gardens when you think about it—saving life... saving lives. Just imagine being part of all that? Five star, it would be, as a certain person would say...

The herb garden was bloody cool as hell too. That'll be next—I'm going to grow food. What a project that'll be. And the meadow of course. Dad thought the meadow was a brill idea but questioned if we really had the space. I need land. Maybe I'll be a secret planter—like Banksy and his secret graffiti art. A guerrilla gardener. 'Plantsy' I could be called. It could be for everybody. I could climb into military bases and plant poppies, or old people's homes, schools, prisons and derelict land and plant flowers and vegetables. New kinds of crop circles. Dad told me about someone called Adam Purple (not real name—he apparently always wore something purple); can you believe they destroyed his 'earthwork' Garden of Eden that he spent years creating in the lower east side of New York City where buildings had been knocked down? I must tell Kamal about him.

Dad had asked if I wanted to bring Kamal or Poppy along to the Kew Gardens trip, but what would be the point in... well, I've explained all that. My head was full of birds and plants and trees for weeks after. Stupidly, I did find myself thinking that Kamal and Poppy would have loved that day; Poppy would have learned so many more names of plants and trees and Kamal would have relished the Latin words and the global politics side of it all. We could have learned a load of stuff together. I had to face that I missed Poppy. There you are, I've said it. To be totally honest, I realised I actually yearned to see her, never mind missed her. It was obvious because I lay awake in bed at night, detecting the signal from my heart above the din of the white noise. She'd forget about me soon, I hoped. That would make it easier.

Did I mention my dad screaming my name from the garden the morning after we got home from Kew? "Oliver! Quick! You've got to get down here now!"

I pulled on a sweatshirt and danced my bare feet down the stairs to the back door. I stopped, held its frame, and squinted to see what Dad was on about. He was in my patch, his head by now hung low and his hands over his eyes.

"What? What Dad? Has someone dug up my garden?"

I ran to the gate, clanging it open, and leapt down the steps to where he was. Then I saw...

"Myosotis," was all he said. The forget-me-nots. I walked towards him and put my arm round him. "They're beautiful, son. She chose them, didn't she? Lily chose them?"

"She planted them."

"She should be here to see them, then. Doesn't make sense. My little girl should be here."

And he shook in my arms for a good few minutes.

"I could move them down to the bottom. They could be the start of the meadow. Lily's started off the meadow you see, Dad? Let's think of them like that." Then a voice from the patio said,

"When daisies pied, and violets blue

And lady-smocks all silver-white,

And cuckoo-buds of yellow hue

Do paint the meadows with delight..."

Kamal false-shivered with glee when my dad said, through sniffs, "Ranunculus repens."

"This is like living in a parallel universe," I said. "I presume that's a poem and Ranunc whatever it is, is Latin for one of those—"

"It's a double translation if you will: cuckoo-buds is buttercup, and Ranunculus—"

"You've perked up, Dad. I tell you, yous two are too clever for your own good." Needless to say, this was music to Kamal's ears.

"Love's Labour's Lost, Act V scene (ii)." Dad egged him on:

"Brilliant, Kamal, brilliant!" He took one last sniff, wiped his eyes with the heals of his hands and his sleeve under his nose before continuing, "'Do paint the meadows with delight.' Shakespeare. Wonderful. He was a keen gardener, you know, Kamal?"

"As sure as night follows day, that is a certain truth. Ah to be amongst such learned folk. All of this dear day could I pass with you fine fellows."

And he did... spend all day with us that is. Kamal took a photo of Dad and me next to the new forget-me-nots and I took one of him with his nose in a snapdragon, then we all read up on how to create a wildflower meadow area.

By the way, even though Kamal has decided now he wants to study English (not History) and Politics at Oxford University and he 'hasn't got time for frivolous diversions', he still couldn't resist the school play, and has got us both involved in the next one. It's a version of *A Midsummer Night's Dream* by William Shakespeare. I'm playing Peter Quince, a carpenter (and helping with the painting of the backdrop which is a wood) and Kamal got the part of Bottom. He has to wear a donkey's head for part of the time, so, he says, he won't have to work on his facial expressions and can hide behind the mask.

No matter how many activities I have in my life, some people just never get out of your head. They just won't go. You have to squeeze your brain with the pain of it. They ambush your quiet when you're least expecting it. Nurse Celia, Thomas Diamond. Kamal, Poppy, Lily.

I sense Lily in quite a few places other than the special table. I certainly sense her all over the house and garden. Seeing the rose bush, the unpruned pink polyanthus she planted, always makes me smile. Mam even wrote her name in massive letters on the kitchen wall. She used sparkly pink stickers. I thought it was a bit too big at first, but I suppose even if the letters were bigger than the house, they couldn't reflect how much that name means to us all.

By the way, this might sound strange, but now, it's not just when I look at a photo or my locket or play 'Sweet Baby, Sleep' that I see my little sister's face smiling a proper smile. I see it a fair bit—when I'm playing other tunes or listening to music or just when I'm looking at a bird or gazing into a stream, or at stars and trees. I suppose really she's dancing in my head the whole time, whether it's a slow waltz or rock 'n' roll. Uncle Francis was right after all—she's always there.

Fairy Rose.

Stargazer Lily.

Forget-Me-Not.

Always with me.

Printed in Great Britain
by Amazon.co.uk, Ltd.,
Marston Gate.